The Unreliables

When The Only One You Can Trust Doesn't Exist

Katherine Nichols

Black Rose Writing | Texas

ISBN: 978-1-68433-888-7
PUBLISHED BY BLACK ROSE WRITING
www.blackrosewriting.com

Printed in the United States of America
Suggested Retail Price (SRP) $19.95

The Unreliables is printed in Garamond

*As a planet-friendly publisher, Black Rose Writing does its best to eliminate unnecessary waste to reduce paper usage and energy costs, while never compromising the reading experience. As a result, the final word count vs. page count may not meet common expectations.

As always, my reliability depends on the love and support of my family, especially my beautiful grandchildren—Carson, Holland, Quinn, and Heidi.

The Unreliables

Chapter I

One minute I was standing in the produce department comparing prices of seasonal fruit. The next, I was sitting in the middle of the cereal aisle surrounded by boxes of honey and oat GoldieOs, rolling blueberries, and uniformed personnel.

The time between those events was a blur. I know I pushed my cart past the mangos and peaches to the dairy display and stopped in front of an unending sea of yogurt. Incapable of deciding what I wanted, I gripped the handle so tightly my knuckles whitened.

Once a person who weighed her options and made calm rational choices, I was unprepared for this recent version of myself, someone for whom the smallest decisions had become monumental. Should I get out of bed and face the day or crawl back under the covers and wait for nightfall? Did I want to wear sandals or tennis shoes?

And now, would it be Greek or regular? Despite the cool air emanating from the refrigerated shelves, beads of sweat gathered at the base of my neck. I backed away from the counter and cut my cart hard to the right, speeding toward the wine section.

I was so fixed on the gleaming oasis of deep reds and pristine whites and bubbly pinks that I failed to notice the giant cardboard bumblebee perched atop neatly stacked boxes in the middle of the aisle. If it had been any other brand, even any other variety, I might have made it safely to the checkout line. But those little golden bits of grain, coated with tiny droplets of honey, filled me with a thick glaze of despair that morphed into rage.

My next moment of clarity was staring up at the round, flushed face of the manager.

"Please, Miss." His voice drifted downward as if from a great distance. "Are you able to get up or should I call someone?"

Faced with another impossible decision, I could only shake my head before grabbing one of the cereal boxes and crushing it against my chest.

"I'm perfectly fine," I said, as I struggled to my feet. "It's just that I forgot the cereal. It was the only thing he asked for. And now I really need to get home, so he won't have to...."

But I had no memory of what he wouldn't have to do. I did, however, remember there was no reason for me to hurry because there would be no husband waiting for me. That husband was gone, and I was the reason for his death.

•   •   •

"I'm sorry, Andy," I mumbled, eyes closed against the throbbing in my brain.

After much sobbing and apparently some foul language on my part as store security tried to separate me from the Goldies, I ended up in the manager's office. He coaxed me into giving him the number of Andy Freeman, my best friend since college.

He paid for the berries and multiple boxes of damaged cereal and convinced the poor guard I posed no threat to the public. Then he gently guided me to his car, drove me home, and settled me on the sofa.

"You don't have anything to be sorry about. Just lie there while I fix us something to make it all better." He walked to the kitchen, where I could hear him rummaging in the cabinets.

Now an attorney, he had once been an English major like me. We met as undergraduates, and he was the first person to encourage me to become a writer. He helped me develop my risqué story about a young woman who falls for a handsome con man and loses everything, including her virginity. And he suggested I transform my protagonist, Garnet Rivers, from victim to avenger. It was Andy who insisted I submit the manuscript for *Hidden Jewels* to a long list of agencies.

I was shocked when Wanda Everett of the Everett Literary Agency offered me a contract and even more surprised when the book sold, as did the second and third novels in what became the Garnet Rivers series. I was working on the fourth when someone shot and killed Michael—my husband of one year, two months, and twelve days—on his way home from the grocery store. And now it was Andy, armed only with humor and determination, who kept me from surrendering to the darkness inside me.

"Doctor Feel Good to the rescue." His cheerful voice pulled me back to the not-so-cheerful present.

"Come on," he urged, holding out an icy glass. "It's your favorite, lemon vodka with a twist and a smidgen more vodka."

I pushed myself into an upright position, accepted the drink, and took a generous swallow. "How bad was I?"

"Not so bad." Still standing, he stirred the ice with his finger, then took a sip. "But it would probably be a good idea if you did your shopping elsewhere from now on, at least until they lift the restraining order." He sat beside me on the sofa and put his arm around me. "What happened back there? All I could get out of the store manager was something about a scuffle over cereal. And the security guard refused to repeat what you said to him when he tried to get you to stop flinging boxes around. He did mention getting slammed by a grocery cart."

"Jesus," I sighed. "Honestly, the last thing I remember is seeing that giant bee stuck on top of a mountain of..." I closed my eyes against the memory and whispered, "GoldieOs, the oat and honey ones."

His look of bewilderment disappeared. "Oh, that." He moved closer, and I rested my head on his shoulder. "You have to let it go."

I nodded but suspected he knew I wouldn't be able to let go of the guilt I felt about being the reason Michael had been in the path of his murderer.

"Well," he continued. "At least the store wasn't too crowded."

"Oh, God, I hadn't thought about that. If you-know-who finds out what happened, I'll never hear the end of it."

We both knew it was my stepmother Barb who would flip out if news of my break with reality got back to her. She started nagging me about seeing a therapist a week after Michael died and hadn't let up for the past eight months.

"You should be safe. I don't see Barb dishing dirt with the checkout girl. Hell, does she even go to the grocery store?"

"Only if the housekeeper's sick. And then only Whole Foods."

His phone sounded the opening refrain to "It's Raining Men." He dug it from his back pocket. "It's Paul," he explained with a smile. "Give me just a minute."

Paul was Andy's partner in the law firm and in life. As my friend left the room, I fought against the stab of envy I felt at the look on his face. Once I had experienced that same joyful lift in spirits at the unexpected interruption of a call from the man I loved.

"I'm at Kara's," he said.

I wasn't trying to listen, his voice boomed from the other room. After a long pause, he lowered his volume, and all I could make out were a few "Oh no's" and one or two groans before he said, "Thanks for letting me know." He ended the call and rejoined me on the sofa.

"Is Paul okay?"

"Paul's fine," he answered without looking at me.

I watched as he became engrossed with his cell phone.

"Oh, shit," he whispered, staring at his screen.

"What?" I tried to see what was causing his concern, but he blocked my view with his hand.

A woman screamed, "Don't touch me, you son of a bitch," followed by several stronger epithets. Her mounting hysteria made it difficult to understand the rest of her diatribe, but one thing was clear. The voice of that woman who was spewing a stream of impressive profanities belonged to me.

Chapter 2

I played and replayed the YouTube of me losing it in the grocery store at least ten times before Andy wrestled the phone from my hand and took it with him to the kitchen, where he fixed another round of drinks.

Even without the actual footage of the incident, all I had to do to see it again was close my eyes. The image of me, wild curly brown hair sticking out Medusa-like, slamming into the display island, was indelibly etched in my brain. As was the part where the security guard tried to restrain me from running the cart over the fallen boxes, back and forth until the floor was littered with torn cardboard and ground oats.

Mercifully, Andy returned with vodka before I got to the most disturbing portion when I rammed my buggy repeatedly into both the guard and the store manager.

I snatched the drink from his hand before asking the question I didn't want answered. "How many hits has it gotten?"

"Not counting the ten or eleven times you played it, a little over two hundred. Which isn't too bad considering it's only been up for about five hours."

"Not too bad? Holy shit, Andy, I don't want it to go viral. What kind of person records something like this?"

"The asshole kind."

"But why me? Do you think someone's been tracking me, waiting for the chance to make me look like a lunatic?" As soon as the words left my mouth, I realized how much like a lunatic I sounded.

"Like a stalker? I doubt it. I bet one of your rabid fans is working on a tell-all documentary on the woman behind your slutty heroine."

"I've told you a hundred times; Garnet is not slutty. She's a strong woman with a healthy sexuality. She—never mind. Can we find out who posted it and beg them to take it down?"

"You can message them or comment on the video, but there's no guarantee they'll respond. Probably not a good idea anyway, though, since whoever put it out there would most likely enjoy knowing it was bugging you. But I wouldn't worry. The shelf life for personal embarrassment videos is a short one. And it's not like you're some celebrity flashing her hoo-ha getting out of the backseat of a limo."

"I'm not sure a little hoo-ha flashing might not be better than giving the world a front-row seat to the *Kara Dolan Story: Maniac on a Rampage.*" I held the cold glass against my forehead.

"You're not a maniac. You're a good woman trying to get through one of the worst things that can happen to anybody, a nice person who needs to give herself a break. I know how you feel about talking to somebody, and I consider myself pretty damn good at this best friend thing, but it might be time to bring in a professional."

Before I reminded him I had no intention of sitting down with some stranger who would smile and nod, then prescribe mind-numbing drugs, the doorbell rang.

"Sit. I'll get it," he said.

A wave of exhaustion rolled over me, and I wished I'd told Andy to tell my visitor I was resting. But he was already in the foyer, opening the door before I thought of it.

"What a lovely surprise." Andy's voice, loud and full of false cheer, echoed down the short hallway, sending a shot of dread up my spine. "Kara," he called, reverting to the Southern accent that signaled he was laying on the faux charm. "Guess who it is?"

"For God's sake." My stepmother's voice preceded her entrance into the room.

Fifteen years my father's junior, Barb could have been the poster girl for an active-over-fifty-retirement-community. I pictured an enlarged glossy photo of her outside the model home. With sunlight glinting off her shiny blonde bob and a tennis racket poised for slamming the ball down her opponent's throat, she would draw hordes of seniors looking for their personal Shangri-La.

As she stood over me, I trembled when I noticed she had left home without combing her hair or applying makeup. Although her Botoxed forehead remained uncrinkled, the fierceness in her eyes and the arms-crossed-over-the-chest stance radiated disapproval.

Andy stood behind her and shrugged.

I resisted the urge to kill the rest of my drink and placed it on the end table instead. Then I rose to greet her.

"Hey, Barb." I gave her the stiff-shouldered hug we settled on as our preferred method of greeting, noticing she was even stiffer than usual.

"I believe you two know each other."

She wrinkled her straight little nose before stretching her lips into a smile. "Mr. Freeman, isn't it?"

"Please, it's Andy." He extended his hand. "Always a pleasure."

She offered him a quick fingertip touch, then pulled back. The two had met last year at the first and only Thanksgiving dinner Michael and I hosted, and they hadn't exactly taken to each other. Barb had trouble dealing with what she called "Andy's unconventional lifestyle," and he had trouble dealing with what he referred to as her state of being "a stone-cold bitch."

"To what do we owe the pleasure of your company?" I asked, trying not to giggle at Andy, who was making faces behind her back.

"I wish it were a pleasure visit." She strode to the chair across from the sofa and flounced down in it, leaving the two of us standing in the middle of the room. "I was hoping we could speak in *private*."

"No problem. I've got some errands to run, so I'll head out and leave the two of you—"

I grabbed his arm and squeezed hard. "Don't be silly." With my back to my stepmother, I glared at him and mouthed, "Don't go."

Turning to Barb, I added, "Andy and I are besties. We share everything. Right, Andy?"

"Right." He sighed. "Unless Barb wants to tell you something naughty, like how her sex life with your dad is going. Then I'd be more than happy to let you two have a little girl talk."

She rolled her eyes. "I suppose it doesn't matter. It's about that thing we've been talking about."

Our main topic of discussion had been how much she wanted me to see a therapist. More accurately, she'd been telling me about the benefits of seeing a professional mental health specialist, and I'd been ignoring her.

"How about something to drink, Barb? Wine or something a bit stronger?" Andy suggested.

"It's a little early for me. Do you have any diet ginger ale?"

"You sit." I pushed him out of the way. "I'll get it."

He frowned but sat on the sofa across from Barb.

"How about you, Andy? Can I freshen your drink?"

"Does the Tin Man have a hollow wienie?"

Stifling my laughter, I grabbed our glasses and took them to the kitchen. I decided Andy and I needed to keep our wits about us in the face of another onslaught from Barb about my desperate need of counseling, so I added a touch of tonic to our drinks. Then I poured Barb a glass of high-caloric ginger ale.

When I returned, he was regaling her with a story about a friend's fortieth birthday party and had just reached the part about cutting into the X-rated cake.

"Barb told me she's concerned about your well-being. And I told her how sweet that was." He raised his glass. "To Barb and her everlasting sweetness." I tapped my drink against his. My stepmother ignored our tribute and took a healthy sip of sugar-laden soda.

"Seriously, Kara. I think you know why I'm here." She paused to cast a suspicious glance at the bubbly liquid, then gulped down a third of the beverage.

"I'm not sure," I lied. "I mean, we talk about so many things."

"Please. You know how worried your father and I have been about you. And now that the whole world can see how, how, uh, how troubled you are, we can't ignore the problem anymore."

"The whole world?" I'd been expecting her familiar refrain about how selfish it was of me to make my father worry so much and how could I not see how important it was for me to get help. But this wasn't that. As unlikely as it was my very non-technological stepmother had been surfing the web and stumbled onto my debut, I began to suspect she knew about the video.

"Maybe not the world but certainly my entire tennis team."

So, one of those skinny bitches had somehow seen me on YouTube and rushed to share the good news with Barb. I picked up my glass and gulped the remainder of my drink, wishing I'd gone with more vodka.

Chapter 3

When my stepmother threatened to show the video to my father, I capitulated. It wasn't fear of his disapproval or of embarrassing him. And it had nothing to do with worrying about jeopardizing our relationship since after my mother's death, we barely had one. As a ten-year-old, I assumed it was his distaste for me rather than his all-consuming grief and survivor's guilt that made him disappear from my life. Now I understood how easy it could be to get lost in loss.

We hadn't experienced a handholding kumbaya moment, but I had begun to see my father in a different light. He seemed proud of my success as an author although I doubted he read any of my books. And for the first time in my adult life, I hoped we might find a way to connect. The sight of me devolving into an out-of-control supermarket freak would most likely end that possibility.

So, I let Barb make an appointment for me with Dr. Simon Riley, a psychiatrist who specialized in grief. I was skeptical of someone who sought the company of depressed losers, but she assured me he had impeccable credentials.

"And Tiffany says he's absolutely wonderful."

"Who the hell is Tiffany?"

"Tiffany Elliott from my tennis team."

"Oh, well, if she's on your tennis team, then it's okay you shared my mental health with her."

"There's no need to get nasty, dear. Tiffany is brand new. And, honestly, I can't believe we got so lucky. At UCLA, she ranked number four. She moved to Atlanta from Charleston, so don't worry about her being a West Coast liberal. Frankly, you should be thankful to her since she's the one who spotted you on YouTube."

"Yes, Barb. I am deeply indebted to the woman already."

"I'm serious. Any of the other girls would have spread the news throughout the entire club. But Tiffany's not someone who enjoys airing dirty laundry. She's very discreet."

"Exactly how does this woman know the good doctor? Because if she has her own mental issues, I'm not sure we should trust her recommendation."

"She knew him when he was in a different line of work." Barb dusted invisible debris off her black pants.

"What kind of work?"

She crossed, then uncrossed her legs. "All right, already. He was a priest."

"A what?"

"I know you don't like priests, but everyone says he's very down to earth, not at all holier than thou."

There was no reason to point out he had to be a good deal holier than me or to explain that I didn't dislike priests. I just didn't trust them. But I was also drawn to them.

Early in my relationship with Michael, I revealed my odd obsession with priests after he confessed he was a lapsed Catholic. I told him how their piety incited me with the need to bare my soul and reveal all my dirty little secrets in a sensual cleansing of spirit. How their denial of the flesh made them conversely desirable, as if they'd thrown down some sexual gauntlet.

He laughed and said he pitied any priest I decided to seduce. Then we resumed dealing with our own desires.

As this was not something I cared to discuss, I went along with Barb's plan, while formulating one of my own. I would see the doctor a few times, convince him I was progressing appropriately on the grief continuum and get him to sign off on my improved mental health, then return to my life. I injected a note of enthusiasm into my voice when Barb called to say she had booked a session for the next week.

•   •   •

Since my husband's death, I rarely slept through the night. Snatched from warm dreams of my pre-loss life, those happy images vaporized as I bolted awake. With traces of tears on my cheeks, I would lie there shivering, unable to return to sleep.

On the day of my appointment, I woke up a little after 4:00 a.m. It wasn't because frigid hands yanked me from my walk through the park with Michael. It was because of the unearthly howls coming from my back yard.

I'm not terrified of dogs to the point of being phobic, but I do respect the beasts. This one was a ferocious-looking German shepherd named Rex. Both his owner, my eighty-six-year-old neighbor Ira Portman, and Michael, who loved animals, had assured me he was a good boy with a gentle disposition. Even Andy chimed in, calling me a wuss. But I kept a safe distance from the creature.

From my bedroom window, I spotted the dog. Illuminated by his back-porch light, his frantic cries had stopped. He stood in total silence, with his muzzle pointed toward the far corner of my yard. His stillness frightened me more than his furor. I followed his gaze to the thicket of ivy outside my fence. The leaves rippled, then closed behind the path of whatever had disturbed the greenery and sent Rex into spasms of fury.

I hurried downstairs to the kitchen and stepped onto the deck. At the sound of the sliding glass door, the dog whimpered and turned toward me. He stared at me for several seconds, as if trying to share some primal form of communication. Possibly sensing my inability to understand him, he looked away first, then loped off and disappeared through his doggy entrance.

Other than the low buzz of cicadas, there was nothing. A veil of uneasiness settled over me, and I hurried inside. I couldn't shake the feeling the video of me flipping out at the grocery store hadn't been random at all. Sometime around seven I fell asleep, troubled by dreams of shadowy figures lurking on the edge of my property.

•　　•　　•

At 8:30 my alarm jarred me awake. Still rattled from my moment with Rex, I rummaged through my underwear drawer until I found the can of pepper spray Andy had given me for Christmas. I held it tight as I checked each room for signs of an intruder. I looked out the window to see if the dog was outside. He wasn't nor was there any sign of an unwanted visitor.

I tried to convince myself I was being paranoid, but when I left the house, I stuck the can in my purse.

I arrived thirty minutes early with paperwork printed from the doctor's website. The more straight-forward section of the form, the generic sort you find on most physicians' checklists, was a breeze. A bit of an overachiever, I enjoyed saying no to all the negative factors, such as smoking, heart disease, and high blood pressure. I fudged a little on the question about alcohol consumption. How could I say how many drinks I consumed on an average week when I no longer knew what such a week looked like?

The mental health section was more of a challenge. If I responded honestly to questions, such as what brings you to therapy and what do you expect to get from the experience, I would have said my overbearing stepmother and getting my overbearing stepmother off my back. But then the doctor might conclude I was being resistant and double-down on making me normal again. And wasn't that a hopeless cause? My normal disappeared when Michael died.

So, I accepted the role of cooperative patient. I gritted my teeth and provided the kind of answers someone who believes in the possibility of life after loss might give. I admitted to having trouble sleeping and experiencing mild depression and anxiety. I explained my situation under "additional comments."

> An unknown assailant shot and killed my husband, who was on his way to the grocery store because we were almost out of his favorite cereal, and I forgot to pick up a box.

I could have added what a fine person Michael was. How he brought me coffee in bed every morning and always over-tipped, even if the service was lousy. I could have written about his volunteer work at the shelter for homeless vets and our plan to collaborate on telling the stories of those forgotten soldiers. Then I would have to explain how I never looked at any of Michael's notes and how that failure compounded my guilt, but the space was too limited for a rambling pity-party.

When I stepped into the doctor's office, a collage of beiges and browns overwhelmed me—walls, carpet, furniture. I suspected the design was intended to lull potentially violent clients into a compliant frame of mind. A broad-shouldered woman who looked to be in her mid-thirties sat behind a desk, partially camouflaged by the earthy shades of her tanned skin and caramel-colored hair. Fingers flying over the keyboard, she remained glued to the screen in front of her.

I cleared my throat. She continued typing.

After waiting a few seconds, I said, "Excuse me" and dropped my folder beside her computer.

She held up an index finger, sighed and turned toward me, lips set in an expression of irritation bordering on hostility. Her features settled so quickly into a mask of ennui I thought I had imagined the antagonism. Or could this be the initial part of my consultation, a test to see if I sensed malice when it wasn't there?

Determined not to fall for any possible tricks of the analysis trade, I plastered a bright smile on my face and said, "I'm Kara Dolan here to—"

"He's with someone now but shouldn't be much longer. Please, take a seat."

I sat on one of the straight-back leather chairs and fidgeted with the hem of my skirt, wishing I'd gone with slacks in case I had to lie down on a couch. I had the irrational need to make this woman, who seemed to find me annoying, change her mind, to see my charming self. Before I could mount my campaign to win her over, she returned to her screen.

I flipped through a stack of *Psychology Today* magazines on the coffee table and selected one featuring an article on how to choose a therapist. I'd just gotten to the part about how a person's relationship with her physician requires a kind of chaste intimacy when I heard movement from the inner office. A door closed with a soft thud—probably a privacy exit to stop the loonies from mingling.

Seconds later, the door on my side opened.

"Sorry to keep you waiting, Mrs. Dolan."

I gasped and closed my eyes. This deep, solemn voice was so like the one that had flowed throughout the church, casting oil on a sea of shuddering sobs. It blanketed us with comfort as we said our final goodbyes to Michael at his funeral.

Chapter 4

"Are you all right, Mrs. Dolan?"

I opened my eyes, no longer in the sanctuary where the soothing voice offered false comfort.

"Yes, I am. All right, that is and Mrs. Dolan. Only it's Kara, please." Michael's farewell party faded.

"It's nice to meet you." He extended his hand.

I wondered if I should shake it and what it might say about me when I didn't.

"I'm Dr. Riley." No first name for him, I noted—chaste, but not particularly intimate. "Please, come in."

Larger than I expected, the room featured a worn Persian rug in dark shades of rose and blue covering most of the hardwood floor. The obligatory therapy couch sat across from a wall of bookshelves, filled with titles like *Narrative Means to Therapeutic Ends* and *Diagnostic and Statistical Manual of Mental Illness.*

Dr. Riley was handsome in that conventional, non-threatening way only men of a certain age can pull off. Dark hair threaded with enough silver to give him credibility, deep-set brown eyes below a furrowed forehead, high-bridged nose, straight white teeth that suggested a keen awareness of personal hygiene.

Those teeth flashed in a well-practiced professional smile. "Please have a seat while I review your file." He motioned to a black leather chair, then brushed past me to sit on the other side of his desk, leaving a trail of musky aftershave in his wake.

Nodding, I gave him my own practiced smile, intended to radiate sanity and self-control, then sat quietly as he began reading through my information.

I imagined him as a black-robed figure peering through a crack in the sliding window of a confessional booth.

Although he was nothing like my husband, something about the intensity of his expression made me think of Michael, specifically the night we ended up in bed together. Naked and breathless, I had been filled with the need to validate our physical intimacy with the exchange of as many details about ourselves as we could fit into the time we weren't exploring each other's bodies.

"Mrs. Dolan?" The rich tones of my confessor interrupted my carnal thoughts, and a rush of heat ignited my cheeks.

"Sorry. I'm afraid I've been a bit out of it since, uh...." I still had trouble saying the words aloud, difficulty choosing between *since Michael died* or *since I lost my husband* or more dramatically *since the murder*.

"Perfectly natural reaction, compounded by the circumstances of your husband's death."

He smiled again and paused long enough for me to anticipate his next question, the one everyone had been asking me for the past eight months. The question those of us who have been torn apart by grief come to dread.

How are you?

The first few times someone asked me, I gave the inquiry the careful consideration I assumed it deserved. I was angry and sad and inexplicably overridden with shame. The idea of performing ordinary activities like brushing my teeth or fixing a sandwich overwhelmed me. I didn't want to be alone, but I couldn't stand being around anyone. I was drowning in sand.

After a few unsuccessful attempts to put these emotions into words, I came to understand the question was rhetorical. And I answered I was fine, yes, really.

But that wasn't what Dr. Riley wanted to know. Not exactly.

He asked, "Where are you right this minute on the grief spectrum?"

I had to stop my go-to reply of *I feel fine* when I realized he'd slipped me a trick question. I caught myself and said, "I'm not sure what you mean."

"People grieve in different ways. Most follow the five stages: denial, anger, bargaining, depression, acceptance. Some doctors view them as linear, but I don't think it's as simple as that. My theory is you can be depressed and angry at the same time. And that you could accept your situation one day and try to bargain away your pain the next. I prefer asking my patients where they are at the exact moment I ask the question."

"Right now?" I stalled. "Well, I guess you could say I'm not on any spectrum." I watched him for signs of disappointment or frustration, but he only nodded and scribbled more notes, giving me time to revise my response. Did I sound cold-hearted, as if my love had been too weak to register on some stupid scale?

"That's not quite right," I added. "It's just that five stages aren't enough. There should be one for being numb." And for being too exhausted to turn over in bed. And one for crazy echoes of partial conversations no one else can hear.

The scratch of his pen across the paper was the only sound in the room. Jesus, what was the man writing and would he ever speak to me again? Well, two could play at the quiet game; I determined not to be the one to break the silence.

After what seemed like forever, he looked up but said nothing. He kept his face neutral, impossible to read. I blinked first.

"Is that okay? Numbness, I mean. Because I don't always feel that way. Sometimes I'm pissed, really pissed." *Like now, sitting here with Mr. Stoneface.*

"Hmm, hmm," he murmured, adding another notation.

I expected him to ask who had angered me and had the reasonable answer ready. I was furious with Michael's murderer and bitter toward the police who had given up on finding the killer. But it was difficult to direct anger at anonymous sources. So, if I were being totally transparent, which I had no intention of being, I would have said it was my husband who filled me with inexplicable rage.

I had to hand it to Riley, though. He wasn't predictable. He ignored my admission of anger and said, "I see you're a published author. Are you currently working on another novel?"

I envisioned the first few chapters of the fourth Garnet Rivers novel I hadn't touched since Michael's death and almost admitted I might never return to it.

Instead, I lied. "I am, actually. I'm not sure where it's going, though. But I'll get there. I always do." I tried to stop talking, but something about his demeanor stimulated elaboration.

"I'm playing around with having my main character fall in love with a police detective, which would be a problem because she isn't exactly a law-abiding citizen." I smiled at the absurdity of my rebellious protagonist being attracted to a cop.

"That's very interesting."

Unsure if he meant my fake plot line or something deeper, I resumed my dissembling. "I hope so. I mean, I hope my readers will like it. I've been lucky so far. Because Garnet does things most women—most of my readers are women—want to do but are afraid to try. At least, I think that's the reason, but who knows?"

I stopped for breath, expecting him to offer an opinion about my popularity with ordinary women who wished they weren't and to ask me if I belonged to that group, but he only nodded. A trickle of sweat slipped between my shoulder blades.

"And there's the project my husband and I were working on. Sort of a human-interest piece about the homeless center where he volunteered, something he said might not change the whole world but could improve our corner of it. Michael was like that, idealistic and somewhat unrealistic, but very determined. It will be challenging to finish it without him, especially since it's my first attempt at non-fiction. But he had already done a lot of the groundwork: interviews, data collecting, stuff like that. And I've been doing a little research on my own, too."

My only research had been to Google St. Cecilia's and homelessness among veterans. And I'd been unable to retain much of it.

I feared I might erupt into what my grandmother would have called a hissy-fit if the doctor continued his silence. Thankfully, I noticed a slight uptick of his brows at the mention of the unrealized writing project.

"Tackling something like that on your own might be very stressful. But picking up with something not quite as taxing, perhaps lighter, could be a very effective way to cope with your grief."

I was trying not to take offense at his patronizing tone when a whisper in my ear stopped me.

Isn't it amazing how Dr. Know-it-all assumes he can kiss it and make it all better?

I whipped my head from side to side, searching for the source of the unknown, yet somehow familiar, voice.

"Are you all right?"

If you were, you'd be lying on the beach sucking on a pina colada.

From the expression on his face, it was obvious he hadn't been included in the conversation. I kept my eyes fixed on a spot on the wall behind him and said, "I'm good, thanks. You could be right. Sticking with the familiar might help me cope."

Now I was the one slinging bullshit because I agreed with my invisible friend. Insinuating I wasn't up to the task of fulfilling a promise to my husband was beyond condescending—unless it was true. But no. It wasn't true, and I would prove it. I would write that damn story.

"That's excellent."

"And you should know, I've already started coping—all over the place, actually. People say I'm quite the coper."

"Mmm, hmm. It sounds that way. As I said, establishing a routine is a positive step. But I would think writing could be solitary work, lonely even."

"I guess."

"I'd like to help you develop some new routines, establish some patterns that are less isolating. Perhaps get you involved with a support group."

I shuddered as I remembered the grief counseling session Barb had talked me into attending. I had tried to empathize with stories of loss from the ten or so damaged women surrounding me. Instead of identifying with their pain, however, I found myself floating above the circle, wondering what I could have in common with this broken little group.

The only piece of wisdom I took from that visit was that the death of a loved one permanently changes a person. The violence of my loss had turned me into someone I no longer recognized.

My expression must have reflected my lack of enthusiasm for the idea.

"We don't have to rush into anything." He paused to thumb through my paperwork. "The anxiety and depression you're experiencing is perfectly normal. Some even have bouts of extreme paranoia. They feel as if someone is watching them or that others are out to get them. I'd like to prescribe a mild antidepressant as well as an anti-anxiety prescription. You'll take both in the evening. The combination will make you feel more like yourself, plus it will help you sleep better."

Unable to remember what being myself was like, I allowed the idea of sleeping through the night to seduce me into abandoning my aversion to taking medication. I eagerly bobbed my head up and down.

"Good. We'll get you started and schedule a follow-up visit to see how you're doing." He reached for a spiral notepad on the corner of his desk. I questioned his use of paper instead of computer and decided it might have something to do with confidentiality.

I pictured him sleeping with the notebook under his pillow.

"I don't have an opening at ten. Would next Monday at 1:00 work?"

I smiled and said what a cooperative patient would say. "Whatever you think is best."

"Very good." He stood and came from behind the desk. "Remember, Kara, the grieving process skews thinking. It's like driving through a black, winding tunnel. I want to help you navigate your path and guide you toward the light. I can keep you from ending up in a very dark place." He put his hand on my back and ushered me to the privacy exit. Before he closed the door, he added, "All you have to do is trust me."

Chapter 5

Sun streamed through the leaves, creating a brilliant blind spot across my windshield. I slowed down, sat up taller, and adjusted the visor. Dr. Riley hadn't been as intrusive as I expected. Despite my distrust of anti-everything meds, he had been successful in getting me to agree to taking drugs. At least, I kept quiet about my most recent neurosis, the voice in my head. Still, our session had been so unsettling I raced to my car and drove with no thought of my destination.

After what must have been about twenty minutes, I arrived at the one spot Michael's memory hadn't overshadowed, a place where I might be safe from my disturbed psyche—Briarpatch Book Shop. Tucked in a strip shopping center in downtown Woodstock, the store was the site of the launch for all three of my Garnet Rivers books.

I parked directly in front, experiencing the same rush as six years ago when *Hidden Jewels* was first released. Like today, I arrived a little after eleven. Then I was psyched about seeing my name on the shelf beside my favorite authors. Now it was because I needed a place to hide from the intensity of emotions still lingering from my visit with Riley.

I was halfway out of the car when my cell vibrated. It was Andy, probably calling to see how I fared with the good doctor. I considered hitting *ignore* but knew he would keep trying until I answered.

"Hey." I never worried about injecting simulated cheer into my greeting to him. He didn't need or expect it and wouldn't have bought it if I had tried to sound lighthearted.

"How's my little celebrity this morning? Did the doctor cleanse you of all evil thoughts and reshape you into an upstanding citizen?"

"Can I call you back? I'm busy right now."

"Oh, my God. Are you still with Dr. Who's-it? Is he holding you against your will? Shout *pineapple* if the answer's yes and I'll come break you out."

"Hold the Cavalry," I responded. "I'm just doing a little shopping."

"If you say so. But don't think you're going to escape a thorough cross-examination about your soon-to-be-all better mental health. Love you."

He hung up before I could return the sentiment.

I stuck the phone back in my purse and was close to the entrance of the store when a gust of cool air brought the hair on my arms into an upright position. Only it wasn't a breeze. It was more of a sensory signal alerting me something was off. I pivoted, then tried to look nonchalant while surveying the cars in the lot.

If someone was stealing glances at me, he had disappeared. More likely I was reacting to Riley's suggestion that people in situations like mine had episodes of paranoia. Maybe that explained my early morning unease when I made eye contact with Rex. And it could explain why I'd heard a voice that Riley hadn't.

I rubbed against the rising goosebumps, then entered the bookstore. The bell above the door announced my presence. From behind the register, a white-haired woman wearing wire-rimmed glasses and a big smile welcomed me.

"Good morning. Let me know if I can help you."

I smiled and told her I was just looking. Usually, I take my time meandering through new releases. Today, I went straight to the mystery section.

My last book, *The River Runs Red*, was released over a year ago, but the owner still displayed a copy on the shelf next to other stories with kick-ass female protagonists. I removed it and admired the cover. Below the title, cascading water swirled in between sharp-edged boulders where a woman's torn, blood-stained dress dangled from an overhanging branch.

In the bottom right-hand corner, K.E. Conway appeared in bold black letters and underneath that in smaller print was a banner reading *Another Garnet Rivers Adventure*. My agent insisted initials made me mysterious. I traced each letter with my index finger, marveling at how seeing my name on the cover of a book never failed to amaze me.

Also, although I fought the idea at first, I never tired of looking at myself on the back. The photographer performed a minor feat of magic by capturing a natural smile instead of my usual grimace. My dark brown curls glistened with highlights—some real, some photo-shopped—and framed my face, enhancing blue eyes shining with pre-murder hopefulness.

Before meeting Michael, being published was everything to me. I wasn't the kind of girl who saw what she wanted and simply took it. Too polite to push my way to the front of the line, by the time I got there, women like Garnet had emptied the shelves. But the night I met my husband, I hadn't been my usual well-mannered self.

●   ●   ●

Sitting across from the accountant Barb had coerced me into meeting, I fantasized about how my heroine would have handled my date's assertion that most females needed professional help managing money, and I was no different. I drew a complete blank as my intrepid avenger would never have been browbeaten into spending an evening with such an insipid ass.

Apparently, my date mistook the glazed expression in my eyes as an invitation to the squeeze my knee.

I slapped his hand, and dark red wine sloshed into his ravioli. I slid from the table as he was trying to sop up the liquid with a roll.

I removed two twenties from my wallet, crumpled them into a ball and dropped them in the soupy pasta mix. "Manage that, asshole."

Then I turned and walked toward the exit, careening into Michael. We didn't fall together like the stars of a cute-meet romance-movie. Instead of melting into his arms, I bounced off the door frame and slammed into him, catching my heel in the cuff of his pants. I lost my shoe, missed the step, and was on my way down. He caught me by my stretchy-braided belt and I bungeed for a second before stumbling against him.

"Are you alright?"

After I assured him I was fine, he released me and stooped to pick up my shoe. Before I could answer, he dropped to one knee and held out the high-heeled pump, Prince Charming style.

Although I was not the Cinderella type, I found the gesture charming and rested my hand on his shoulder as I eased into the slipper. When he stood, I leaned close to him to thank him and introduce myself. If I'd been my Kara-self, that might have been the end of the story. I would have been too afraid of rejection to ask a handsome stranger to join me for a drink. But Garnet never imagined any man would refuse an invitation from her, so she asked Michael.

It was also Garnet who, after several drinks, brought him back to my apartment, and Garnet who led him straight to the bedroom where she began undressing him before he returned the favor. But during the early stages of touching and kissing, my alter-ego vanished. It might have been my sexy heroine who got Michael into my bed, but I was the one who kept him there.

•   •   •

Memories of our first encounter left me feeling hollow. I tried to fill the emptiness by buying four novels from local authors and a copy of *Cold as Ice,* the second book in the Garnet series. More from superstition than ego, I never leave a bookstore without purchasing at least one of my own books.

On the way to the car, a sliver of my earlier uneasiness returned, as if I brushed against an invisible spider web. I reached into my purse and closed my fingers around the can of pepper spray, certain I would find someone standing behind me. But there was only an extremely pregnant woman, dragging her protesting toddler by the arm. I hated to admit it even to myself, but Barb might have a point about my shaky state of being.

As I opened my car door, the voice returned. It was soft and sultry and so real it tickled my ear. This time, I knew who it belonged to.

I don't trust anything but my instincts. They never let me down.

I dropped my rape-whistle key chain and whipped my head in the direction of my heroine's words, half expecting to see her standing there, "raven hair cascading over her shoulders and grazing the top of her firm breasts."

There was no one. I scrambled to pick up the keys, hopped into the car, and slammed the door. I often imagined how Garnet would sound with the velvety, just-been-ravished voice I had assigned her. But I'd never *heard* her speak.

I closed my eyes and tried to picture the pages of *Hidden Jewels,* the book that contained the advice my character had so unexpectedly delivered. Mind-thumbing through the novel, I called up the scene. In search of a dangerous blood-diamond smuggler, she seduced an Interpol agent. While they were lying together after having hot sex that faded to black before I ventured into the messy technical details of intercourse, he suggested they work together and promised she could trust him.

Other than falling into bed with Michael, I seldom relied on instincts. And even then, it was Garnet who dictated the scene. Only that wasn't completely true. I let her take over for me the night I met my husband, but I'd chosen when I wanted to be back in charge.

This was different. Today, she came unbidden and in control.

Shaken at the realization my creation had made an auditory appearance, I wondered if the rest of my characters would soon chime like a Greek chorus. Garnet's lover would have a deeply seductive tone, but how would her abusive father sound?

I was so absorbed in the possibilities, I almost forgot to stop at the drugstore. Despite my initial resistance to medicating my grief into submission, I thought it might not be a bad idea to lie back and let modern pharmaceuticals work their magic. My heroine's sexy whisper, as she delivered my lines, affirmed the possibility I might need heavy drugs.

When the pharmacist handed me the little white bags full of pills and warnings, I stuffed them in my purse as quickly as possible and hurried to the exit. In my haste to avoid running into someone I knew, I ran into someone I didn't: a heavy-set man in dark sunglasses. He attempted to walk through the sliding glass door at the same time I did. The collision was nothing like my encounter with Michael, but we did become entangled. In the process of untangling, the contents of my purse and his shopping bag ended up on the floor.

"Whoa there, sistuh. Where you goin' in such a rush?"

The low, rumbling voice with its northern undertones was disorienting, as if I'd been transported to the Jersey shore.

If the man scrambling to retrieve his purchases had once been a Guido, those days were long gone. In some distant past, his back and shoulders could have been worthy of being oiled and exposed on a crowded beach. Now, a layer of fat rippled beneath his thin polyester golf shirt. A beam of fluorescent light bounced off the top of his head where shiny, pink scalp had conquered whatever thick gelled hair might have once reigned. He was just another unsuspecting obstacle the universe seemed to enjoy throwing in my path. This time, neither Garnet nor I were in the mood for romance.

"It was my fault. I should have been paying attention." I took a quick inventory to make sure I hadn't missed picking up an expensive lipstick or a Macy's coupon. That's when I noticed the name on the prescriptions wasn't mine. Before I could read more than the first two initials, R and U, he snatched it out of my hands.

"Looks like we might have gotten our stuff all mixed up." His thick caterpillar eyebrows wriggled as he thumbed through the bags in his oversized paw. "Here we go." He held up my prescriptions and added, "I think these are yours."

My fingers brushed across his furry knuckles as I backed away.

"Thank you," I said and fast-walked out of the store. It wasn't until I was in the parking lot that I became aware I'd been holding my breath. I rationalized my overreaction to this stranger as nothing more than a reflection of the paranoia Riley had mentioned, heightened by the impossibility of Garnet speaking to me.

That logic didn't stop me from turning to see which way he had gone. I should have been reassured when I didn't see him behind me or anywhere else. But the idea a man of his bulk had disappeared from an open lot made me pick up my pace.

Chapter 6

By the time I reached the townhouse my husband and I bought two months before our first anniversary, I was less distressed than disheartened, as if I'd surrendered—to what I couldn't say.

I entered through the kitchen, ignoring the high-tech alarm system Michael had installed. The week after his funeral, I disarmed it and never bothered trying to reset it. Voices drifting from the living room startled me. But it was only the host of *Family Feud,* revving up the rivalry between opposing sides, coming from the TV I left on more often than not. I trudged upstairs.

On the way my shoulder brushed against one of the framed pictures of me and Michael that lined the stairwell in crooked clusters. Compulsive about perfectly aligned arrangements, I hadn't been able to bring myself to touch, much less straighten, these images of the life I once had.

Some were candid shots of me: cooking, writing, sitting in the sun. Others were professional: engagement photos of a happy couple, a few wedding pictures. The happiness we exuded was a jeering reminder of what I lost, so I kept my eyes fixed on the top stair when I passed them.

Today I felt compelled to look at my favorite. Taken at the beach on the last day of our honeymoon, Michael's hair was longer than usual, flipping up just below his ears. He smiles at the camera with his arm around my waist. I'm smiling, too, but not at the camera. Wild curls blowing away from my face, I'm looking up at my new husband as if there were no one else in the world.

The frame was out of line with neighboring pictures, but when I reached out to adjust it, I hesitated, then placed a fingertip on Michael's cheek and traced his upturned lips.

The cool glass encasing this memory warmed under my touch, and I drew back my hand. The air didn't turn pink and fuzzy, but there was a lightness around me as if I'd ascended to a higher altitude, one that made me dizzy. I shut my eyes and when I opened them, the sensation vanished.

Instead of going straight to the guest room, I walked to the bedroom Michael and I once shared and sat on the king-sized bed, trying to determine if what I'd felt was real or imagined. I didn't believe in communication with the dead but had been jealous of people who did. Several women in my one-time only grief group told stories of times when their lost loved ones came to them with unspoken messages from the Great Beyond. One claimed she had seen her husband pulling weeds in the garden. Another caught her son's reflection in her backyard pond.

Their special recollections saddened me at first, filled me with sorrow at my failure to be someone who demanded eternal devotion. Then they had angered me. Surely, I deserved at least a nod from my departed husband. I decided the women were the victims of a self-perpetuated hoax.

Had my hostility deafened me to Michael's voice or worse, frightened him away? Was I too closed-up to possibilities beyond what I could understand? What did it matter when I couldn't handle those that I did?

I smoothed the floral spread Michael had protested purchasing. It was too frilly, too feminine. He gave in easily, though, as he had in so many things. I pressed my palm on the spot where he had slept, thinking that, like the picture, it might ignite some change in the room and in me. But it held no warmth, and the atmosphere remained the same.

Next, I went to the guestroom. The bed there was smaller and less comfortable than the king-size one. But the space beside me had been so vast, I feared I might lose myself in it.

Fighting the urge to return to my unmade bed, I tugged the sheet and blanket into place, then pulled the comforter over it. I tossed decorative pillows at the headboard and stepped back. I read the simple action of tidying your sleeping area sets a positive tone for the day. The act did nothing to improve my mood, but I thought I would slip this detail into my next session with Dr. Riley as evidence of the new and improved me.

My stomach growled, reminding me I skipped breakfast. I scrambled and ate the last two eggs in my refrigerator and was loading the dishwasher when disco queen Donna Summers began singing "She works hard for the money." It was my agent.

"Hey, Wan—"

"Kara, have you looked at the comments on your site?"

As usual, she wasted no time with pleasantries. Before Michael's death, I found her businesslike manner unnerving. Now I liked the way she got directly to the point.

"I was just getting ready to."

I tempered my lie by opening my laptop and logging in. Sparkling jewels in various shades of red were sprinkled throughout the home page where the picture from my book cover appeared along with a brief bio, the covers of my novels, and a link to the blog that had been an area of contention between us, as I considered it a waste of valuable writing time.

"Why would anyone want to read my inspiration for creating Garnet or what I have for brunch?"

"It's important to connect with the people who love your books, especially the women who need a Garnet in their lives," Wanda responded.

Even though I had known she was playing to my weakness, her reference to readers who needed to relate to someone who didn't take crap from anyone, worked. Probably because I knew exactly how they felt.

Turned out blogging wasn't easy. It was difficult developing content that engaged fans without flooding them with trivia. Wanda assured me I didn't need to post daily or even weekly, just frequently enough to remind fans I cared.

"And if you run out of ideas, I'll put Todd on it." Poor Todd, as everyone referred to him, had been her assistant for years. Tall and slender with a receding hairline, he had the look of an anemic English professor from a BBC mystery set in Oxford or Cambridge or some other lofty academic location. Rumor had it he started work on a literary novel during his post-graduate days and was well into five hundred pages with no end in sight.

Wanda kept him busy reading submissions and occasionally put him in charge of coordinating book launches and other author events. The few times I'd met him he'd been polite, but distant. And even though she insisted he loved my writing, I got a slightly condescending vibe from him, like he was more than a little offended at having to represent work with absolutely no literary value.

I declined my agent's offer to let him help with my blog and wrote posts explaining that while I had created the character, she had taken on a life of her own. I confessed that sometimes it was as if she were telling her own story. I didn't share that there were times when I couldn't remember writing the escapades that appeared on my screen. And I would not be adding the recent tidbit of Garnet whispering not-so-sweet nothings into my ear.

Most of the time, I enjoyed the comments and requests for advice on everything from fashion to sex. As K.E. Conway, I was at a loss about how to respond to these queries. But Garnet knew, and she seemed to love helping readers decide what to wear to attract sexy lovers or dump unfaithful ones.

Like most people with an online presence, I received plenty of negative feedback.

Some of my more conservative fans wanted Garnet to clean up her act. Usually, this category of critics was prissy, but polite.

I really like Garnet, but couldn't she be a little less promiscuous?

I was also polite in my answers to these comments, explaining that my character was beyond labels. That her mission was to free women from judgment. If they persisted in church-lady rebukes, I blocked them.

Others were nastier.

Why do you keep mentioning Garnet's full, heaving breasts? Sounds like a personal problem. Could it be somebody needs a boob job?

I resisted sending what I considered my perfectly adequate measurements and blocked those kinds because it made me feel good.

"All right," I said. "I'm in. What am I looking for?"

"Scroll down to yesterday's posts and look for GarNetted."

"Okay, give me a minute." I found and read the response.

Ive tolerated your silence long enough. Now your trying my patience.

Your just being selfish. Your not the only one in pain you know.

"Well, she's definitely not an English major."

"Forget the goddamn grammar. It's the crazy that worries me. I think you should block her."

Although the tone was strident, the reference to pain made it hard for me to dismiss the comment. My angry commenter had a point. All-consuming grief is selfish. But if I shared it with others, I would have to let some of it go, and that would be too much like letting go of Michael.

"The part about me being selfish is pretty snarky," I said.

"Keep scrolling. There's more."

Dont you care about Garnet and the people who need her?
Its time someone reminded you of your duty. Why should your suffering
be more important than other peoples.

"The woman needs to get a life."

"I'm not so sure GarNetted is female."

Wanda warned me Garnet's blatant sexuality might attract an undesirable element—readers who used my heroine to stoke their fantasies, who blurred the line between character and author. And the messages lacked any hint of femininity. Especially the one reminding me about my *duty*.

"Either way, we need to do something about it. I say block him or her or whatever." She cleared her throat before adding, "Unless you have gotten into the fourth book. In that case, you could give the sick-o a little hint about your next story."

Not known for her patience, Wanda had been uncharacteristically sensitive about my lack of progress. She hadn't pushed for details or sent reminders of upcoming deadlines.

"I'm still working out the plotline."

"That's fine, hon. At least, you've gotten started."

"I suppose so, but I'm thinking of making some changes."

"Changes?" I could hear the frown in her voice. "I guess you could mix it up a little. Let Garnet fall for somebody. But don't change her too much or forget what your audience wants."

"I'm not talking about Garnet. I meant it might be time for me to make some changes in my life. Maybe switch careers altogether."

"Sweetie, being a writer's not a career; it's a condition. But it's too soon for you to be making big decisions or changes. I still think you should block GarNetted. Better yet, I can put Todd on it."

"No, I'll handle it." No reason to further agitate the woman with the possibility I might honor my promise to Michael and try my hand at non-fiction. "I can use the diversion."

"Speaking of diversion. I'll send you all I've got on the Roswell Crime Family?"

Shit! I'd completely forgotten the two-week workshop Wanda had talked me into teaching. When she first brought up what she called "an opportunity to expand my reading audience," I explained I didn't have the experience or patience to be a teacher. She assured me the group of mystery writers was looking more for a guide—someone to encourage them in their writing journey. I didn't see myself as that either but agreed to give it a try.

After Michael's death, Wanda offered to cancel the workshop, but I'd been trying to convince everyone, including myself, I was doing better. That there'd been a break in the fog of grief surrounding me. So, I told her I was looking forward to exploring the art of mystery writing with aspiring authors.

"No, I'm good to go," I lied for the second time in less than thirty minutes. "But thanks."

"No problem. And I'm going to keep an eye on that weirdo." I thanked her for being on top of the situation and hung up.

Not quite ready to deal with the unpleasant comments, I read through some of my own posts, stopping at the one I'd written after Michael and I eloped. Most of the responses were congratulatory ones from readers delighted by our run-away romance. Some of my fans confused me with my protagonist and assumed I would continue the series incorporating my marriage into the mix. They seemed to be unaware of the awkward nature of mixing my sex life with Garnet's or of the basic differences between the two of us. I had been puzzling over how to deal with the issue when Michael's death made it unnecessary.

At a loss for the best way to share how my husband's death had affected me, I had written a short message explaining he had been the victim of a shooting and provided links to the news stories about his murder.

Today, I began re-reading pages of so-sorry postings. Most were uncomplicated, but kind and didn't require a response.

Many included multiple emojis: crying faces, broken hearts, angels. All the silly little images on the page were jarring at first. Then I realized the women sent them to express sympathy and try to provide comfort, the online equivalent to chicken casseroles and pound cake.

The only comfort I'd found lately was the liquid kind, but when I checked the clock, it was only a little after one. If I started in on the wine this early on a Friday afternoon, I'd be teetering on the edge of a lost weekend.

Instead of alcohol, I turned to caffeine and made a cup of strong coffee. Then I began considering how I should respond to my disgruntled fan. The trick was to ignore the nasty tone of the message and write something reassuring. I needed to take the position that GarNetted enjoyed my work and was so eager to read the next book he'd become overly agitated. The problem was that I wasn't sure there was going to be another Garnet mystery.

It didn't seem like a good idea to mention that bit of information, though. I considered and rejected repeating the plot I fabricated for Dr. Riley. Misleading my therapist didn't bother me. It was his job to see through patient deception. But there was no satisfactory justification for being dishonest with a loyal reader. No, I would have to walk the line between tempered honesty and outright deceitfulness. Three drafts later, I came up with what I hoped would fit the bill.

> *It means the world to me that Garnet's fans miss her. I've been rethinking my original concept for her next adventure and have some serious rewriting ahead of me. Because my readers are so important to me, I want it to be perfect.*
>
> *I might need more of your patience.*
> *Thank you for loving Garnet as much as I do.*

I kept this exchange private, pretending it was to shield GarNetted from the ire of my more devoted readers. And in part, it was. But it was also to protect myself from the possibility those devotees might smell blood and turn on me.

Chapter 7

Monday morning, I caught my reflection in the mirrored walls of the rec center. The director had converted a dance studio into a makeshift classroom; the result was unsettling. Where willowy ballerinas should have been twirling, men and women drifted in and sat in ancient student desks arranged in neat rows. Once in place, they began setting up laptops or opening notebooks—all but one white-haired woman in the middle row. Instead of writing tools, she removed a ball of yarn from a canvas bag.

My anti-depressant had done nothing to improve my outlook, and I silently cursed Wanda for getting me into this situation. It didn't help that the lady began knitting and purling with the terrifying enthusiasm of Madam Defarge, Dicken's bloodthirsty French citizen. As heads rolled around her, the bitter harpy gleefully shouted, "Guillotine."

It was also distressing that I now realized the list I'd pulled from the internet, *Icebreakers That Don't Suck,* did. Guaranteed to be fun and funny, questions like "What kind of vegetable would you be?" or "What season are you and why?" were neither.

Cold beads of sweat gathered at my hairline, and I considered telling the group their instructor had come down with swine flu, but not to worry. A refund check was already in the mail.

Whenever I'm in front of a hostile audience, I imagine myself naked and poof! Goodbye hostility, hello happy.

Gripping the edge of the desk, I scanned the room to see if anyone else had heard Garnet's quip, one from my last novel when she explained how she dealt with a bunch of redneck meth dealers while solving the murder of a young girl.

It appeared nobody had. That didn't stop her suggestion I strip naked from bringing heat to my face and neck. I took deep, calming breaths and read through the opening speech I prepared late last night. Words that sounded confident and wise when I delivered them in front of my bathroom mirror became pompous and lame underneath the harsh fluorescent lights.

I shoved the paper aside and faced the class. Seemingly unaware of my existence, they kept laughing and talking.

"Good morning, everyone."

An eerie silence fell over the room as twenty-two—if my roster was accurate—pairs of eyes homed in on me. I squirmed under the particularly intense stare of a woman wearing tortoise-shell glasses. Something was oddly familiar about her, but I couldn't recall if we'd met. Her smooth brown hair framed a slender face; a few creases on her forehead and mouth suggested she was at least fifty, maybe older. Nothing was extraordinary about her appearance, except for an edgy wariness, as if she was in on a secret.

Now that I had everyone's attention, I no longer wanted it, but I decided all I could do was move on. Stepping from behind the scuffed wooden desk, I ad-libbed.

"Welcome, fellow writers." Totally cheesy, but no one groaned outwardly. "I'm Kara Dolan, aka K.E. Conway, author of the Garnet Rivers series. When my agent informed me the Roswell Crime Family was looking for someone to teach them about the art of mystery writing, I didn't think she meant me."

A few polite chuckles rippled through the group.

"I explained I wasn't qualified as a teacher, and my novels weren't exactly art. But she can be very persuasive, an excellent quality in an agent. So, I accepted your group's gracious offer, and now I'm looking forward to getting to know you through your writing."

I paused to smile and make eye contact. A good portion of the group looked like retirees; the rest were of indeterminate age and status. The thing I feared they might have in common was that they were all turning to me for inspiration.

I thumbed through my notes until I found the printouts from a site entitled "Selective Quotes on Detective Fiction."

"I don't know about any of you, but I didn't choose to be a mystery writer. I planned on writing literature with a capital *L*. But these dead bodies just kept showing up in my stories."

The laughter was less forced.

"The creator of Philo Vance, one of the first amateur sleuths, said, 'There must be a corpse in a detective novel, and the deader the corpse the better.' So, I embraced my identity as a mystery writer. More important, I stopped apologizing for it. I adopted the philosophy of the French author Jeanne Patrick Manchette: 'The crime novel is the great moral literature of our time.'"

Encouraged by the smiles, nods, and note taking, I continued.

"I don't see my novels as 'moral literature.' And reality isn't made up of tidy endings. In reality, many mysteries never get solved. As authors, though, we make our own rules. We can expose evil and set things right. Because that's what people want, isn't it? What they need?"

Surprised at the intensity of my delivery, the image of Michael, lying lifeless in the store parking lot, came to me. How would an author go about making that better? I shook my head and changed the subject.

"Enough about me and my writing. I want you to tell me why you chose to write about murder and mayhem."

There was a brief silence, then a silver-haired man near the back caught my eye, and I pounced.

I nodded in his direction. "Please introduce yourself and your motive for exploring the dark side of humanity."

He hesitated a second before saying he was Howard Pemberton, a retired homicide detective. "People told me I should write about what I'm familiar with. Unfortunately, I know a bit about real-life crimes that didn't get solved, bad guys that got away with murder. But in my book, the good guys always win."

Hands shot up like quills on a porcupine as they began sharing stories that ran the gamut between falling in love with the Hardy Boys to developing an obsession with missing mafia figures.

While they talked, I stole a glance at the prompt I found on a creative writing site.

Describe your favorite place. Explain why it's important to you. Include how going there changes you.

I was about to end the discussion and ask the class to respond to the tired, but safe topic when the sound of soft, throaty laughter stopped me.

Are you asking people to talk about their happy places in public? You are a naughty girl.

I suppressed a giggle; then it hit me my creation had gone rogue, inserting opinions I hadn't given her. It was possible I was coming unhinged. Possibly a subject for Dr. Riley if I kept my next appointment with him. But for now, I had to admit, Garnet had a point. I ditched the topic and went a little rogue myself.

"I would guess most of you have a project you're working on, and I respect that. After this one, I won't be assigning random writing prompts, but I'd like to get to know each of you beyond the usual *My name is* and *I enjoy knitting*." I smiled at Madame Defarge. She didn't drop a stitch. I continued. "What I would like is a slow reveal. I want you to create a short mystery starring you."

Varying levels of confusion flitted across the faces in front of me, and I couldn't blame them. I didn't know where the idea had come from, much less how to clarify it.

A tiny woman with faded blonde hair held in place by a girlish headband raised her hand. She had been quiet during the earlier discussion, swiveling back and forth in reaction to the comments of her colleagues as if they were players in a tennis match. I nodded to her.

"What if there's nothing mysterious about you?" she asked.

"Good question."

If not for my husband's murder, my story would have been wonderfully uncomplicated, maybe even dull. "Sorry, I'm still learning names. Yours is?"

"Betty. Betty Frazier. And my life is an open book."

More like an unopened one, gathering dust on the shelf.

Garnet had returned, along with her signature snarkiness. As usual, my heroine was right. Betty was remarkably unremarkable. I shook my head to clear my protagonist from my mind.

"I don't believe you," I fibbed. "I bet there's more to your story than you realize. But no worries. I'm not asking you to dig into your psyches for deep, dark secrets. Although I do love a juicy secret."

A few people snickered, but Betty's expression stayed pained.

"You can write about anything you want. An event that changed your viewpoint about someone or something you believed in. Or a time when you wish you could undo your actions or take action. And it doesn't have to be true."

"Basically then, you're asking us to lie to you?" The question, which sounded more like an indictment than a request for clarification, came from the woman I thought I'd seen before. "I'm Louisa Carter. Unless you want me to make up an alias." She removed her glasses and narrowed her eyes.

Several students chuckled, but I didn't think Louisa Carter was a person to be taken lightly.

I cleared my throat and responded, "No, please use your real names. And isn't fiction stylized lying to reveal the truth? That's why the fiction we write can disclose more about us than if we were writing an autobiography."

I held my breath, anticipating more hostility, but Louisa seemed satisfied.

A boy from the back of the class spoke up. "Is it okay to use our laptops?"

"Since we don't have access to a printer, we'll have to go old school. My handwriting is the worst, but I like paper and ink for journaling. I had the most beautiful brass pen. It's silly but writing with it inspired me. Sadly, I lost it." No need to mention my inspiration had disappeared as well.

After the publication of my second novel, Michael gave me the pen, insisting I needed something more elegant for my book signings. When I confessed I lost his gift, he smiled and promised to buy me a Montblanc when I completed the Garnet series.

The room had grown still during my mental side-trip. I forced a smile and asked if there were any more questions. Other than a few about required length and format, there were none. I told the class to begin, adding they were free to leave when they completed the assignment, mostly because "free to leave" had an official ring to them.

While I watched, everyone fell into various rhythms. Some erupted into bursts of energetic scrawling; others chewed on the end of their pens before dragging them across the page.

As they struggled with the heavy lifting of transforming thoughts to words, I remembered my favorite high school teacher. Rather than take the role of bystander when we wrote, she joined in. But when I picked up my own pen, my mind remained as blank as the paper in front of me.

Students began dropping off their work, and I made a point to smile at each one, even Louisa, who graced me with a slight upturn of her lips. When they were all gone, I put the papers in a folder and stuffed them into my red leather briefcase. Then I gathered the rest of my things and shut off the lights. I closed the door harder than I intended, surprised at the way the sound reverberated down the darkened hallway.

The regular rec center classes were on a quarterly hiatus. No hip-hop moms or Mahjong players accompanying me. Unnerved by the sudden quiet, a light sensation tickled the back of my neck. I fought the impulse to make a run for the exit. Instead, I kept my pace to a speed-walk and didn't slow down until I was halfway across the lot.

I barely noticed the dark clouds hanging low overhead as I fumbled in my purse for my keys. Just as I slid behind the wheel, the sky burst, and raindrops pelted my windshield, turning the landscape into a softer, grayer version of itself. When I turned on the wipers, my world dissolved into a smear of oil and dirt. I thought of Michael and wondered if passing time would do the same to my memories of the life we'd had together. Blur them until I could no longer summon the ghost-touch of his hand on mine or hear the echo of his laughter.

Chapter 8

It was after twelve when I reached my drive. The rain had stopped, leaving a sparkling clarity in its wake. I pulled into the garage, then checked the mail. As I shuffled through fliers and coupon books, I came across an envelope from Saint Cecilia's Hospitality Home, the shelter where Michael had volunteered.

I pitched the advertisements in the trash and was about to toss the letter as well when I remembered the veterans who had come to pay their respects at the funeral. Despite their shabby clothes and weathered faces, there had been a quiet dignity about them.

Michael encouraged me to join him when he served meals at the decaying, but stately Victorian home converted into the shelter. I questioned what I might offer as a volunteer, and he said the men at Saint Cecilia's didn't need much more than acknowledgment. I never went.

I set the letter aside, planning to donate in Michael's name, then put my briefcase on a kitchen chair. As I stood at the counter eating the last protein bar, I heard staccato hammering from the tree outside my sunroom.

Easing the sliding door open, I stepped onto the small glassed-in area Michael designated as my "safe space for writing." It had been months since I'd been in there. With its warm lighting and unrelieved cheerfulness, it had become alien to me, too full of lost possibilities. But it offered the best vantage point for catching sight of the pileated woodpecker we named Woody Peckerhead.

Most of the time, the noisy creature stayed hidden in the woods behind our property. But the previous winter, he drummed on the tree below our bedroom window before dawn. For over a week, he pecked and squawked, claiming his territory and driving us crazy. Then he disappeared. We were afraid the hawk that shadowed our neighborhood had taken him out. I hadn't thought of him at all after Michael died.

And here he was, drilling deep into the same tree. His crimson-capped head bobbed back and forth until he found whatever he was looking for. Then he spread his wings and flew away. As I moved toward the door, I bumped against the antique desk Michael had given me on our first and only Christmas together. A thick layer of dust covered it like a shroud.

Pricked with needles of guilt, I hurried back to the kitchen and tore off a wad of paper towels. Then I rummaged underneath the sink until I located the furniture polish. Restoring the shine on the desktop gave me more satisfaction than I expected, so I got the glass cleaner and rubbed at streaks until my shoulders ached.

When I finished, I stepped back and closed my eyes, breathing in the comforting blend of lemon with a hint of engine oil and the pungent scent of ammonia. When I opened them, brilliant rays of sunshine shot through my streak-free windows. The beams provided backlighting for wind-whipped clouds. An urgency I hadn't experienced in a very long time came over me. Unsure if it was satisfaction from having accomplished something or mind-muscle memory from being near my desk, a powerful need overwhelmed me.

This sudden renewal differed from the personal kind that drives a writer to her computer and keeps her chained there for hours. I wasn't ready for that. Although I didn't expect to be wowed by the class submission, I was surprisingly eager to peek into the inner lives of the group, however ordinary they might be.

After retrieving the student introductions from my briefcase, I grabbed a soda from the fridge and returned to the desk. I spread the papers across the glossy desktop and stared at them. How would a seasoned professional begin? Should I use an alphabetical system or arrange them by length with the shorter ones on top? Since I had no clue, I decided to make a game of it. With closed eyes, I rifled through the pages before making my selection.

I landed on Betty Frazier's, the mousy little woman whose life held no mystery. Our brief exchange had left me with low expectations, and the title, *My Secret,* did nothing to raise them:

People think I'm quiet and shy and mostly I guess I am. But once a month when the moon is full—

I stopped and sighed. Was she seriously going to write about a werewolf? Technically, supernatural creatures had as much right to be in crime fiction as human monsters did, but personally, I was over them. Determined not to let my bias affect my opinion of her work, I read on and discovered Betty's submission wasn't based in the paranormal realm at all.

•　　　•　　　•

I plan my escape. I already have my bag packed. Only one for a quick getaway. And I have a credit card in my name. I have maps and brochures for places like Costa Rica and Honduras. And some day whether the moon is full or not, he'll look for me, but I won't be there.

•　　　•　　　•

Despite the exotic destinations along her escape route, the passage evoked more despair than hopefulness. I read it again. Was she sending me a coded message for help? Or had she given me exactly what I'd asked for, revealed who she was through the voice of an anonymous narrator?

I held the paper up to the light and tilted it, thinking if I looked at it from a different angle, it might give me a better insight. It didn't. But the glint of sunlight that bounced off the wedding ring I still wore was illuminating. A symbol of love, it kept me locked in the past. Unlike Betty's narrator, I had no desire to escape.

You wanted a mystery; you got a mystery. Leave it at that, I thought.

So, I didn't write a note asking if she needed someone to talk to or help her make a run for it. Instead, I wrote at the bottom of the page: "Excellent use of details. Love the full moon."

I picked one from the top of the stack. It was an elaborate account of a woman who discovered she was descended from royalty but couldn't reveal her identity for fear of being assassinated.

The rest fell into predictable categories. Several students wrote about secret super-powers: mind reading, time travel, and a racy one about x-ray vision. A few were spies. I smiled when I read Howard Pemberton's account of a police detective who was also a well-known author.

I hesitated when I came to Louisa's paper, unsure what to expect from this woman I had an unexplained connection with. But her story provided no clue to a shared past. Instead, she created a tale about a secret shopper. Although I was amused by her original treatment of the topic and her stylish prose, I sensed she was hiding behind her humor, holding back a much more important part of herself. And even though I knew it was ridiculous to have expected some sort of grand revelation, disappointment washed over me.

After I finished reading Louisa's, a short story with a dominatrix made me uncomfortable until I realized it was about a video game. The last one was folded and stapled. I loosened it with my nail. The name in the right-hand corner was Nina Stevens.

•　　　•　　　•

Amelia woke to the squeal of the garage door. It was a little after midnight, which meant he would be stumbling, but not falling down drunk. For her plan to work, he had to be totally wasted. And she needed it to be tonight. No more putting it off like that lame Prince Hamlet.

She hated that loser. His one purpose in his whole stupid life was to get revenge on his uncle for killing his dad. But when he got the perfect chance, he wimped out because of a religious technicality.

Amelia would not be a Hamlet-style wienie. If good old Randy wasn't drunk enough, she would keep the beers coming until he passed out. Then all she had to do was light the cigarette and—

She heard the thud of the garage door and sat at the table, waiting for him to stagger in, stinking of liquor and smoke.

Minutes ticked by, and he still didn't show. She held her breath as she entered the garage. Half-expecting him to jump out and grab her, she moved cautiously toward the car where she saw a figure slumped behind the wheel. It was Randy, passed out with the motor running. Closed-up nice and tight. Unlike Shakespeare's sad prince, she didn't even need a sharp, pointy object. All she had to do was walk away and shut the door behind her.

Later, Amelia would ask herself why she'd done it. Why she reached in and turned off the engine. She cursed herself for being such a coward and vowed that next time would be different because she would be totally committed. She would trust her instincts because they never let her down.

•   •   •

I released the paper with its pale-blue lines and neatly written script and sat back as it drifted to the stone-tiled floor. Then I closed my eyes and pictured my workshop group, trying to put a face to the name Nina Stevens. Other than Howard, Louisa, and Betty, the faces were gauzy and blurred as if they were part of a half-forgotten dream.

The content of Nina's story was disturbing taken on its own. But her direct reference to Garnet's philosophy—*I don't trust anything but my instincts. They never let me down*—was creepy as hell and too on point to be coincidental. Was it a confession or a plan? And if her nod to Garnet indicated she agreed not only with my character's viewpoint but also with her actions, my dream class might become a nightmare.

Chapter 9

After over an hour debating whether Nina's story was dark wishful thinking or the blueprint for a murder, I called Andy. He answered on the first ring.

"I was about to start checking local facilities to see if the doc had you committed," he said.

"Shows what you know. Dr. Riley says I'm handling my difficult situation quite nicely, thank you. But forget that for now. I need your legal expertise about something a woman in my workshop wrote. It would be better if you read it yourself. Can you stop by on your way home? I'll cook dinner for you."

"What a lovely offer, but I'm still getting over the unfortunate fried chicken incident."

"That was over a year ago, and it was a tiny grease fire. And when I said cook dinner, I meant order Chinese."

"Sorry, but Paul's got an awards hoopla tonight at one of the charities he supports. It's not easy being married to such a good man. I could stop by after, but I can't guarantee my sobriety. What about tomorrow morning? Come to my office early, and I'll have your favorite bagel waiting for you."

I explained my workshop started at 10:00. Since he was on the way, we agreed to meet at 8:30. Less than a minute after we ended the call, my phone vibrated. I picked up before the opening notes of a ringtone sounded.

"Cinnamon raisin with cream cheese," I said. But instead of my friend apologizing for forgetting what my favorite bagel was, there was only a rustling sound. "Wait. Who is this?"

A dry, hacking cough seized the person on the other end, giving me enough time to note the call came from an unknown number.

"Sorry, but I don't respond to telephone soli—"

"I'm not trying to sell you anything, Mrs. Dolan. I was a friend of your husband, and I have something for you: a warning. Watch your back."

"Do what?" I gasped, but the line was dead. I stared at the phone without moving, trying to determine if I was more scared than angry. His voice was deep and halting, as if rusty from disuse, but I didn't detect hostility. And he said he was Michael's friend. I couldn't, however, picture any of his friends telling me to "watch my back." Was the call really a warning or could it have been a cruel prank? Had he mentioned my husband's name to trick me into trusting him or to taunt me somehow?

As always, the thought of his death underscored how alone I was. Before the call, that knowledge had made me lonely, but not fearful. Now, I wasn't just solitary; I was vulnerable.

I tried resetting the security alarm and cursed myself for being so inattentive when the service man reviewed the steps and for lying about knowing how the damn thing worked. I ransacked the catch-all drawer in the kitchen and the desk in the upstairs office in search of the instructions. After almost an hour, I gave up, poured myself a glass of wine, and sat on the sofa in the den.

I channel surfed until I found *House Hunters*. The show usually distracted me with its never-ending supply of annoying couples bickering over natural light and location. Tonight, I couldn't concentrate on the importance of an eastward facing lot.

A second glass of wine didn't help, but I knew if I went to bed this early, I'd never fall asleep. Then I remembered the miracle pills Dr. Riley had prescribed.

The list of side effects was daunting, everything from irritability and headaches to loss of memory and muscle weakness. It was also contradictory: drowsiness and insomnia or diarrhea and constipation. I tossed the paper aside, poured half a glass of wine, and popped a pill. I had just swallowed when I caught the "avoid alcohol" label.

•   •   •

Traffic was light, and I made it to the square in downtown Marietta a little after eight. Although the city has over sixty thousand people, the area surrounding Andy's office had an aw-shucks small-town feeling. Clusters of jonquils lined the stone walkway. They lifted their faces to the sun in cheerful defiance of the fickle nature of southern springs, smirking at me with flowering audacity. Groggy from waking at 5:30 after a night of moving from one disturbing dream to another, I wanted to snap off their perky little heads.

I resisted the impulse and thought of my decision to dismiss my mystery call as a prank, one not worth mentioning to Andy. There was no reason to overwhelm my friend with details of the ongoing and possibly unbelievable drama in my life.

Originally part of a high-powered law firm, he had grown tired of long hours and office politics. He and Paul started a personal injury practice in a renovated bungalow within walking distance of the courthouse. With its fresh coat of white paint, shiny black shutters, and bright red door, the house, much like its owner, exuded down-home charm. Not quite as down-home was the gold Escalade parked out front. When I remarked on the extravagance of the vehicle, he said it wasn't just about transportation. It was about image. Clients liked the idea their attorney could afford expensive stuff. They assumed his success would translate into cash for them. Besides, he added, it was pre-owned.

I ignored the roaring lion-head doorknocker and rang the bell, then walked into what Andy called the parlor. The walls were painted a non-threatening bluish gray. Behind the reception desk, an ornately framed mirror took up most of the space. He had positioned it there so that the first thing prospective clients saw was their own image outlined in filigreed gold, another not-so-subtle hint of the riches awaiting them if they allowed him to handle their claim.

It was too early for his assistant to be in, and Paul was out of town. So, I headed straight for the stairs. What had once been a guest bedroom was his partner's office; the master was Andy's.

Built-in shelves lined the walls. Like Dr. Riley's collection, many of the titles were on Andy's chosen profession. But the three thick ones centered on the top shelf—*Georgia Rules of Evidence*, *Official Code of Georgia Annotated*, and *Georgia School Laws*—weren't professional treatises at all. I knew from personal experience the covers were fake and concealed a crystal liquor carafe and two highball glasses.

A stack of papers on top of the inbox threatened to topple onto an armchair already covered with piles of books and a half-eaten jelly doughnut.

Andy was standing at the window when I tapped on the open door.

"Am I in the right place for legal advice?"

"It's not that security guard, is it? Because he accepted two primo Braves tickets in exchange for his agreement not to press charges."

"Nobody's suing me," I assured him as he wrapped me in a hug.

He plucked the pastry from the top of the books, moved them to the floor, and motioned me toward the cleared space, then sat behind his desk.

"Bite?" he asked, holding out the doughnut. I shook my head and watched him finish it off.

Andy's round face was as smooth and unlined as it had been in college. Despite a diet of bakery goods, frozen entrees and alcohol, his slightly receding hairline was the only indication he wasn't completely immune to the passing of time.

"Don't think I forgot your bagel." He shifted some papers around. I know it's here somewhere."

I assured him I wasn't hungry.

He squinted and frameless glasses slid down his nose. "There's something different about you. What is it? No, don't tell me. I've got it. You're not an abject picture of sorrow." He glanced at his watch. "Are you day-drinking? Because it's not even nine o'clock, but what the hell. Pull out the flask and I'll join you."

"I'm not drunk, you fool."

I did feel a little light-headed, though. It could have been my renewed interest in something other than grief combined with the prescriptions from Riley. Normally, Andy and I overshare, but I was unexpectedly reticent to talk about either possibility. I was afraid admitting how much I was enjoying my workshop might jinx it. My motive for keeping the medication to myself was more complicated.

Well-balanced, self-sufficient people are supposed to power through anything life throws at them. That kind of person doesn't need pills to blunt the edges of grief or supply the strength needed to get out of bed. I didn't want to admit I no longer belonged to that segment of the population, wasn't sure I ever had, and was beginning to hate them.

"Did you say you wanted me to read a writing sample from one of your Roswell criminals?" He snorted. "I cannot wrap my head around you teaching how to tie a shoe, what's less conveying writing wisdom on innocent or guilty people."

"The Roswell Crime Family. But they're not criminals. They just write about crime. And I'll have you know I have a real knack for education. Anyway." I handed him Nina's story. "Check this out and tell me what you think."

He pushed his glasses up and read. When he finished, he looked at me, then reread it.

"Girl says she's committed. Sounds like she should *be* committed." He put the paper face down. "What in God's name was the assignment? Write something that will scare the bejesus out of the teacher? And that 'trusting instinct' crap? Please, tell me that's not a Garnet reference."

"It's definitely a Garnet reference. And the prompt was pretty tame, or at least I thought it was. I asked the group to introduce themselves, to reveal themselves through their writing. It didn't matter if it was true or not. I'm hoping Nina enjoys shocking people, that she's not some kind of sociopath. This doesn't sound like something a sociopath would write, does it?"

"That's the thing about sociopaths," he began. "They look and act like you and me. More like you, actually."

"Ha, ha. But seriously. Is there something I should do? I mean, if she really does kill somebody, am I in trouble for not warning the police?"

"Involving them would certainly put a damper on the rest of your happy little workshop. And I doubt the cops would do more than talk to Nina. Probably not even that. Have you thought about toning down your assignments? What's wrong with *My Summer Vacation*?"

"Not helpful."

"You did the right thing keeping your comments on the writing itself. Maybe she wanted to rattle you. Make you question her reliability just for the hell of it. You know how kids these days can be."

I didn't point out neither of us knew anything about kids these days or any others.

"It's the reference to your work that bothers me. She might be fixated on you."

"Or perhaps she's just a reader with good taste. Garnet fans aren't particularly dangerous." I thought of GarNetted. "Not usually, anyway."

Chapter 10

A breeze ruffled through the leaves as I walked to my car. Ivory blossoms fluttered around me. In addition to the lovely flower petals, the gust of wind whisked up a pungent odor. It was an interesting combination of rotting fish and dirty socks, the hallmark smell of the Bradford pear trees lining the sidewalk.

This contradiction of senses never failed to unsettle me. Michael, who had known much more about gardening and landscaping than I did, said it was nature's warning not to be deceived by the looks of what he called a blooming nightmare. He explained how the Bradfords were so prolific they had become a curse on the environment.

"If people would just pay attention to what nature is trying to tell us, we wouldn't be in such a mess," he lamented.

At the time, I'd been amused at his indignation. Now I wondered if I might be missing a similar warning about human nature. Was there a whiff of true evil beneath Nina's passage? Were GarNetted's messages more than a fan letting off steam?

I shook petals from my hair and clothing before getting in the car. Andy's attempt to reassure me about Nina hadn't helped. I still had no idea whether I should approach her about what she'd written or ignore it. I didn't even know what she looked like. Then I remembered what Andy had said about her reliability and realized I had stumbled onto what might be a "teachable moment."

I made it to the center before nine. Instead of going to my classroom, I checked in with the main office and asked the secretary if I could have access to a computer and a printer. She logged me into the system and, starting with Poe, I compiled a list of authors and their unreliable narrators. I had no clue how well-read my group of aspiring writers was but decided to assume they would recognize at least some of my selections.

It was comforting to be in familiar territory after an evening filled with uncharted terrain. I might not know much about dealing with nasty online comments or conspiring to commit murder, but I knew my way around authors and literary devices.

I remembered Andy's comment about how I wasn't my usual sad sack self. It was possible teaching had influenced my change from despair to something else—apprehension or anticipation. Most likely a mixture of the two.

When I reached the classroom, many of the students were seated. My knitting enthusiast ignored my entrance and kept click-clacking along. I stashed my things underneath the teacher's desk and began writing on the whiteboard.

> Some novels and stories have what we call an unreliable narrator. What does this mean and how might such a narrator affect a reader's perception?

As the remaining participants took their seats, I studied the faces of the women, searching for signs of homicidal tendencies. But if Andy was right—and I suspected he was—there would be no visible signs of madness.

Rather than call the roll, I tore a piece of paper from a legal pad and requested students sign in. This would give me an informal seating chart I could use to match names to faces. While they passed the sheet, I directed them to the board and asked them to jot down their thoughts on the subject. Then I stood behind them while they wrote.

The list was halfway around the room when a girl with unnaturally dark hair rushed in. Mascara smears below her heavily lined brown eyes gave her a haunted look, providing a startling contrast to the sparkling diamond on the side of her nose. She wore a sleeveless, oversized black sweatshirt that dwarfed her tiny frame, and at least three inches of her upper left arm was tattooed with what I thought were Chinese letters.

She sat in the back row, then dug in her bulky canvas satchel, pulled out a spiral notebook, and dropped the bag to the floor. When the list came to her, I strolled by and watched her scrawl her name at the bottom: Nina Stevens.

As she read the prompt, a smile spread slowly across her pale face. Unlike some members of the class, there was no confusion, no hesitancy at all. She immediately began writing.

After about five minutes, I requested that they put their work aside.

"First, I want to thank you for sharing your personal mysteries with me. They were quite imaginative." I glanced at Nina, but she kept her eyes on her paper.

"Second, the reason I asked you to define the term unreliable narrator is that some of you did an excellent job using this device. Could someone give me your definition, please?"

Silence descended. I surveyed the room, purposely avoiding Nina. Then I consulted the column of signatures on my list and was in the process of making a random selection when I heard a familiar voice.

"It means the person telling the story can't be trusted," Louisa Carter announced. "Like when you write about a secret that may or may not be true."

She had replaced the beige sweater set with pastel pink over navy slacks. With her glasses perched atop her head, she seemed younger than before and less imposing.

"That's exactly right," I nodded and smiled. "Several of you used this technique in your submission. Can anyone explain why?"

This time I looked directly at Nina. But she was occupied with picking black polish off her fingernails.

Once again, the silence intimidated me. "Okay, then. If you did make your storyteller less than honest, you're in good company. And not just your classmates." My admittedly blatant attempt at pandering was rewarded with a few weak smiles.

"Many well-known writers chose to make their narrators untrustworthy. Can you name an author like this and what they wrote?"

Instead of enduring another round of ear-splitting silence, I consulted the list and called on Howard Pemberton.

"How about you, Mr. Pemberton?"

One of the few men, he sat near the back, not far from Nina. His silver hair gleamed under the fluorescent bulb, highlighting the dark blush spreading from his cheeks to the top of his tightly buttoned shirt. Feeling like a bully teacher who calls on the shyest kid in the class just because she can, I was about to move on when he spoke.

"I think the young man from Salinger's *Catcher in the Rye* would qualify. Don't you?" he asked.

"Holden Caulfield. He's a perfect example." I followed up with a quick summary of the novel, reassuring both Howard and myself that I knew my stuff.

He nodded his approval, and several hands shot up. None of them belonged to Nina. I picked a girl wearing a *Nevertheless, she persisted* t-shirt.

"Would the novel with the drunk woman on the train count?"

Before I could answer, a young woman called out, "*Girl on a Train*! I loved that movie. You mean it was a book, too?"

A sleepy-looking boy in the back row sat up and asked, "What about that bat-shit crazy guy who hears heartbeats under the floorboard?"

Someone called out, "Tell-Tale Heart."

And they were off. We spent the next thirty minutes discussing everything from *Gone Girl* and *Fight Club* to the works of Dickens and Welty. After a brief debate on the overall effectiveness of an unreliable narrator—some enjoyed getting inside the head of the flawed storyteller; others felt betrayed—I told them I wanted them to begin working on an extended piece of fiction.

"A short story, a series of journal entries, or letters would be great. You can start a novel or revise one you've already written. But first, I want you to consider three elements."

I moved to the board and wrote: Genre, Audience, Voice.

After defining the terms, I asked if there were more questions.

With her paisley writing accessories, she was more a happy housewife than the tortured soul from her excerpt.

"Ms. Frazier, right?"

"Betty's fine." She spoke so softly I had to move closer. "My genre is romance, but doesn't that mean my audience is anyone who likes to read romances?"

"Not exactly. Are you going to write about teenage girls who fall in love with creatures of the night? Or two people in their sixties who reconnect after years of being apart? See the difference?"

"One's hot, and one's not," a man sitting near the window offered. Several students chuckled.

"Yes, but which one?" I countered, provoking more laughter. "Answer that and you'll have your audience."

I returned to Betty, who smiled and nodded.

"We'll devote most of tomorrow's time to your personal writing, so bring it and your laptops with you. Your only homework is to take a close look at your opening paragraph. Ask yourself if it would keep a reader turning pages. Does it set the tone you want? Is it too descriptive? Not descriptive enough? Make the changes you think it needs, but save the original, so we can see what you've done." I waited for questions, but no one seemed confused.

"I'd like to close the class with another short prompt." I glanced at my notes and the topic I selected in response to Andy's suggestion to go with a subject with less possibility for drama: *Where would you go if you could go anywhere in the world? Why?*

But I ditched it and wrote:

Choose a time in your life when you made a decision you regretted.

I read aloud and wondered where it had come from, then explained it was designed to get them thinking. "Write whatever comes into your mind without worrying whether it makes sense."

No one appeared confused or anxious. I couldn't tell if it was because I'd inspired them to be spontaneous or if they'd accepted their instructor was unbalanced.

"When you finish, turn in your paper. Then you may leave." *You may leave?* What was it about being in front of a captive audience that made people sound so pretentious?

From behind my desk, I watched their faces as they wrote, searching for clues to their writing process. Or as Michael put it, their kaleidoscope faces.

Michael coined the phrase one afternoon last September. He came home early and found me at my writing desk. "Did you know that when you write, your face is like a kaleidoscope?"

I was so absorbed in the beginning of my fourth Garnet novel, the one I hadn't touched since his death, I didn't hear him open the door to the sunroom.

"A kaleidoscope?"

"All these emotions light up your face so quickly I have just enough time to think I recognize one, and then it morphs into something entirely different. It's beautiful, but a little scary."

I hit save before getting up and crossing the room to stand in front of him. Brushing my fingertips across his lips, I stood on my tiptoes and whispered, "Surely, you're not afraid of me?"

I tugged on his earlobe with my teeth, then trailed kisses along his jawline. I spent the next hour or so demonstrating how very unfrightening I could be.

A cough from the back of the room brought me back to the present, where Louisa scowled, holding her pen so firmly her knuckles whitened. Betty chewed her lower lip and tapped her foot. Howard stopped occasionally to gaze at the ceiling. Nina leaned low over her paper, a dark curtain of hair falling across her face.

Observing them while they were lost in their own stories made me feel voyeuristic, as if I'd caught them in an intimate act. I knew I should look away but couldn't. It seemed wrong that I had a glimpse at something beautiful and secret without their permission. Or had I projected my own magical experience when I wrote onto them? Did that mean I might have mistaken the mystical for something darker. Perhaps even sinister.

•　　•　　•

"Ms. Dolan? Are you okay?"

It was Howard Pemberton, a concerned look deepening the creases on his face.

"Sorry." I gave him my reassuring smile, one I had perfected from overuse. "Guess I was lost in thought. And it's Kara. How can I help you?"

"I wanted to say how much I appreciate you letting us work on independent projects. I heard some of the other workshops were on the frou-frou side. You know, describing the taste of rain or pretending you're a frog."

"Thanks for saying that. And I'm looking forward to hearing more about your project, about everyone's ideas," I said, a little surprised at the sincerity of my statement, considering my original reluctance to teach the class.

Within a few minutes, most of the students dropped off their assignments and left the classroom. Only Louisa and Nina remained behind, leaving me to speculate about what it would be like to be alone with one of them. While she wasn't exactly warm and fuzzy, Louisa's initial hostility—if it had really been that—seemed to have lessened. But I doubted she was the kind of woman who would want to hang around and chat. Nina didn't seem like the chatty type either, which was good since that whole maybe-she's-a-murderer-thing didn't make her too appealing.

Louisa finished first and brought her paper to me.

"I enjoyed reading about your secret shopper." I felt awkward but really wanted her to like me. I wanted everyone in the class to like me and had the unpleasant feeling she didn't.

Andy insisted I was desperate for unanimous approval. He said only village idiots were beloved by all. He would have scoffed at the unnaturally wide smile plastered across my face.

Louisa shrugged and murmured a quiet thank you, then turned and walked out the door. Apparently, she wasn't too keen on my please-like-me-grin either.

Now it was just me and Nina. I squirmed in my seat and straightened the already perfectly aligned stack of papers in front of me. I started to erase the whiteboard, but the idea of turning my back on her changed my mind.

Within minutes of Louisa's departure, Nina stopped writing and dropped her paper on my desk. I struggled to offer a comment that didn't sound like what it was—an attempt to win her favor. When had my need for acceptance become so desperate, I was willing to woo a self-admitted aspiring murderess?

I was still trying to come up with pleasant banter when she spoke.

"So why haven't you told the class who you really are?"

Her accusatory tone startled me, and I had no idea what she meant. "Who I am?" I repeated.

"You know." She leaned over the desk. "Garnet."

"Oh, that." I smiled. She didn't. "You mean about me being the author of the Garnet Rivers series. I was worried you all would suspect the class was going to be nothing but one long book promotion. It's more important to—"

"I get it, but I'm not talking about that. I'm talking about who you really are—Garnet."

"Me, Garnet? Hardly. She's not afraid of anything. Me? I get nervous on escalators."

"Whatever. She's cool. The way she doesn't take any shit from anyone. The way she follows her own code, dealing out punishment to men who deserve it. What's that thing she says? You know, when she's got some douche bag cornered?"

"*I'm not afraid to get a little blood under my fingernails. But if you make me break a nail, I'm really going to be pissed,*" I repeated Garnet's favorite tag line.

"That's it. Blood under her fingernails. God, I love that line."

Chapter II

Despite my exchange with Nina or maybe because of it, I buzzed with unexpected energy. For the first time in months, I was excited, interested in something not directly related to my own personal loss. And while most people would consider my eagerness to read student writing pitiable, for me it provided a much-needed sense of purpose.

It also made me hungry. With nothing at home to eat and no one to eat it with, I picked up a combo from Wendy's and decided to have a private picnic with myself. Instinctively, I headed to a park not too far from home, a spot where Michael and I had frequently stopped.

My tires dug into the gravel as I parked near our favorite bench. Instead of getting out, I sat clutching the steering wheel. Memories settled over me like fog. A woman pushing a stroller passed in front of the car, and I relaxed my grip. The fog lifted but left a crippling despair in its place. I backed out and drove toward home.

French fry aroma wafted up from the grease-stained bag in the passenger seat, but I had lost my appetite. I sucked most of my soda through a straw, finishing it by the time I pulled into my garage. Once inside, I sat at my kitchen table, choked down a few fries, then tossed the rest in the garbage. After taking a bite of my cold burger, I started to pitch it as well, but stopped when I thought of Rex.

Our late-night encounter had made me rethink my relationship with the animal. Maybe what I assumed had been his intense distaste for me, growling and gnashing his teeth if I got too close to his property line, had been the result of my fear. I wouldn't have taken it personally since I did know his breed was conditioned to stand guard over their territory, but the damn dog loved my husband. The sight of him would stop Rex mid-snarl. He would shoot me one last wild-eyed warning before wagging his entire body at Michael's approach. I'd watch as the ferocious brute stuck his muzzle through the rails so Michael could stroke his thick fur.

"Just let him sniff your hand," he would urge as he scratched behind the dog's ears. "Let him get to know you."

I had always resisted becoming better acquainted with the beast, and now that Michael was gone, I rarely ventured farther than the deck outside the sunroom.

Still holding the hamburger, I slipped the meat out and dropped the bun in the trash. Then I rinsed off the ketchup and mustard before drying the patty with a paper towel.

Peeking through the wooden blinds on my kitchen window, I could see Rex, still barking as he ran back and forth along the perimeter of his property. When I opened the door to the deck, he froze, then lunged toward the fence, and stood quietly, sniffing in my direction.

He stared as I began descending the steps. His tail raised up in a half-wag, then dropped in what I assumed was doggy disappointment.

"Sorry, buddy." I lowered the pitch of my voice the way Michael had recommended, assuring me dogs responded better to lower tones. "It's just me."

Rex turned his head, a quizzical expression on his regal face, and I braced for an onslaught of thunderous growls. But he stayed silent, and I tentatively resumed my advance. A few feet from the fence, I held the sodden hamburger patty in front of me, hoping I hadn't washed away the tantalizing scent of prepackaged meat.

"I brought you something." I had no idea if dogs recognized smiling as a sign of friendship, but I stretched my lips into a broad grin. "A peace offering."

I broke the burger into three pieces and held up the smallest one. Rex snapped to attention. I took another step, then lobbed the treat over the fence, high enough not to startle him. A blur of movement in my direction sent me scrambling, despite the sturdy structure between us. Springing upward, he snatched the meat from the air and swallowed it in one smooth motion.

"Good boy," I crooned, almost as pleased with him as I was with my own brave self. "How about another bite?"

He sat, tail wagging expectantly. This time I move a little closer before throwing the treat. Once again, he grabbed it before it reached the ground, but rather than return to his seated position, he moved cautiously in my direction. I dangled the last of the burger, and he snatched it without so much as brushing a single razor-sharp tooth against my skin.

He stuck his silky nose between the posts and whined. I reached toward him and stroked it with my index finger. Then he leaned against the fence, and I scratched his ear. Groaning softly, he wriggled his behind and pushed against my hand.

"You really are a good boy, aren't you?" I continued petting him until a squirrel scampered across his yard, and he darted off in pursuit.

I stepped back and sniffed my hands, detecting the pungent, slightly musky smell of my new buddy. Then I realized this was more than the scent of dog. It was the smell of victory.

Rex and I weren't besties, but I had taken the first step toward conquering my fear. And I had done it without Michael. That wasn't entirely accurate. While my husband hadn't been there, he'd been with me. Garnet would have said knowing how to ease into my new relationship with Rex had come from trusting my instincts. But it was more than that. Letting myself feel, rather than think, had given me the kind of confidence Michael once had in me. Maybe still had in me.

I was almost to the deck steps before I remembered the rustling leaves on the spot where Rex had focused. I turned away from the house and walked along the perimeter of the fence until I reached the thicket of ivy where something had agitated my new friend.

There was no trace of whatever disturbed the greenery, and I was in the process of returning to the house when I caught a glimpse of something white in the undergrowth. It was too far to reach from my side of the fence and too filled with the possibility of snakes or spiders for me to climb over to investigate. I looked around the yard and noticed a rake one of the neighborhood association grounds crew must have left propped against the oak tree.

I used it to part the leaves until the object of interest was completely exposed. I hadn't been wrong in my assumption: no raccoon or opossum had scurried into the underbrush. The creature who had disturbed both mine and Rex's sleep had walked on two legs. And whoever it was had left a crushed cigarette butt behind.

Relying on my television CSI training, I hurried back to the kitchen where I retrieved a plastic bag and ice tongs, then returned to the evidence. Using the tongs, I nudged it into the baggie and took a closer look. The lettering on what remained of the cigarette identified it as a Dunhill. The coat of arms next to the name branded it as fancy.

Half an hour later, I was still wandering from room to room checking and rechecking the locks on doors and windows. Then I called Andy to tell him about my discovery, but it went to voicemail.

"Hey, Andy. It's me. I hate to keep bothering you, but I was wondering if you could stop by on your way home. I found something kind of weird in the backyard. Not exactly in the yard, but by the fence. I think it's still my property. Anyway, I need your opinion, please. Okay then. Bye."

I placed the baggie holding the offending object on a paper plate on the coffee table. Whoever had left it had taken the time to grind it out, so at least, my creep wasn't a firebug. And he might not even be mine. He could have been watching my neighbor's house or even a rich teenager who'd swiped a pack of daddy's most likely very expensive cigarettes.

Whoever he was, he was a real buzz kill. The high from my victory with Rex had vanished, leaving me tired and defeated.

Defeat is a state of mind. I prefer New York.

I jumped at the sound of Garnet's voice, unsure which novel she was quoting or if I'd even written her latest tip. Either way, it was irritating, mostly because she was right. I could choose to tremble like some helpless damsel in distress or I could woman up.

Chapter 12

I decided womaning up would be easier with a glass of wine in my hand, so I took it and my briefcase to the sofa in the den and removed the folder with the class responses to regret.

Nina's was on the top of the pile, but I set it aside and pulled one from the middle of the stack. I don't know what I expected. My idea for writing about regrets came out of nowhere. But the candor of their confessions surprised me. Even the predictable submissions—overindulging in alcohol, callous remarks to loved ones, failure to take advantage of opportunities—were painfully honest.

Howard had done it Sinatra-style beginning with *Regrets, I've had a few, but then again too few to mention.* He added a very personal account of losing the first woman he loved because he couldn't tell her how he felt.

True to form, I annoyed Louisa with my choice of topic.

•   •   •

Regrets are pointless. Why waste time thinking about what you should have said, what you might have done, what could have been—all these sad little thoughts can take a person the wrong way on a one-way street? And for what? What's lost can't be regained.

•   •   •

I shook my head and jotted down some inane comment about how powerful her street metaphor was. Louisa's despair was contagious, and I needed more wine. After refilling my glass, I returned to the papers, saving Nina's for last.

•　　　•　　　•

My mother warned me my biggest regret in life would be my golden dragon. She's fierce with orange flames erupting from her snarling lips at the top of my right shoulder blade. Her body twists down my lower back. Her scaly tail disappears at the base of my spine. I suppose I may wish I hadn't gotten her someday. But I don't think so because the fire she sends across my flesh burns away pain.

The blaze I regret is different. That one destroyed everything in its path, leaving only piles of ashes waiting to be blasted by the fiery breath of the wind.

•　　　•　　　•

Once again, Nina left me with more questions than answers. What had her dragon purified? Was her story memory or fabrication or a combination of the two? Had her destructive fire been real or symbolic? Did it matter?

I found myself identifying with this young writer. I made my living writing about a character whose actions mimicked my own fantasies. A wild woman who often blurred the line between imagination and reality. That could explain why I switched topics at the last minute, abandoning the safety of descriptive writing for the treacherous territory of truth. Asking people to reveal regrets is like requesting they stand naked in front of a packed auditorium, then commanding them to peel away thin strips of skin.

Nina had been willing to do that, and while I didn't understand what her truth was, I felt I knew her better. In her first story, her fictional character hadn't been able to stand by and watch someone, even a man she hated, die. Was this new submission more reality-based? Did she follow through with her plan to destroy the drunken abuser in her life? And if I discovered she had, what should I do about it?

What should you do about one less predator in the world? Set off fireworks and start the party.

Garnet spoke in her inside voice—inside my head—but her words were powerful. I didn't like to think about what I might do if I found Michael's killer slumped behind the wheel in a smoke-filled garage. Would I turn off the engine? Or would I slip away with a smile on my face?

• • •

The sound of distant pounding, like someone at the door demanding to be let in, was only the echo from a dull thudding at my temples. The light from the lamp on the end table shone too brightly. I covered my eyes, trying to calculate how long I'd been sleeping, then peeked at my watch. Seven-fifteen. The last time I checked it was a little after three, right before I called Andy. Or was that when I started reading the papers on regret?

I shifted to an upright position, sending several pages fluttering to the floor. The room tilted, and I steadied myself. An almost-empty wineglass sat next to a completely empty bottle of Merlot, which I hate. I only bought the damn stuff to curtail my alcohol intake.

I retrieved the fallen papers and stacked them on the table, then walked to the kitchen to check my phone. Andy had texted to say he was tied up in court but would stop by later.

My throat was sandpaper; I needed water so badly I turned on the faucet and drank directly from the tap. I splashed some onto my face and stood looking at my reflection. The woman staring back at me bore no resemblance to the photo on the book jackets of my novels. This one was pale, with dark circles under swollen eyes. My hair was tangled, a damp strand matted to the hollow of my cheek.

Standing in the cool air of the open refrigerator, I tried to piece together the moments before I fell asleep. Passed out was more accurate, but I didn't remember drinking enough wine to render me unconscious. The printed warning on my magic pills flashed in front of me. Was this what mixing the meds and alcohol looked like?

I filled a glass with ice, added ginger ale, gulped it down, and poured another. Halfway through it, the doorbell rang. I was on my way to answer it when I heard the hinges squeak.

"It's me," Andy called from the foyer.

"I'm in the kitchen."

"That meeting was a little slice of heaven. I am so ready for a drink. What have you—Yikes! Looks like you already had one or half a dozen. Whatever you're having, I want something else. Seriously, Kara, you don't look well."

"I don't feel well. Too much wine and not enough food, I guess." Although I still didn't remember having more than two glasses.

"Sit down and rest. Uncle Andy's here to make it all better." He opened the refrigerator and stared at the sparsely filled shelves. "Just as I suspected. That's why I ordered Thai on the way over. It should arrive shortly."

He took a beer and pulled his phone from his pocket. "I need to give Paul a quick call."

"Say hi for me," I said and hurried to dispose of the empty wine bottle.

"Thai Heaven," he said, settling on the sofa. "Don't you love that name? Thai Heaven. I never get tired of saying it. It sounds like a specialty massage parlor, one that covers you in coconut oil and curry before you get your happy ending."

"That's because it's Thai House, not heaven. I think Thai Heaven *is* a massage parlor."

"I'm pretty sure you're wrong. But tell me, please, what is driving you to drink?"

"It started the other night when Rex was howling—"

"Rex? Who is this Rex and how did you make him howl?"

"What? Oh, for God's sake. Rex is my neighbor's German Shepherd, and I didn't do anything." I summarized my first encounter with the dog, omitting the moment when our eyes met, and we'd shared a connection. Andy was a tolerant man but telling him about my special canine experience might push the envelope too far. When I got to the part where I shared my lunch with the good boy, he interrupted.

"Hold the phone. You mean you dangled meat in front of that frothing beast, as I believe you once referred to him, and he didn't take off your hand up to the wrist. Or was it hound from hell?"

"You were right. I was a wuss. Now if you'll let me finish, please." I told him about checking out the spot where I thought I'd seen something or someone duck between the trees and concluded with finding the cigarette butt. Then I produced the paper plate.

His bland expression disappointed me. When he glanced at the evidence and shrugged, I wanted to smack him.

"It's definitely a cigarette butt. I'm sure, however, you would concede there are many plausible reasons for it to be in your backyard."

"I hate it when you do that. Go all fuck-wad lawyer on me, especially while you're drinking my beer."

The front doorbell rang, and he jumped from his seat. "Thai Heaven to the rescue."

I rested my head against the sofa, fighting tears of frustration. I didn't need my smart-ass friend to point out the many possible explanations for the appearance of that random butt. What I needed was for him to validate my fear someone had been watching me. Because I was much less afraid of some voyeuristic creep staring at me from the woods than I was at the possibility I had hopped on the fast train to Paranoiaville—next stop Delusion Junction.

"Truce? I bear offerings of peace," he said, holding out the grease-stained brown bags. "I didn't mean to be a jerk. Let's talk after we eat."

He spread out containers of food while I put paper plates and silverware on the table.

"I am sorry about before," Andy said between noodles. "I wasn't trying to be a jackass. Guess it comes naturally for us fuck-wad lawyer types."

"I may have been a little harsh."

"Not at all. I love it when you talk dirty. And your theory makes as much sense as any of my hypotheticals. I have a friend on the force. I can ask him to schedule a patrol car to include your street. That should make any unwanted visitors think twice about loitering in the forest with a lit cigarette. In the meantime, keep your alarm system armed."

"About that." I confessed I'd never reset it, bracing myself for a lecture with at least one story about a girl who neglected to lock her door. His favorite involved a serial killer with a propensity for decapitation. I suspected it was grossly exaggerated. Surprisingly, he only sighed and promised to help me with it before he left.

"I almost forgot," he said as we were clearing the table. "I did some digging around on Nina Stevens. Girl's got no criminal record. In fact, she graduated from Grady High at the head of her class and was headed to UGA on a full scholastic scholarship. But she never went. She dropped off the radar for over a year before enrolling in a tech school. I couldn't find anything about where she was or what she was doing, so I ran background on her family. Parents divorced ten years ago; the dad disappeared. Her mother remarried when Nina was twelve."

Andy packed up left-overs and took another beer from the fridge.

"Guy the mom hooked up with was a real piece of work. Mostly small-time stuff: check-kiting, bar fights, plus quite a few domestic battery calls. The month after she graduated, he messed up bad. Got drunk, fell asleep in the recliner with a smoking cigarette and lit up the whole house. Nina was at a friend's. The fire department showed up in time to drag him out with some nasty burns, but nothing life-threatening. The mother wasn't so lucky. She didn't make it. He's two years in on a ten-year sentence for involuntary manslaughter, but with good behavior, the son of a bitch could get out in three."

Chapter 13

I struggled to hide my emotions. Andy's news provided the basis for the anger and remorse this young girl expressed. But had it been regret over not being there for her mother, or was it because the wrong person died in an inferno Nina had created?

Empathy for her loss, coupled with an unwillingness to involve Andy in an ethical issue, kept me from sharing the second paper. Nor did I tell him about my anonymous caller because it seemed trivial after hearing what had happened to Nina and her mother. My reticence to discuss recent disturbing events also had more than a little to do with my fear he might not believe me. And when you looked at it logically, I wouldn't have blamed him.

"Don't worry," he said. "If you need to put on your Nancy Drew outfit, I'll be your loyal sidekick but not the butch one. What was her name? Charlie? No, it was George. I want to be the gal who likes chocolate and shopping. Until then, let's look at your alarm."

We spent the next half hour reactivating my security system. He suggested I should bolster it with outdoor cameras, but I insisted that wasn't necessary and sent him on his way.

After he left, my phone began buzzing. Another unknown number, possibly the man who'd told me to watch my back. I considered ignoring the call, but something—Garnet might have called it instinct—made me answer. This time I would be prepared. I would tell that asshole exactly where he could go.

"Mrs. Dolan?" The caller had the smooth bass of a deejay on an easy-listening station. Not the raspy caller with his vague, but ominous, warning.

"Uh, I uh, yes. This is she. Who is this?"

"My name is Lucas Montgomery. First, I want to say you have my deepest condolences for the loss of your husband." Now his voice was less rhythm and blues and more host of a call-in show offering advice to the lovelorn. "I apologize for not getting in touch with you sooner. I was waiting to see if there was any progress on your husband's murder, but that's no excuse."

I appreciated that he didn't ask how I was doing. Not only did I appreciate not having to give my standard "I'm-fine" lie, but I also welcomed the way he wasn't tiptoeing around my feelings like so many people who seemed to think sweet euphemisms were comforting. My husband hadn't passed away or departed or gone gently into that good night. He had bled out after being shot three times at close range.

"Thank you. Lucas Montgomery, you said?"

Ooh. This guy's got that porn-star vibe. You know, when you combine the name of your first pet with the street you lived on when you were a kid.

I grew up on Crabapple Avenue and the only pet I had was Malcolm, a depressed canary I inherited from my grandmother. I didn't imagine Malcolm Crabapple would be packing them in at the Pink Pony.

"That's right. Please call me Lucas."

Thanks to Garnet, images of Magic Mike snapping out of tear-away pants distracted me for a second. "Well, Lucas, I'm afraid I don't recognize the name."

"We've never met. Your husband and I were working together on a series of articles about Saint Cecilia's for the *Journal*."

"You're a reporter?" For months after Michael's death, the press plagued me. The story of a grieving widow, combined with an unsolved murder, made good copy. I refused to speak to any of them and thought they'd given up. "I have no intention of talking about my husband's murder. Now if you'll excuse me—"

"Please, Mrs. Dolan. Let me explain. I don't want to interview you. I'm writing about the stories of the men at the shelter and how they ended up there. Michael was helping me."

Too tired to attempt a polite response, I took a page from Garnet's book—no, my book although I felt less in control every day—and said, "Really? He never mentioned you."

"No, he wouldn't have. You see, we discovered an, uh, unusual situation at Saint Cecilia's."

"Unusual how?"

"I'd rather not discuss it over the phone. But I'm certain Michael's murder was connected to it."

"The police never mentioned any of this." My jaw tightened and my pulse quickened because I had never accepted a random twist of fate had struck down the man I loved. Was it possible my intuition would be validated, and was I sure I wanted it to be?

"They don't have all the answers. They're not even asking the right questions."

"I'm sorry, but how I can help?"

"It's more about how we can help each other. If we could meet in person, I'll explain it all to you."

"Explain what? I had no idea my husband was working with you."

"That's what I'm worried about. What scares me is what the people who killed your husband *think* you know."

After Lucas's comment about people who thought I knew something I shouldn't, we agreed to lunch the next day at the OK Café, a popular diner off the expressway near downtown Atlanta. Although the location wasn't convenient, it reduced the likelihood I might run into anyone I knew.

I spent over an hour online reading about Lucas Montgomery. An investigative reporter for a small paper in Florida, he accepted a job with the *Atlanta Journal Constitution* a year ago.

Besides traditional reporting, he wrote a blog. His latest posts highlighted the shameful way the nation had treated our vets in the past and in the differences in the current treatment of the men and women who'd served their country. He included statistics on drug abuse and its relation to the high rate of suicides among veterans.

The picture next to his byline, an attractive African American man, looked harmless enough. A remarkably precise hairline accentuated his smooth forehead and well-groomed brows. From the photo it was difficult to determine his age, but I guessed he was in his mid-thirties. Behind black, square-framed glasses, his light brown eyes were serious, and his unsmiling lips emphasized the gravity of his subject.

I skimmed through several of the stories until I came across a reference to Saint Cecilia's. Titled "Tossed Aside," the article revealed what life had been like for one of the men who had spent two tours in Vietnam and faced a different battle when he returned home. This time, he fought against alcohol. His wife and son became collateral damage in that war. After he lost them, he surrendered to his addiction. The country he defended offered him little help, and he ended up alone on the streets. Saint Cecilia's had given him a chance to change his life.

Lucas's style was straight-forward and compelling. The discovery that the stranger I had agreed to get together with was a good writer was irrationally reassuring. Nina Stevens wrote well, too, and she was quite possibly a sociopath. Or maybe, like me, she was a victim of her circumstances.

Regardless, she and the rest of the workshop would be expecting me to have some pearls of wisdom for my next class. Not only did I have none, but I was too tired to come up with anything creative. Once again, I thought of my high school teacher. She liked to put us in groups to work on developing peer review skills. The way Nina handled herself in a small group should give me additional insights into her personality. It might even offer clues to determine her genre—fiction, memoir, or true confession.

The first notes of the theme song for one of the late-night shows trumpeted through the room. Since Michael's death, in addition to waking up in the middle of the night, I hadn't been able to fall asleep until well after midnight. Thanks to Dr. Riley, I only had to pop a pill and drift into oblivion. I turned off the TV and did a final re-check of the locks. After washing my face and brushing my teeth, I drew back the curtains on the bedroom window. There was no sign of Rex. Either he'd abandoned his post willingly or been trapped inside by a closed doggy door. I hoped he had made his rounds and decided all was well for the evening.

Chapter 14

Groggy and disoriented, I woke to what I thought was my alarm. But when I reached to shut it off, I discovered I hadn't set it. The sound I awoke to had been familiar—a hollow chu-chung like the metallic clang of a prison door shutting or a judge's gavel echoing through a courtroom. The deep bass voice that signaled the start of *Law & Order* came to me from the downstairs TV, the one I always turned off before going to bed. The same way I would have sworn I'd done last night.

I held my breath, certain I would hear footsteps plodding up the stairs. Except for the murmurs of my favorite on-screen detectives, the house was quiet. I slipped from under the covers, careful not to let my feet land heavy on the carpet, and crouched down in search of something to defend myself with. Beside the box marked winter boots, I saw the five-pound hand weights I bought to build up my sagging biceps. I took one out and shifted it from hand to hand, considering the best way to weaponize it.

The most threatening stance would be to hold it in front of me with both hands. I tiptoed forward and eased into the hallway. Nobody lunged at me, so I kept my back to the wall and scooted toward the master bedroom. I slipped through the half-closed door, peeked in, and found it empty. Of course, an insane serial killer might have been lurking in the shower, but I wasn't about to become a hapless victim by opening the curtain to be mutilated and washed down the drain.

I took the stairs like an old person, slowly and deliberately, a step at a time. A glimpse of myself in the mirror—bedhead hair tufting in opposite directions, a smudge of mascara under my eyes, lime-green hand weight jutting ahead of me—made me glad Dr. Riley wasn't around to see me. After slinking through the downstairs, room by room, I determined I was alone in the house. But that didn't mean I had been alone the entire evening. Someone could have waited until I was asleep to, to what?

What kind of devious plan included turning on somebody's television? I considered the possibility my conversation with Lucas had contributed to the confusion, causing me to recall an event that never happened. It was more likely, however, that the meds my therapist had prescribed impaired my ability to separate action from inaction, reality from imagination. That realization, while less disturbing than the alternate home-invader theory, wasn't reassuring.

My adrenaline high disappeared, leaving behind a pounding headache. I turned to coffee, hoping the caffeine would offer relief. It didn't. A second cup and two aspirin wrapped the thudding in cotton but did nothing to alleviate the general malaise that had descended over me. Frustrated, I began to question the effectiveness of my new prescriptions. Wasn't I supposed to start feeling cheerier? Unless this anxiety was one of the many side effects I skimmed over.

Possibly, I just needed something to eat. I settled on a carton of Greek yogurt that was only a week past the expiration date and ate it standing at the sink. A thin shelf of dark clouds rested above the pine trees beyond my fence. Oddly, the prospect of a gloomy day didn't bother me. Since Michael's death, it was the bright, sunny days with their stark contrast to my own mood that left me feeling out of touch with the world.

I tossed the container in the trash, fixed a third cup of coffee, and took it with me to the den, where my laptop lay on the sofa, then sorted through emails, answering the few that mattered.

I thought of GarNetted and wondered if my friend had accepted my explanation or was silently simmering before boiling over with more vitriol? A quick look at the new comments answered my question.

> *What the fuck does "rethinking the concept" mean? You know what I think? I think you dont give a shit about the people who got you where you are today. Or should I say where you were? Bring Garnet back fast or you could be rethinking a lot of things. Like that sweet little life you have in that cutie-pie townhouse.*

GarNetted's latest comment angered more than frightened me, and I almost hit delete. Instead, I copied the message into an email to Wanda and assured her

I was fine and didn't think I needed to contact the police but would if things got weirder. Seconds after hitting send, I received an automatic response telling me she was away from the office and would get back to me as soon as possible.

I resisted the impulse to respond to GarNetted's blistering post with a nasty retort and rose above the situation, blocking him instead.

My ex-fan's description of my boring home disturbed me, so I ran a word search in my blog to see if I'd ever mentioned buying a townhouse with Michael. I hadn't. I told myself I could have said something about it in a radio interview or somewhere on social media. But I knew that wasn't true.

•   •   •

My hands were still shaking when I got to the rec center. Determined to keep it together, I walked at a leisurely pace from the car to the classroom and smiled at participants as they entered.

When it was time to start, I did a quick head count and came up one short. My missing student was Nina.

I began without her. "I appreciate your willingness to tackle my unconventional get-to-know-you assignment. And I was relieved taking this class didn't show up as anyone's regret." Encouraged by a few polite twitters, I continued. "I'll be returning your work later. For now, I want to try something different."

I asked them to take out their opening paragraphs and explained my plan for peer reviews. After reading my list of groupings, I helped arrange desks. Then I instructed everyone to exchange papers and read them, placing check marks by lines that stood out to them, until each one had been reviewed by each group member.

I moved around, returning their assignments and answering questions and almost missed it when Nina slipped into the room. Head down, dark hair half covering her face, she moved toward the spot where her desk had been and stopped. She wore the same oversized sweatshirt with missing sleeves. There were no mascara trails down her cheeks today, but she was paler if possible, and had a haunted look about her. She backed up and leaned against the wall.

Fearful she might flee, I hurried to her side.

"We moved the desks to make it easier to do peer reviews. You're with that group over there." I pointed to where Howard, Louisa, and Betty were sitting.

"You mean this is a group thing? Because I'm totally not into that."

"I don't blame you, but this more of a way to get comfortable sharing your writing. Please, give it a try, and if you hate it, we can look at some possible alternatives." Not that I had any such options since I hadn't been prepared for rebellion.

Still upset over GarNetted's nastiness, I didn't trust my emotional state. The edginess I was beginning to attribute to my new medication, made me worry how I might react if Nina refused to go along with the plan.

I exhaled with relief when she shrugged and took the desk next to Louisa. I put the four of them together because of the strength of their writing. At the sight of Nina's hostile face and Louisa's stern glare, I questioned my decision. If the two turned against me, I could be in serious trouble.

After I passed out papers, I began moving among the groups to gauge the pace of their progress. With only a few minutes left, I told them to continue with their projects at home and be prepared to read their work within their groups the next day.

As my students—only three days and I already thought of them as mine—prepared to leave, I gathered my things. When Nina passed my desk, she gave me a nod so slight I might have imagined it, but she didn't ask for an alternate assignment. And I couldn't be sure because it disappeared so quickly, but I think Louisa Carter smiled.

Chapter 15

Atlanta's morning traffic was always sluggish, with unpredictable backups and the occasional sweet spot where cars zipped along at thirty miles an hour. After eleven, the stop and go rhythm usually switched to slow, but steady. Today was more steady than slow, and I arrived at the café a good fifteen minutes early for my meeting with Montgomery. I found a parking place close to the entrance of the yellow building with its perky rooftop outlined in bright red.

Before leaving the car, I checked my phone and was a little surprised to find I had an email from Todd.

Wanda's not well. Not sure if it's a virus or food poisoning, but I'm manning the office. GarNetted's latest comment, or should I say threat, is absolutely appalling. I agree we should wait to bring in the police. But if anything else happens, call me directly, and I'll take care of it.

The idea of Todd riding in on a white horse to save me from a digital scoundrel would have made me laugh if I hadn't been so creeped out. And I couldn't remember a time when Wanda had been too sick to show up for work. On my way to the entrance, I decided the timing of my upcoming meeting would be a welcome distraction.

The second I entered the hallway leading to the hostess stand, a blend of the nostalgic with the modern lay ahead of me. Well-lit, wood-slated ceilings contrasted with the checkered tile floor. The seating arrangement included shiny red leather booths and a counter equipped with cushioned stools.

A smiling waitress in fifties attire—white uniform and apron trimmed in bright blue with a matching crown cap—greeted me. "Welcome to the OK Café. Booth or counter?"

Before I could answer, I felt a tap on my shoulder, followed by the deep, buttery-smooth voice of my caller from the previous night.

"Mrs. Dolan? I'm Lucas Montgomery."

Well, well, well. Not exactly the bump and grind kind of guy. More like Clark Kent, the mocha chocolata version.

I silently cursed Garnet while trying to stop imagining him in tights. The picture from the article provided an accurate image of the reporter, but the man standing behind me had an electric energy no photo could capture. Nor could it properly represent the depth of his light brown eyes or the texture of his dark, smooth skin.

"I recognized you from the follow-up articles about your husband's death."

"It's Kara." I tried to recall an article with my picture and decided it must have been the one taken at Michael's funeral.

"Table for two?" the server asked. Without waiting for a response, she said, "Right this way, please," and led us to a small booth by the window.

Despite the bright morning sun streaming over us, I couldn't escape the feeling being with him was shady. There was an intimacy about it that caused me to squirm in my seat, as if being alone with such an attractive man meant I was cheating on my dead husband.

He seemed to sense my discomfort. "Would you rather have a bigger booth?"

I shook my head. "This is fine."

She smiled and placed menus on the table.

"Just coffee for me," I said.

"Coffee's good," he agreed.

As soon as she left, he began. "I met Michael a little over a year ago, the same time Saint Cecilia's had purchased a nearby building and turned it into a small clinic to help their clientele. I was interviewing some of the vets who hang out there, and he was helping Sister Mary Alice create a program to monitor the progress of the men. He included everything from how often they checked in to the center to the meds they were taking—or supposed to be taking."

I was going to ask what he meant by "supposed to be" when the waitress returned with our coffee. Lucas poured cream in his cup and stirred. I added sweetener to mine and waited to see if he would address my unasked question. He did.

"Tracking their medication regimen was especially important to Sister Mary Alice since they're primarily funded by grant money and had just received a sizeable one from a pharmaceutical group." He sipped his coffee.

"Why would big pharma be interested in a center for homeless vets? Where's the profit?"

"I wondered the same thing myself. The company line is that they want to give back to the people who sacrificed so much for their country, blah, blah, blah. But I suspected it might be an opportunity to use the men as guinea pigs for experimental drug testing."

"Is that even legal?"

"I was looking into that when I met Michael. Your husband was a great guy, but you know that."

With my throat too tight to speak, I could only nod and study the Formica tabletop.

"It's not always easy to get people who've been living on the streets to talk to you. That's especially true of some of the veterans I run into. Some of them suffer from PTSD; others just don't trust regular folks, the kind who enjoy sitting in judgment. But Michael had a gift. He treated them like friends. No, that's not right. He was their friend. They shared pieces of their lives with him, even let him record them. He told me you agreed to work with us on transforming their words into compelling stories."

"I did. Only he never said you were part of the project. That *we* would be working together." Although it bothered me that Michael had never mentioned anything at all about Lucas, I was warming up to the idea of collaborating with him. "Doesn't matter, though, since I haven't done much to follow up with my promise." And I feared I never would.

"Not your fault. If I'd gotten in touch with you sooner, we might have encouraged each other. My only excuse is that I was trying to work through some questions I had on the events that led up to the night of the shooting. I've been talking with one guy in particular, Clive, the unofficial leader of the group. He and Michael were close. Because he trusted your husband, he was willing to help get the others to talk to me. Otherwise, I'm not sure how much of their stories I would have heard."

He stopped and I wondered if we were thinking the same thing. That if not for him, Michael might still be alive.

"But it was Clive who put us onto something unusual about the men on anti-psychotic medications. The reactions to the drugs were erratic. Sometimes they would be so wasted they had trouble talking. Other times, they were high as kites, hallucinating even. He was especially worried about a buddy of his, Benny Rodriguez; everybody calls him Aftershock. He got so bad they admitted him to the hospital. A variance like that isn't odd in a population where the medication is self-administered. But at St. Cecilia's, the staff was meticulous about monitoring patients with severe conditions."

The waitress came with offers of refills. He moved his cup closer; I covered mine. My level of agitation had been on the rise during the conversation, and I most definitely did not need another shot of caffeine.

"Technically, the center falls under the jurisdiction of the head of the area diocese, but the hospital is owned by a private company. Sister Mary Alice handled the daily operations and interactions with the veterans. Her responsibilities included administering medication to the men in the trial, as well as some who were too disoriented to stay on a schedule. Clive and the nun were tight. She told Michael how hard it was for her to keep track of everything without a better system. Anything would have been an improvement over hers—color-coded spiral notebooks. So, Michael created a program for her and had just started entering the information when he was killed."

Despite my approval of his straightforward approach to my husband's death, the brutality of his statement made me flinch.

"I'm sorry, Mrs. Do—I mean Kara. All the time I spend with cops and other reporters is turning me into an insensitive ass. Although my mother might argue I started out as one."

When he smiled, his eyes crinkled at the corner.

"It's okay. Please, go on."

"The day before the shooting, Michael called to set up a meeting. Said he'd come across something he thought I should see. I got hung up at the paper and texted I was running behind. Turns out he didn't have the time to wait."

Neither of us spoke, as he poured more cream in his coffee. I stared out the window where a white-haired couple I'd guess to be in their mid-to-late seventies, walked arm-in-arm to their car.

"Did you see him, uh, after?"

"No. The police were already there when I arrived. I told them about our meeting. Later, I gave a statement, explaining he was looking into some irregularities at the center. I clued them in on our suspicion that something wasn't quite right with the care the men were getting. They suggested I report it to the Veterans' Affairs folks. Guess they didn't think shabby treatment of vets was important enough to kill someone over."

"On the phone you said you were worried about some people thinking I know more than I do. What did you mean by that?"

"I'm not exactly sure. I hoped I'd get more specifics from Clive, but nobody's seen him since the shooting. I've been trying to locate him, but he's disappeared."

"What about Sister Mary Alice? Have you talked to her?"

He removed his glasses and rubbed the bridge of his nose. "I would have, but it seems the poor woman took a bad fall a few days after Michael's murder. The story was there's a loose board on the rectory stairs, and she was in a hurry."

"But she's okay, right? We can still talk to her."

"Unfortunately not. She was unconscious when they found her. Doctors suspected it was a concussion. They kept her at the hospital to run tests but never got the chance. She had a stroke. Then she slipped into a coma and never regained consciousness. She died last week."

Chapter 16

On the drive home, I replayed my conversation with Lucas, mulling over the possibility Michael's murder and Sister Mary Alice's accident were connected. As I slid out from behind the wheel, a wave of dizziness overcame me. I leaned against the window for a second before regaining my equilibrium.

My headache medication, promising eight to ten hours of relief, failed around hour five, and I was afraid to take more without eating something. But I was already a bit queasy, and the thought of food made my stomach lurch. So, I took an icepack and lay down on the sofa, enjoying the quiet. Too quiet, I realized, sitting upright. It was time for the local news update, but there was no perky blonde anchor relating the latest political debacle.

Like switching it off in the evenings, turning on the television as soon as I came downstairs became such a habit I seldom had a definitive memory of it. I knew it was on this morning, so had I gotten confused and switched it off before leaving? Had I started mixing up my days and nights? I closed my eyes and pictured the list of side effects from my meds. Forgetfulness was near the top. Regardless, the damn thing was off now, and all I could hear was my pulse beating in my temples.

Ice against my forehead, I went straight for the television and tuned into the home shopping network. Then I rummaged through my pantry until I found crackers and a jar of peanut butter. I wasn't hungry but needed something to accompany the wine I'd prescribed to settle both my stomach and nerves.

I stood at the counter and choked down the makeshift meal. The throbbing in my head subsided, and I was no longer nauseated. So, I took my laptop and the Riesling to the sunroom.

It was as quiet outside as it was in. I hadn't felt so totally alone since the evening after Michael's funeral. Barb and my dad tried to talk me into going home with them, and Andy volunteered to stay with me, but I insisted I was fine. And I had been at first until a mudslide of solitude buried me.

It wasn't as if I was afraid of being by myself. I lived independently for years. But now, without Michael, I was incomplete.

In need of fresh air, I opened a window. A splash of color announced the return of my redheaded friend. Instead of flying to his favorite tree, however, he perched on the fence with his beak pointed in my direction. Regal and ridiculous at the same time, he made me smile.

"What's that, Mr. Peckerhead? You think I'm being a self-centered shit, sitting around moaning and groaning about how pitiful I am when I should be trying to find out who killed Michael?"

He didn't answer, but I sensed birdlike approval as I began my research into Saint Cecilia's Hospitality Home. I discovered it was one of the few shelters with specific resources for veterans. Their mission was "to provide support and assistance on the road to self-sufficiency."

The good news was that Atlanta had experienced some success in reducing the number of vets living on the streets. The not-so-good news was that while homelessness was a common denominator, it wasn't always the biggest challenge facing this group. Substance abuse, especially for those suffering from PTSD, ranked higher than the general population and getting treatment could be difficult.

The really bad news was the increasingly high suicide rate of this population, something Lucas touched on in his series. His article, however, omitted statistics on the topic as it related to Saint Cecelia's.

Both my mood and the afternoon darkened. A rumble of thunder underscored my mental turmoil. A breeze sifted through the screen and brought with it the earthy heaviness of rain. I'd been so absorbed in my research I hadn't noticed it was after six. More surprising, I forgot to finish my glass of wine.

I closed my laptop and the window, then went to the kitchen and made a sandwich, which I proceeded to eat in front of the TV. The evening news was too dismal, so I channel-surfed, stopping when I hit a close-up of Liz Taylor telling Paul Newman she feels like a cat on a hot tin roof. He says she should jump, then adds that cats do it all the time and survive the fall.

Like much of the advice in old movies, these lines from *Cat on a Hot Tin Roof* bordered on the absurd. Cats can get killed leaping off into the unknown. But how long can they dance on that sizzling roof before they jump, or someone pushes them?

•   •   •

I woke to the tune of Wanda's ringtone, wondering why she would call me in the middle of the night. A quick glance at my watch revealed it was only a little after nine. Paul and Liz had yielded to a black and white classic I didn't recognize. Not wanting my agent to know I'd been dozing instead of writing, I tried to sound alert.

"Hey, Wanda," I croaked. "What's shaking?"

"Jesus, Kara. I've been trying to get you for hours. I was about to call the cops. Did you say *What's shaking?* Are you drunk?"

"I'm perfectly sober." *Why did people always think I was drunk?* "I left my phone in another room. Aren't you supposed to be home recovering? Todd said—"

"Todd's an idiot. Honestly, that boy would like nothing better than to step over my still-warm body and slip his scrawny ass behind my desk. I might not be a hundred percent, but I'm not about to leave that pretentious little twit in charge. Especially not when some sick perv is threatening you."

First Todd, now Wanda. I began to doubt the wisdom of sharing my former fan's obscene comment. "Don't worry. I've taken care of it. GarNetted is officially blocked."

"Good, but he's not done with you, I'm afraid. Check your Twitter profile."

"Hold on a second." I switched screens and reread my last post.

Garnet is on a short break, but will return soon, sassier and sexier than ever.

GarNetted retweeted my message and added to it.

Doesnt look like a short break. Maybe KC has lost her nerve #disappointedwithdolan

What followed were replies and retweets, offering theories on my lack of inspiration and the YouTube link to my supermarket breakdown. Most recently the creep included my mystery workshop in his litany of grievances, disparaging both my legitimacy as a teacher—he said I sucked in that department, and I had to agree—and my motivation for leading the group—sheer unmitigated greed, which I did not agree with.

Even more disturbing to me than the hateful content were the handles: Veronica Beaumont, Chelsea Alexander, Chance Taylor, Troy Vandergriff. All were in the Garnet Rivers series.

"I can't believe people would use characters from my books to slam me like this. Isn't there something we can do to stop these assholes?"

"I sent Todd to talk to the tech guys. They told him Twitter has been working on deleting fake accounts, but their priority is filtering out Russian bots. Dealing with antagonistic readers stealing names from novels is pretty low on their list. The good news is you're not trending."

"Does that mean there's nothing we can do? We just have to sit back and take it?"

"I didn't say that, but we don't want to get in a pissing contest with a bunch of cowardly trolls. Or most likely, one pissant asshole with several accounts. We'll get rid of the obvious ones. That won't stop others from popping up, but it will slow them down. It's not as bad as it could be since most of your fans aren't exactly members of the Twitter generation. For those that are, you could always tweet a few teasers about the book you're working on. That would stimulate some positive chatter."

She paused, probably in the hope I'd react enthusiastically to the idea of giving my readers provocative hints about my heroine's upcoming naughtiness. When I didn't react at all, she continued.

"Anyway, Todd can take care of blocking the worst of them, if you—"

"No, I want to do it. And I'll write that teaser, too." It surprised me how much I wanted to personally eliminate my detractors. Even more of a shock was the stirring of excitement I experienced at bringing Garnet back.

"You will? That's fantastic!" My stoic agent sounded like a giddy schoolgirl but only for a second. Then she said, "There's something else we need to consider. GarNetted may be more than a pissed-off nut job from Bumfuck, USA. The jerk might be someone you know."

Wanda's explanation of the social media blitzkrieg someone had designed to destroy me had been unnerving enough without the added possibility I might know the person hell-bent on taking me down. And while *destroy* might be too strong a word, if my reputation as a writer was ruined, what would I have left?

I took great pleasure in clicking on the names of my tormentors and blocking them from my life—my Twitter life, that is. Less pleasurable was coming up with the tweet on Garnet's next escapade. Since I'd already fed Dr. Riley a load of crap about how I planned to have my protagonist become involved with a law enforcement agent, I decided it would be easier to keep track of one lie. After five attempts, I came up with a version that managed to be intriguing without locking me into a plot commitment.

When a sexy detective ends up in Garnet's bed, you can expect more than sparks to fly.

The rest of the evening was a wine-induced blur, ending with me taking my meds. Just before I slipped into unconsciousness, I wondered what I had done to make someone angry enough to go after me. And whether this online campaign might bleed into my real life.

●　　　●　　　●

Sitting behind the old wooden desk in the rec center gave me what I suspected was a false sense of security, especially when I had to consider the possibility a workshop participant could be my online tormentor.

I'd done nothing to prepare for today, so I went with group work again. A moment of inspiration came to me. I asked everyone to mark favorite passages in their classmates' writing, then return the papers to their creators, who would then choose two lines from the piece to share with the class.

While the assignment wasn't particularly new or creative, the intent behind it was. I planned to study my aspiring authors as they read aloud to determine who might secretly hate me. My plan would be useless if Andy was correct in his assertion that sociopaths wore masks of normalcy, but it was the only one I had.

When everyone seemed to have finished, I asked for volunteers. A young man in a sweater at least a size and a half too small raised his hand. He strode to my desk and began emoting. Approximately ten lines later, he stopped and bounded back to his seat.

The class continued. Even Madame Defarge—who was really Bernadine Culpepper, a seemingly harmless resident from an assisted living community—dropped her knitting needles and read a brief passage. I was so engrossed in looking for something that would lead me to the dark soul of my antagonist, I barely registered what anyone was saying. But I concluded only a few of them had the capacity to write as poorly as my Twitter terrorist. Unless that person was so good, he or she could assume the persona of a terrible writer, in which case I was screwed.

When Betty Frasier read, most people leaned toward her. I had no idea if their body language signaled genuine interest or was a reaction to her whisper-soft voice. Nor did I know if the vacant space in front of my desk meant everyone had shared or that no one wanted to follow her.

While scanning the room to see if anyone needed individual encouragement, I caught sight of a woman seated in the very back. A heavy-set man blocked my full view of her. If she hadn't been tapping the toe of her dangerously high heels, I might not have noticed her at all. I scooted sideways to get a better look and assess how to coax her into sharing.

Before I could think of the right words, the burly guy inched to the left, and I glimpsed shiny black hair falling across an expanse of smooth, pale skin. I hopped to my feet and saw what I'd taken for partial nudity was only a fashionable off-the-shoulder knit top in a deep shade of crimson. The thick dark curls cascading over her porcelain collarbone stunned me with their familiarity, as did the poreless skin, hollow cheeks, and dazzling green eyes.

She slipped from her desk and tossed her hair back. Without thinking, I mirrored the action. When she smoothed her skirt, I followed suit. But when she took a step in my direction, I backed into my chair. The sound it made hitting the desk broke the spell, and I returned my attention to my students, who were giving me varying levels of confused looks.

"You okay, Ms. D?" the boy in the tight sweater asked.

"I'm fine," I said as I sat. "Guess I was overwhelmed with everyone's writing." I attempted a smile, but the sight of Garnet walking toward the door caused my lips to tremble too much to complete the effort.

She had no such problem. When Garnet reached the exit, she stopped and looked over her shoulder. Then she shot me her trademark smile: the icy one that never failed to strike cold fear in the heart of anyone who stood in her way.

Chapter 17

By the time I reached home, I convinced myself Garnet's appearance was the direct result of stress from the escalating complications in my life.

On my way to check the mail, I reassured myself I wasn't baying-at-the-moon crazy. "It's not as if I called on her and asked her to read her favorite lines to the class."

Probably a good thing, since Garnet would most likely have picked something risqué. Possibly an excerpt from *The River Runs Red* when she offered advice to a friend who kept making terrible choices in men: *If you have to wait for your prince to come, you're not doing it right.*

"Hey, Kara."

I jumped, then noticed Ira and Rex coming back from their early afternoon walk.

"Didn't mean to spook you." He gave me a concerned look; the dog whined in sympathy.

"Not your fault. I was daydreaming." Daytime nightmaring was more like it, but oversharing with my neighbor would be a waste of his time. I held my hand out to Rex and asked, "How are you guys doing?" He sniffed, then licked it.

"Well, what about that? He's taken quite a liking to you."

I knelt until we were eye level and scratched behind his ears. "You're a good boy, aren't you?"

He pawed the air and moved closer, so I could have easier access to the sweet spot. After a few seconds, I stood.

"I was hoping to catch you," Ira said. "I don't want to scare you, but a little after nine this morning, Rex started going ape-shit. I stepped out on the back porch, but if somebody was there, they'd already run off."

Known for being a one-man neighborhood watch, he rained down justice on the mailbox-smashing middle-school gangsters. Their parents paid for the damage, and the three boys spent a month doing hard yard labor under Ira's supervision. And he caught the old lady who'd been stealing packages from porches. Turned out she was senile rather than larcenous, but still.

"You think someone might have been out back?" *A shadowy figure smoking a cigarette while watching me?*

"I doubt it. Most likely it was just some raccoon hell bent on getting Rex riled up. Wanted to let you know so you could make sure your alarm is on." He started toward his house.

"Wait," I said, louder than intended. Ira stopped and Rex snapped to attention. I shared my story about seeing someone on the other of the fence, including the cigarette butt I'd found.

"Probably some kid sneaking out for a smoke. But if you see or hear anything that doesn't seem right, lock yourself in the bedroom, dial 911, then call me. In the meantime, Rex and I will stand lookout."

At the sound of his name, his ears shot up. He glanced at his owner, then turned those soulful eyes to me. Once again, the intensity of his stare made me feel as if we had a connection, that he wanted to tell me something.

Although Ira's advice was troubling, I found his rational response to what others might have found crazy comforting.

It was only a little after three, which meant much of the afternoon and all the evening loomed ahead. When I'd been a writing writer, this emptiness would have thrilled me. Hours of imagining possibilities and bringing them to life with nothing more than language. Now, I was restless and tired at the same time. And I wanted a drink.

Despite Andy's enthusiasm for it, day-drinking scared me, especially this early. And today I had the unexpected and almost unrecognizable need to accomplish something. Fearful of finding a host of more characters from the Garnet series tweeting insults, I steered clear of Twitter and turned to an area that offered me more control: tomorrow's class.

•　　•　　•

"We're going to discuss some of the more practical issues of getting published—querying agents."

I filled most of last night reading up on the ever-elusive perfect way to catch an agent's attention and arrived at the rec center early to make copies of what I found. After spending twenty minutes going over the materials, answering questions, I volunteered to read query letters from those brave enough to write them. Then I sent them back to their groups and told them to pick up where they had left off the day before.

Nina seemed less hostile about working with others, and Louisa exhibited no signs of distaste toward me. Betty and Howard were their comfortingly compliant selves. And Garnet appeared to be skipping school.

The time I hadn't spent on reviewing the art of query-letter writing, I devoted to reading about the differences between sociopaths (the anti-social condition I had suspected my online tormentor suffered from) and psychopaths (the anti-social condition I hoped he or she didn't have).

I discovered the psychiatric community avoided labeling patients as either, and arm-chair mental health people insisted it was difficult to tell the difference between the two. Sociopaths had weak consciences; psychopaths had none. Both lacked empathy and were manipulative and narcissistic. Neither were destined to be cold-blooded killers, but psychopaths were more likely to choose violence to get what they wanted. Most of the articles stressed that only three percent of men and one percent of women had verifiable anti-social disorders, but those statistics were higher in prison populations.

The low probability of my encountering such people in or out of jail did little to reassure me. Like the lottery, someone has to win. In my case, someone had to lose, and it was as likely to be me as it was to be some other loser. I continued scanning student faces but found no clues to who might have a proclivity for violence.

Class ended, and all but Howard packed up and shuffled off.

"Have you got a minute?" he asked.

"Of course."

He came forward and scooted a desk close to mine.

"I don't like to butt in people's business," he began. "But I'm worried about a member of my group."

"Okay." I was hesitant, too, and wished I'd paid more attention to the four-page handout from the Writers Club on expectations of guest instructors. Was I bound by some sort of literary Hippocratic Oath? Or was I more of a confessor—a person free to listen and suggest penance, then keep her mouth shut?

"Louisa and I both noticed it, but we decided I should be the one to talk to you."

Not a big surprise. "Okay, I'm listening."

"It's Nina. We don't really know her all that well, but we've seen some changes in her behavior. Louisa's especially concerned what with her experience with this sort of thing and all."

He paused, possibly realizing I had no idea what he was talking about when he referred to Betty's and Louisa's issues. I wasn't aware of the relationship they had before joining the workshop. Whatever had troubled him, he shrugged it off and continued.

"We're afraid Nina has depression. Not just a bad mood. The dark kind people don't come back from."

I almost shared my own concerns but wasn't sure he knew as much about Nina's background as I did. And I didn't want to admit how I'd gotten the information.

"What has she done or said that makes you think that?"

"Other than the tone of her writing, there's nothing I can put my finger on, and the two of us confronting her might backfire. I know it's a lot to ask, but since Nina thinks so highly of you and your opinions, we hoped you might talk to her."

It took several seconds for me to recover from the shock the girl held me in such high regard. "Are you sure you about that? About her valuing my opinion?"

He nodded. "She's shared more during this workshop than she has during her time with our critique group. A dam inside her burst and started spilling out all these words and emotions. And the stuff is good. I just wish it wasn't so damned scary." A slow blush began at his neckline and spread north. "Sorry about the language, but I'd feel awful if I kept my mouth shut and anything bad—something I could have stopped if I spoke up—happened to her. Even worse, I'm not sure if Nina is only dangerous to herself, or if she might be in such a terrible spot she could hurt someone else."

After I promised I would consider talking to the her, he thanked me and left.

I stared at a torn poster of a kitten dangling from a string, wondering if Louisa and Howard were mistaken about Nina's feelings toward me. Instead of admiration, maybe it was fixation. Was she confused or deranged enough that I could be the "someone else" he alluded to? My instincts, however, told me I had nothing to fear from this troubled young writer. But despite Garnet's admonishment to trust them, I'd been so lost in my own dark place, I wasn't sure I could.

I also didn't share Howard's faith in my ability to get Nina to open up and, no matter how hard I tried, I couldn't see myself counseling the young girl. Who was I to give advice for overcoming depression? As for consolation, I had nothing to offer.

Chapter 18

On the way to the car, my phone began buzzing from inside my purse. It was a text from Barb.

Your father's really looking forward to seeing you at dinner tonight.

Shit. I had completely forgotten about her invitation. I didn't even remember agreeing to sit down with my father and stepmother. It would be an evening of awkward smiles and uncomfortable silences with Dad and pointed remarks and masterful interrogations from Barb. But when I checked my calendar, there it was: dinner at 7:00 with B&D.

On the drive home, I tried to pinpoint the exact moment I'd given up attempts to communicate with my father. For years, I thought it had been on my tenth birthday, the one nobody remembered. Since she'd been sick for almost a year, I couldn't blame my mother for the oversight. Instead of hurting my feelings, her omission served as a reminder of all that I would miss when she was gone. Dad was another story. He wasn't dying of cancer, so he received the full force of my pre-adolescent pain and fury.

Mom died three months after that birthday, and on the day of the funeral I stopped speaking to my father. He didn't notice because to him I was interwoven into a tapestry of grief. Aunt Joyce, his sister, came to stay. She tried to facilitate conversation, but I refused to participate. After a few weeks, she gave up and left us to our separate silences.

The effort of maintaining righteous anger became exhausting, and I called a truce from a war he hadn't known I'd declared. After time, he began to take notice of me and made efforts to keep up with my life. By then, we were polite strangers.

From the vantage point of adulthood, I saw it wasn't just my unnoted birthday that created the distance. I understand now that my mother's illness consumed them both and that my relationship with my father had become collateral damage from the long goodbye between a cancer patient and the people left behind. As a child, I lacked the tools to break down the barriers. When he married Barb, who couldn't have been less like my mother if she'd been an entirely different species, the barricade doubled in size.

And now I'd committed to spending an entire evening of staring at the two of them across the emotional void that characterized our relationship.

Thoughts of that emptiness reminded me my cupboards were almost bare, so I pulled into the grocery store, not the one where I attacked both cereal and employees. Inside, I avoided the grain aisle and picked up the basics: eggs, milk, cheese, chocolate, and wine. As I passed the pet section, a German Shepherd who could have been Rex's twin stared at me from a box of bones. Below his handsome face, the tagline read "Special Treats for That Special Friend." When I dropped them into my cart, I heard an increasingly familiar voice.

It's getting bad when the only goodies you're giving out are to a four-legged guy.

"Why don't you mind your own damn business," I snapped loud enough to cause an elderly lady buying cat food to reverse direction and speed away.

I pushed my cart toward the checkout, moving almost as fast as the senior citizen I startled. Unlike her, however, I couldn't avoid the crazy woman shouting at an assortment of pet paraphernalia. Because now that Garnet had evolved into creating her own dialogue and I was responding aloud to it, I was that crazy woman.

•   •   •

Barb smiled as she passed a platter of amorphous orange blobs, oozing with a thin white substance that slid off and formed puddles on the platter. The image of pulsating alien cells under a mad scientist's microscope came to me.

"These are cauliflower chickpea patties topped with Tofutti. The recipe is part of our plan to get in shape the vegetarian way. They're delicious."

I speared one and transferred it to my plate, where it slid back and forth before the sauce congealed enough to anchor it in place.

"And this is quinoa beets and bean salad." I tried to look away as she plopped a glob next to the patty. After helping myself to an innocuous-looking roll—gluten-free, of course—I sawed at the cauliflower clump with my knife, finally separating a miniscule piece from the mass.

"Mmm," I murmured. "It's just as yummy as I expected."

She beamed at me, and I thought I detected a slight upturn of my father's lips. He didn't join in with my damning praise, though. Instead, he sighed and ate a forkful of quinoa.

"Have you finished another one of those sexy books of yours?" She asked between dainty bites of healthy food.

Her dismissive tone annoyed me, but I refused to let her bait me into defending my work. "Almost. But I had to take a break to teach a workshop for a local mystery writers' group."

"Seriously, *you're* teaching?" She snorted, spraying a fine vegetation mist into the air.

"What's so funny? Kara would make an excellent teacher."

She and I both jumped at the unexpected proclamation. Not only had my father joined the conversation without being addressed, but he'd also issued a statement of praise directly contradicting his wife's opinion.

"Thanks. I'm new at it, but it's fun, much more than I expected." Unless you considered the part where one of my students might be planning a murder. I spent the next few minutes elaborating on the workshop and slipping pieces of slime into my napkin.

He seemed genuinely interested, but Barb started fidgeting after the first minute or so. I suspected she wanted to talk about my experience at the psychiatrist's office, and I was right.

"How was Dr. Riley?" she asked when I finished my account of the interesting people in my class.

"So far, so good." I shrugged, then added, "You have got to give me the recipe for this cauliflower and pea stuff."

"They're chickpeas," she corrected. "I knew you would love it, so I copied it for you on an index card. You can add it to that cute little caddie I gave you last Christmas."

Like most of my stepmother's well-intended gifts—the box with grinning chickens painted on the sides and a jewelry case in the shape of a red stiletto—it had been donated to the Salvation Army along with the recipes inside it.

"But you only had one piece. Please, have some more."

"Thanks, but I'm stuffed." I folded the now heavy-laden napkin in my lap, taking care to secure its contents.

"Well, all right, but I hope you saved room for homemade tofu ice cream."

"That sounds delicious, but I honestly cannot eat another bite."

"Really, Kara, you are getting way too thin. Those first ten or twelve pounds you lost needed to go, but now you're practically emaciated. That look might work if you were a model, but obviously that's not the case."

I clinched my fist over my napkin and accidentally squeezed vegetarian goo on my jeans.

"Enough, Barb. If she says she's not hungry, she's not hungry." Dad spoke softly, but there was an edge to his words.

"Well, at least let Lupe make a doggy bag for you." Lupe was their long-suffering housekeeper and, in happier times, her cook.

I agreed and insisted on taking my plate to the kitchen, despite Barb's protests that Lupe would take care of it. I didn't want to risk the contents of my napkin spilling onto her pristine white apron. Plus, I needed a few seconds away from my stepmother's voice.

"Don't worry, Rex," I whispered as I opened the door. "I would never feed you this veggie shit."

From the window over the sink, I could see the top of Lupe's dark red hair peeking out from around the corner where she often hid to sneak a smoke. She reminded me of my stalker, if he existed, and how much better he'd been at disappearing into the shadows. Shivering slightly, I put my dish on the counter, scraped my napkin as clean as I could, and took a deep breath. Then I joined them in the den, where I drank several glasses of tofu-free wine.

Although I wouldn't call the rest of the evening a laugh riot, it wasn't bad. Between the drinking and my diversion skills, Barb forgot her cross-examination about my progress with Dr. Riley, and we talked about almost-normal stuff: investment tips from Dad, fashion advice from my stepmother, smiling and nodding from me.

Still, it felt good to back out of the driveway and head to my safe space, even though it was getting less and less safe.

Chapter 19

I woke after ten the next morning. Under the warm shower spray with one hand against the stall for balance, I once again considered the possibility that drinking while on medication might not be the smartest course of action. But by the time I finished dressing, turning on the TV, and eating a stale blueberry muffin, I rejected that conclusion. The idea of abstaining from alcohol was depressing, and that couldn't be good. I did, however, make a vow to cut back on the wine until I got more accustomed to the meds.

Taking a second cup of coffee along with me, I went to my writing room. Sunlight spilled over the tiled floor and highlighted my desktop where a folder with the first two chapters of my latest Garnet novel lay. In search of inspiration, I picked it up and read it aloud. Unlike the version I'd given Dr. Riley, my heroine wasn't headed toward true love. She was on her way to Senegal to help a former lover discover who was kidnapping girls from the nearby village. I considered developing a romance between my protagonist and her friend but couldn't picture my slinky protagonist naked under mosquito netting.

I left the chapters behind and took my cup to the dishwasher. Despite the coffee, my head still felt foggy. So, I headed to check my mailbox and get some fresh air.

Disappointed at the quiet on Rex's side of the fence, I supposed my new friend must be inside napping. I heard shrieks and laughter from kids playing down the street. Michael and I had planned on having children. We'd speculated about how they might look. Would they have my curly hair and his strong jaw? Would they inherit his calm disposition and my slightly warped sense of humor? I blinked away unshed tears.

When I was within a few feet of the mailbox, I realized it wasn't completely closed. From where I stood, I could only make out the edge of what was blocking the opening. When I reached it, I discovered a rectangular, black cardboard box. My name and address were printed in big block letters. There was no postage or any other markings. Puzzled, I removed it and went inside.

I placed it on the counter and stared. Stories of suspicious white powder that turned out to be anthrax and visions of detached digits made me hesitant to rip into it. While I was debating whether I was being cautious or paranoid, I heard Rex calling from his side of the fence. His barking sounded different today, more eager and friendly. I picked up a handful of treats and left the package behind.

"Hey, buddy," I called from the deck.

He was waiting for me—ears up, tail wagging.

"It's not a burger," I apologized as I stuck the bacon-shaped biscuit through the fence. "But it is better for you. Promotes good dental health and—" He snatched it and wolfed it down before I finished explaining the benefits. He sat on his haunches and grinned.

"I guess you liked it."

I offered the second treat. He accepted it and stayed close to the fence. Like before, he presented his furry nose, and I rubbed it, recognizing the encounter as a gift exchange.

A skittering sound signaled the presence of a fat squirrel running along the fence behind him. He jolted back before propelling himself toward the fluffy-tailed rodent, who taunted him by waiting until the dog was within snapping distance before leaping to the other side and scampering away. Rex yelped as the creature disappeared.

"Better luck next time." But he remained fixated on his escaped prey. I didn't take his inattention personally. In fact, our encounter had lightened my mood.

I returned to the kitchen, picked up the tightly wrapped box, and gently shook it. The contents made a raspy rattle. Too much noise for a fine powder, too scattered to be a thumb or finger. And if it were a bomb, all that shaking would surely have detonated it.

"Screw it," I said. "Just open the damned thing." Someone, however, had gotten overly enthusiastic with mailing tape, so I had to get a knife to slice through it.

Beware of men who tell you good things come in small packages. They're setting you up for disappointment.

This time Garnet was being true to her script, quoting from *The River Runs Red*.

I smiled and eased the lid off. An index card lay on top of tissue paper. I picked it up and read the message.

It's too late to save your husband, but if you want to save yourself, you'll get back to writing your sappy romance novels and stop sticking your nose where it doesn't belong.

I released it and watched it drop to the floor. Anyone who knew Garnet would never have called my books sappy. Hell, they weren't even romance. They were adventure stories about a woman who existed outside the limitations imposed on her by a male-dominated world—a woman who also really liked sex and lots of it.

Snap out of it, Kara. This is no time to get sensitive about some stupid attempt at critique. I picked up the card to examine it closer. There was no signature, but I assumed it was a gift from GarNetted. Or was there a hidden psychopath in my workshop group?

With the tip of the knife, I peeled back the tissue paper, revealing a bouquet of Garnet's favorites: red roses. Only the flowers staring up at me weren't dewy or lush like Garnet; they were brittle and decayed, tied together with a thick white ribbon covered in scarlet splatters.

• • •

"Clichéd, but effective," Andy said as he looked at the gruesome bouquet.

In the two hours it had taken him to break away from a client meeting to respond to my distress call, I tried to determine what disturbed me the most about my creepy gift. It was concerning that one of my unhinged fans had my address. I had always known that anyone familiar with the internet could locate me, but I suspected most of my readers satisfied their craving for spontaneity and adventure through Garnet. I hadn't worried about any of them popping in on me. And until now, digital communication had been enough for them.

It wouldn't have been difficult for one of my students to find me either. But I had trouble imagining any of them with the kind of personal hostility toward me to write those hateful posts. I certainly couldn't picture them delivering what amounted to a threat. Besides, as writers, I didn't believe they would be so harsh in their criticism of my work.

It was the mention of my husband's death that hit the hardest. Was it simply a way to get my attention? If so, it had been cruelly effective. And what had the writer meant when he told me to stop sticking my nose where it didn't belong.

There was something other than the content of the message that bothered me, something I couldn't immediately put my finger on. I'd assumed whoever was behind the nasty comments and the sender of the flowers were the same person. After reading the brief note for at least the tenth time, I realized what bothered me. GarNetted didn't use phrases like "sticking your nose where it doesn't belong." And he'd never met an apostrophe he liked. And while his messages were peppered with obscenities, he had never spoken disparagingly about my work. That could mean GarNetted and the one who sent the flowers were different people.

I doubted my ability to incite two fans to the same level of fury. But if I had, could they be connected in a conspiracy designed to drive me crazy? Or since I now seemed to accept conspirators were after me, was I already looney-tunes?

I shared my thoughts with Andy as soon as he arrived, but so far, he'd done little more than read the note and drink beer.

Finally, he said, "The way I see it, this is most likely some weirdo jonesing for a Garnet fix."

"It's a man then?" I remembered my caller with the bad cough.

"Not necessarily, but sending flowers makes me lean in that direction. Of course, it could be a woman trying to confuse you or with a crush on you. Or could be the same one who's been posting all that shit. And that's not good because these were delivered personally. You reactivated your alarm system, right?"

I nodded and tried to ignore the chill that went up my spine as I registered the implication behind Andy's question. "I'm worried my online fan isn't the same person who wrote this note. The style is different, colder. The threat is there, but it's more subtle than the other notes. And much better grammar."

He read the message again but made no comment. This time I didn't try to keep the fear from my voice.

"So, should I be afraid this guy might come after me? And since I don't know what business he wants me to stay out of, how will I stop?"

"People like that are usually cowards, sick fucks who get off scaring anyone they can."

"But what if it's more than that? What if he or she or they know something about what happened to Michael? Oh, God, Andy. What if they decided he was keeping me from writing about Garnet and shot him?"

"Don't get me wrong. The Garnet books are a hell of a read, but motivation for murder? I don't see it."

"I hope you're right."

But if he was right and it wasn't an angry fan or fans, there was a good chance the real stalker had murdered Michael to stop him from sticking his nose into the same unknown area I'd been warned to avoid.

"It wouldn't hurt to tell the cops about your anonymous admirer, though."

"Wouldn't that be extreme?" I pressed the icy glass against my forehead. My last experience with law enforcement involved the two detectives who showed up on my doorstep and destroyed my world. When they closed the case, I was frustrated, but also relieved I would never have to see them again.

"Actually, I think you should do it now. And Wanda, too. I pity the stalker who comes up against that literary harpy."

"Wanda's not a harpy. She's just intense."

"She's not all that literary either, but she is *intense* enough to scare the shit out of ordinary mortals. Why don't you email her while I get the cops?"

"No, I should do it." The opening refrain of "Who Are You?" sounded. Normally, I would let it go to voicemail, but tonight I welcomed anything that might distract Andy from bringing the police into my home.

"Sorry. One of my students said she would get in touch," I lied and checked caller ID. When I saw the name Montgomery, I smiled before faking a resigned expression. "I really need to take this. Grab another beer and sit tight until I get back."

From a safe distance in the hallway, I kept my tone neutral.

"Hope I'm not interrupting anything," Lucas said. "I shouldn't have dropped all that stuff on you all at once. It was insensitive and stupid. Are you okay? I mean, are you doing better processing everything?"

"I haven't really started. Processing, that is. I want to believe Michael's death wasn't meaningless. So, it's hard to tell if what you told me makes sense because it's logical or because I need it to."

"It's not as hopeless as it sounds. As a matter of fact, I may be on to something. I'm waiting to hear back from Clive."

"Are you positive he's dependable? Your article paints a bleak picture of all the poor man's been through."

"You read it?"

"I'm a writer and writers research. I would never go into a meeting without knowing something about the person I might be working with."

"What did you think?"

"I can see why Michael wanted to work with you. And your byline intrigues me." Shit. Was I flirting with him?

"My byline?"

"Yes. Lucas Montgomery sounds uh, well…"

Like a hot male stripper instead of a beautiful brown superhero?

"Stiff." Damn you, Garnet. "I mean formal."

"I have my mother to thank for that. She's an interesting combination of holy-roller and hell-raiser. My full name is Martin Lucas Montgomery. She still calls me Martin Lucas. Martin Lucas Montgomery when she's mad."

"I take it back. It's perfect."

"Thanks. But your husband wanted you involved, too. I hope we can give him that. If you find or notice anything unusual or if you just want to talk, I'm here for you."

I thanked him but wasn't sure how I felt about him being here or there or anywhere for me. Not when merely talking to him on the phone felt adulterous, if it was even possible to be unfaithful to a dead man.

"I'm sensing that wasn't one of your students. It sounded more like more pleasure than business." Andy wiggled his eyebrows and leered suggestively.

His expression brought me back in time to when Michael and I had just started dating. I fell hard from the start but had been afraid talking about him would jinx the relationship. I couldn't, however, hide it from my best friend. He immediately guessed something was going on and had pried the details out of me. Instead of making me fearful, telling him about Michael had been liberating, joyful. The realization I would never feel that way again hit me. My despair must have been visible.

"Hey, I'm just kidding." He wrapped his arm around my shoulders.

"It's not your fault." I said and collapsed against him. He held me until the sobs subsided. "I don't know why I'm crying."

"Well, I do. You're always putting on a brave front when you should let it go. Let other people carry some of the pain for you."

"How am I supposed to do that?"

"You shouldn't be so hard on yourself. Grieving comes with a steep learning curve. As for your mystery caller, you don't have to tell me anything. Unless you want to. In which case I'd be willing to listen."

I laughed, then surprised myself by telling him about my meeting with Lucas and his theory about Michael's murder. When I finished, he closed his eyes and rubbed his forehead.

"That's some serious shit. I was hoping for something less dangerous and a lot sexier."

"Please," I began, but he waved me off.

"I know, I know. You're not ready to think about getting involved with anyone. But it's okay if you have a twinge of interest every now and then. Michael wouldn't have wanted you to shut yourself off forever. Back to the serious part, though. Your friend said he talked to the police, but they need to hear it from you."

"All right. Only not now, please. I'm too worn out to be up half the night explaining everything. I promise I'll do it after class tomorrow."

"I can stick around if you want. We can have a sleepover, do each other's nails."

"Some other time."

"For sure." He grinned and kissed me on the cheek.

I locked the door behind him, then checked and rechecked the alarm system. I put the flowers back in the box and stuck the package on the shelf above my dryer. I wanted a drink but remembered the way I'd felt this morning after my wine-fest at dinner with the folks and decided on hot chocolate.

Cup in hand, I stepped outside and leaned against the railing. There was no sudden movement or insistent barking, but I took no comfort from the stillness. Alone in the dark, I was exposed. I dashed back inside and slammed the door.

Chapter 20

Saturday, I flew into an organizational frenzy. Tearing through closets and drawers, I tossed anything I hadn't worn in a year. Then I stuffed everything in garbage bags and threw them in the backseat of my car.

After my clothing purge, I began scrubbing bathrooms and floors. I kept up this frenetic pace until after midnight, when I took my drugs and passed out.

Sunday, I woke and picked up where I left off, ignoring the shelf with my bouquet and my promise to call Wanda. Around nine that evening, I stopped to make plans for Monday's class.

On my way upstairs, my phone vibrated from inside my pants pocket: Lucas again. My pulse quickened, and I couldn't determine if it was from anticipation or guilt. The still-married lady part of me urged me to ignore him and avoid the inevitable feeling of disloyalty.

"But what if he's found out something about Michael's murder," my rational side posited. "Something that will help make sense of the senselessness of his death?"

I answered before the married lady could counter.

"Is now a good time to talk?" he asked.

"Have you learned more about Sister Mary Alice or Aftershock?"

"They're calling the nun's fall an accident. It may or may not have brought on the stroke. Aftershock is still in the hospital. I don't suppose you've come across any of Michael's records?"

"Nothing." I didn't say I hadn't really looked.

"I promise I'm not giving up," he assured me. "And you'll call me if you find anything, right?" No longer smooth, his voice was higher pitched, almost shrill and tinged with something like urgency.

I said I would, adding to the many lies I'd been telling.

Later, holding the colorful little pills in my palm, I replayed our conversation, wondering if my reservations were valid or the result of this pharmaceutical mix. I was on the edge of sleep when Garnet whispered to me.

> *Beware of soft-spoken men who say they only want what's best for you. They're usually trying to get the better of you.*

Immediately after that unsolicited piece of advice, the same message she delivered to a woman who'd been taken in by a conman in *Cold as Ice*, I remembered my upcoming appointment with Dr. Riley.

•   •   •

The discussion over whether to self-publish or not developed into a debate. We didn't come to a firm conclusion on the topic, but getting the chance to talk about the frustrations of breaking in as an author seemed to make everyone feel better. While I met with students who had query letters to review, the others were free to write or share work with their groups.

With the last critique behind me, I walked around the room. It was the first time I felt comfortable removing the teacher-desk barrier I'd created. I was pleased to see Nina had chosen to participate. I watched the reactions of her group as she read. Howard sat motionless, his brow wrinkled. Louisa chewed on the stem of her glasses. Betty leaned forward, both hands flat on the desktop, studying the young girl's face as if committing it to memory.

When I announced the end of class, several groups, including Nina's, asked if it would be all right if they stayed behind for a bit. I had no idea if rec center rules allowed students to be alone unsupervised. But it wasn't as if I would be leaving a bunch of hormone-crazed teenagers alone in a dark room. And what could they do to me? Revoke my parking privileges? Ban me from Zumba?

"There's no reason you can't hang out as long as you want. I wouldn't go, but I have an appointment I can't miss." I reveled in my newly found rule resistance a few seconds before adding, "Be sure the last person to leave turns off the lights and locks the door."

•   •   •

The receptionist's chair was empty, her desktop free of debris and glistening with a just-polished sheen. Behind it, someone had stuck a hot pink post-it on the entrance to Riley's inner office.

I skirted the desk, careful not to disturb the pristine surface for fear of irritating its occupant should she return and, following the note's instructions, announced my presence by knocking.

Muffled voices came from within, the doctor's and a woman's, possibly the receptionist or another patient. Before I could decide whether to knock again or sit and wait, the door flew open. Riley glared at me from the threshold. His hair was uncombed, and his dark eyes were underscored by even darker circles.

"Mrs. Dolan, you're early." He gave me a stern look and blocked the doorway.

What's with this asshole? You are exactly on time. Obviously, he hates it when women get there before him.

Normally, I would have apologized, accepting blame when I knew it wasn't my fault. With Garnet to back me up, however, I was emboldened. "Our appointment was for 12:30. It's 12:32."

He checked his watch for verification, as if my girl-watch couldn't be trusted, while I tapped my foot impatiently. We stood at an impasse, and I heard a door shut behind him. I craned my neck to see over his shoulder, and he moved just enough to obstruct my view.

"You're absolutely right." He stepped aside. "Please, come in and take a seat."

His earlier dead-calm persona returned so quickly it was disorienting. I had the fleeting thought that might have been his intention—to stay ahead of me by keeping me confused and insecure.

He smoothed his hair and motioned me toward the chair I'd previously occupied. Still bristling over the way he'd greeted me, I took the dominant seat, the one he held court in during my first visit. If he was bothered by my rebellion, he didn't show it. Of course, he had much more practice maintaining a psychological poker face than I had.

"Would you like something to drink? Coffee, tea?"

"Water would be good."

He removed a bottle from the refrigerator by the credenza. Then he filled two glasses. When he gave mine to me, he stumbled, splashing icy water in my lap.

"I'm so sorry." He scrambled for the tissue box on his desk and handed it to me. "Let me get you a refill."

While I dabbed at my dress, he stood with his back to me and poured more water into my cup.

"Please excuse me, but it's been a difficult day. My receptionist had an emergency, and several appointments ran long." He settled into his chair with his spiral notebook in hand and stared at me as I drained my glass. "Dry mouth can be an issue with the medications you're taking."

"My mouth's not dry. I'm just thirsty." I was aware of how petulant I sounded but didn't care. The least the man could do before determining my condition was consult with me.

"I see," he said, scribbling an addition to the growing list of my many neuroses. "Have you noticed any other side effects? Trouble sleeping, drowsiness, stomach issues?"

"I'm actually sleeping much better."

"Okay. How about mood changes?"

"That's better, too. I mean my mood is better."

"How so?"

"Uh, well, I'm not sure how to explain it."

"If you had to rate your mood on a scale from zero to ten, with zero being you have trouble making yourself get up in the morning and ten being you have more energy than any other recent time in your life, where would you fall today?"

He'd done it again—posed another trick question like the first one asking how I felt about my husband's death at *that* exact moment. I hesitated. Obviously, I wasn't going to pick a number under five as that would increase my recommended therapy sessions. If I said nine or ten, Riley would probably suspect I was lying. That left six, seven, or eight.

"Well, if eight is having enough energy to carry me through the day without naps, I'd have to say seven and a half."

"What about stress?"

"You mean like stressful situations?" As in rabid fans or psychotic students, or smoking stalkers?

"Exactly. People or events that increase your anxiety."

Maybe we should stand and salute Captain Obvious.

"Not now, Garnet."

"Could you speak up a little, please? I didn't quite catch that."

Shit. I hadn't meant to throw it. "I said not now or any other time. Nothing stressful here."

"Really?"

I returned his stare, then nodded. "Absolutely."

"Good then. How's that novel coming? The one where your heroine is interested in—no don't tell me—" He flipped through a few pages. "Sorry. Who was she falling for again?"

Although I should have expected it from the way he conducted our first session, his sudden change of topic still caught me off guard. I wondered if psychiatrists were like lawyers who never asked a question if they didn't already know the answer. I considered revising my fake plot to test the theory. Instead, I returned to my original lie.

"A police detective, which would complicate things since Garnet considers most laws suggestions."

"Right. Have you made progress with your work?"

This time I had the odd feeling he knew the answer or at least had a strong suspicion I had made no progress at all. I dismissed the idea after concluding it was my guilty conscience at work. Not some extra-sensory superpower on the part of the doctor.

"It's coming along nicely, thank you." I watched for a reaction—something that would indicate surprise or excitement or one of those side-eyed you're-full-of-crap looks.

"I can't imagine writing fiction. It's one thing to write an article discussing a theory on how the brain works, quite another to create your own personalized microcosm, one populated with purely imaginary citizens. I'd love to hear more about your process."

"My process?"

"Yes. For example, I take handwritten notes, then enter them in my computer. I've heard writers sometimes hand write material before typing it up."

"Oh, that process. Well, I do keep a notepad with me in case something pops into my head, but no. My handwriting sucks, so my story goes directly into my laptop."

"Interesting. And what do you mean when you say, 'it's coming along nicely'? How do you measure progress? For example, when I'm writing about a study I've conducted, the stages are clearly delineated. For you, is chapter completion an indication of expected submission date? Or is it word count? What exactly are the indications your book is coming along nicely?"

His questions were innocent enough, but his tone reminded me of the way kindergarten teachers check on their students' progress.

Who the hell does this prick think he is? Tell him to go fuck himself. On second thought, he's a shrink. Tell him to buy some sexy lingerie for his mother.

The suggestion appealed to me, but open hostility wasn't the best way to get Riley to sign off on my mental health and keep Barb from ratting me out to Dad.

"I don't have any hard and fast technique to measure my progress. It's more like gradual enlightenment. Each scene and every chapter propel my characters toward what eventually becomes the inevitable end."

"I see. Well, however you get there, I'm sure your fans will be thrilled when you finish. Any projections as to when the launch date might be?"

I would have provided him with some vague reference to the completion of my book— sometime after Christmas or late spring or early summer, except a sudden movement behind the doctor stopped me. After her cameo appearance in my workshop, I wouldn't have been shocked to see Garnet there, making rude gestures directed at the solemn man. But the character standing there wasn't one I'd written into existence. This visitor was flesh and blood, with a face as familiar to me as my own. Slowly shaking his head from side to side, index finger held to his lips, Michael stood.

Emitting a sound between a gasp and a sob, I leapt to my feet. The room began spinning, and I fell back, bumping against my chair before plopping down hard on its edge. Teetering there for a second, I lost my battle with gravity and slid to the floor, overcome with dizziness and nausea.

The last thing I remembered was the grasp of familiar fingers clasping my wrist and the citrus scent of Michael's favorite cologne.

Chapter 21

When I returned to myself, I was lying on a plush leather sofa, a cool cloth on my forehead. I picked at the blanket someone had placed over me and tried to piece together earlier events.

"Ah, you're back." The voice came to me from a great distance.

Dr. Riley stood over me, and I remembered the way Michael had seemed to be urging me to keep quiet. Was his appearance the kind of other-worldly message my fellow grief groupers had experienced? If so, I was no longer envious of them. There had been no comfort in seeing him without being able to communicate. Even the touch of his hand on my wrist mocked me with its impossible pressure.

"Please, let me help."

He offered me his arm, as I pushed up on my elbows, but I ignored it and sat on my own, then dropped my feet to the floor.

"Thanks, but I'm good. What happened?"

"I was hoping you could tell me. We were discussing the release date of your novel when you stood and collapsed."

I toyed with telling him my dead husband had been standing behind him to see his reaction. Since it would most likely conclude with my admission to the psych ward, I avoided the subject and asked, "How long was I out?"

"Less than five minutes. And you weren't completely unconscious. Not in the conventional sense. It was more an episode of depersonalization-derealization."

"A what?"

"Doctors used to refer to this disassociation between a person and her surroundings as a fugue state. Usually, the incident is momentary, but it can reoccur frequently over time. Has anything like this ever happened to you before?"

"Not that I remember," I quipped. "Get it? Not that I *remember*? It's a joke. Because if I were having one of those de-whatever episodes, I wouldn't . . . Never mind. No, I haven't."

He walked to a cabinet to the left of his desk and pulled a key from his pocket, then unlocked the door and removed a small bottle of pills. "I'm going to add a stronger anti-anxiety prescription to decrease the likelihood of your having another lapse. Since it's best to take the medication as soon as you have an episode, you should have one now. Starting tomorrow, take one as soon as you wake up. You may experience some disorientation or confusion at first, but that's normal. If you notice any more changes, call me right away."

I accepted the bottle but hesitated before opening it. What if the meds I'd been taking were causing my hallucinations—or whatever they were? Wouldn't adding another pill to the mix make things worse?

Noticing my hesitancy, he shrugged. "Kara, you have to trust me because if you don't…" He left the thought unfinished.

I wanted to reassure him—to say, of course I trusted him—only the words stuck in my throat. I accepted the water and shook the newest member of my medicinal entourage from the bottle. As the pill was going down, I realized Riley's insistence that I trust him hadn't felt like an unfinished thought. It felt like a threat.

•   •   •

As I waited for the garage door to open, I replayed my visit with Riley. When I tried to summon a picture of the apparition I'd immediately recognized as my husband, a gauzy veil blurred his strong jaw and chiseled cheekbones. And I lost him for the second time that day.

I retrieved my briefcase and stepped from the car into the poorly lit garage. That was when I heard it—a deep, wet cough. I whirled around, expecting my intruder to be directly behind me, but there was no one.

"Who's there?" I called, backing away from the sound. There was no answer. "All I have to do is hit the alarm and the cops will be here in minutes."

Of course, I knew a lot of very bad things could happen in minutes. But it didn't matter much since I wasn't sure which combination of buttons would summon them anyway.

I must have fallen into another mini-break from reality because when awareness returned, I was sitting on the steps, slumped against the door to the kitchen, uncertain as to whether I should be more or less terrified that the gaunt, bearded-faced man looking down at me wasn't my husband.

"Are you okay? Can you stand up?" It was the raspy rattle of the caller who warned me to watch my back.

"Who are you and why are you in my garage?" When I reached for the handrail, he extended his thick-veined hand. Without thinking, I took it and was surprised at the strength in his gnarled fingers.

"I hated to scare you, but I couldn't risk anybody seeing me. Clive Scruggs, Mrs. Conroy." He wiped his hand on his pants before offering it to me. I shook it and he continued. "I hoped to meet you at your husband's service, but I didn't get the chance to pay my respects. I'm so sorry for your loss. Michael was one of the finest men I've known."

My foot slipped and I stumbled against him. He stepped back startled, either by my sudden move or possibly our proximity. But when I grabbed his grimy camouflage jacket to steady myself, he kept still. Even from my vantage point on the top step, he towered over me. Underneath the brim of a black cap, his faded blue eyes conveyed what I interpreted as concern, possibly compassion, and I felt tears gathering in mine.

My initial surge of adrenalin had dissolved. In its place something bubbled up from deep inside my brain, but it wasn't my amygdala urging me to choose between fight or flight. It was Barb shrieking in my head:

"Have you lost your mind? It's obvious this guy's a disgusting derelict who plans to rape, rob, and kill you. Not necessarily in that order."

"Shut up," I responded in what I hoped was a whisper. And either I had spoken softly or he was used to being around people who had conversations with invisible companions because he didn't react.

Despite my stepmom's heeding, possibly because of it, I decided to trust Clive and invited him inside.

He blinked when I turned on the lights, and I hit the dimmer. In the garage, the smell of motor oil and gasoline had masked Clive's personal aroma, a pungent mix of body odor and general neglect. I hesitated before pointing to one of my fancy fabric-covered chairs. A deep sense of shame reminded me that if this man had fought for me thousands of miles away in some war no one fully understood, the least I could do offer him a seat.

"Can I get you something to drink? I have coffee, soda, beer?" Way to go, Kara. The man's an alcoholic. What are you going to do if he wants beer?

"Water's fine, thanks." He rescued me from my fear of knocking him off the wagon if he was on it in the first place.

I watched as he finished off the ice water in two long gulps. When I refilled his glass, it dawned on me he might be hungry. But asking him if he wanted something to eat could be tricky. Would he think of it as a handout? I had never been uncomfortable offering food to a guest in my home before. Why should Clive be different?

But he wasn't the same as the people I invited for dinner. None of them looked as if it had been a while since they'd had their last meal. Because our situation was like none I'd experienced, I went with another approach.

"I just remembered I skipped breakfast. That's probably why I got so light-headed in the garage. I'm having a turkey sandwich, and I hate to eat alone. Let me make one for you, too."

"Please, don't go to any trouble."

"You'd be doing me a favor." I took out meat, cheese, pickles, and mayo. After getting the bread out, I noticed Clive squirming in his seat.

"The powder room is down the hall to the right if you need it."

He hopped up and sprinted away, leaving a trail of mildew and perspiration in his wake. Despite my earlier shame at being squeamish, I opened the windows before plucking matches from the drawer and lighting the essential oil candles scattered around the kitchen. Hopefully, he wouldn't take my actions as an attempt to mask his essential oils.

Then I put the sandwiches together—three for him, one for me. The uncharitable thought he might be stealing toiletries crossed my mind, but I pushed it aside.

When Clive returned, he was hatless, thick white hair dampened. His face and hands were clean, and he'd shed his jacket, revealing a Grateful Dead t-shirt.

"Hope it's okay I left my coat in the bathroom. Didn't want to dirty up your nice kitchen."

He waited until I took the first bite before popping an entire square into his mouth, chewing in a slow, forced way that suggested he was exerting a great deal of self-control. When he finished, he thanked me again.

"I should be thanking you, Mr. Scruggs. And not just for rescuing me from another lonely lunch. I should thank you for all you've done for the country. For your service."

He ducked his head for a second, then raised his eyes to mine. "Please, call me Clive. And I did my duty, ma'am. That's all. Like a lot of other guys who weren't as lucky as me."

I hadn't understood what Michael meant when he said the men he worked with didn't need much more than acknowledgement. I did now, and my heart hurt at my failure to go with him to provide that recognition.

I kept my eyes on the table and finished my sandwich about the time he'd done away with his three.

I stood to clear the table, but he insisted on taking the dishes to the sink, where he rinsed and stacked them on the counter.

"I'd put them in the dishwasher for you, but you ladies can be real particular about the way you arrange things."

I tried to imagine this man standing beside a very particular woman, laughing as the two of them playfully squabbled about dish placement.

"Thanks. Now I insist you sit back down and relax while I see what we've got for dessert."

I located an unopened package of Oreos, Michael's favorite, brought it to the table and scattered a few cookies on a paper plate. He scooted them in my direction, and I shook my head.

"You first," I said and waited for him to eat two before asking him to explain the reason for his visit.

"Now that we've gotten better acquainted, can you tell me how you got into my garage and what was so important you had to scare the hell out of me? And who were you hiding from?"

I also wondered if he'd been in touch with Lucas but was inexplicably reluctant to ask.

"I'm awful sorry about scaring you like that. I was gonna hang out under the deck til you got home. Then I saw the window was open and decided it would be safer to hide inside. By the way, you really oughta lock your garage up. It's one of the easiest ways for burglars to get in."

Clive echoed a warning Michael had delivered on multiple occasions after I'd aired it out and forgotten to shut the windows.

"Honey, you're sending an invitation to an open house, where the guests carry off all the good stuff. Or worse, they carry you off."

I realized Clive was still answering my questions.

"I wasn't just hiding for myself. I didn't want *them* to find out you talked to me."

His emphasis on the word lent a note of paranoia to his explanation. How broken was this man sitting in front of me? And how much credence could I place in anything he said? If Lucas had been telling the truth, however, both he and Michael had faith in Clive. Did that make me the broken one?

"I don't understand. Why would anyone be interested in our conversations?"

"I can't tell you that, not yet. But I'm not going to put you in any more danger until I have solid evidence. Evidence I think your husband may have found. Evidence strong enough that it got him killed."

He picked up another cookie, separated it, and nibbled at the creamy white filling, then grinned. "My boy and I used to eat them that way." His smile faded.

"Me, too." I selected one from the plate, dismantled it, and scraped the inside with my teeth. "Please, tell me what you think got Michael killed."

"Did you know about the program your husband and Sister Mary Alice were working on?"

It didn't sound as if he'd been in touch with Lucas, and I became even more eager to discover why Clive had disappeared in the first place. I nodded. "It had something to do with keeping track of medications, right? I'm not sure about anything else."

"Me neither. That was Michael's area. But I'm certain he ran into trouble reconciling the inventory input with the output. I told him about my buddy Aftershock. The guy went off the deep end after a change in his meds. Started reliving Hamburger Hill. What a shit storm. Sorry for the language."

I dismissed his concern with a quick wave of the hand, and he continued.

"You know why they called it Hamburger Hill? Because that goddamn battle chewed men up like ground beef."

He tightened his fists, and I braced for a stronger reaction—pounding or shouting. But he unclasped his hands and returned to his narrative.

"Poor Aftershock couldn't shake it."

He grimaced, and I had no idea whether it was because of his friend's condition or from his probably unintentional play on words or both.

"He'd been doing fine until someone at the clinic talked him into changing meds. About a month later he lost it."

"Do you think they gave him the wrong medication?"

"I'm not sure what the hell they were giving him. That's why Michael started looking into it. He wanted to know how often the patients were getting their medication and what side effects they were having and if there were any positive outcomes."

"So, Michael thought they might be giving your friend a placebo, a substitution for the real thing?"

"I know what you mean by placebo, ma'am," he said, smiling. I felt a blush rising; he seemed not to notice. "That would explain why Aftershock got so bad they locked him up in the psych ward."

"Locked him up? Isn't that kind of extreme?"

"That's what we thought. But it's a good way to keep visitors out. Didn't stop your husband, though. He bought a pair of scrubs, borrowed a name tag from a doctor friend, and walked right up to the nurses' station, holding one of those little computers. Sailed right past security straight into Aftershock's room. Of course, the clinic guards are lax, nothing like a real hospital, but it was still pretty damned impressive."

His face lit up, but quickly dimmed. He shook his head and said, "Didn't learn much. Aftershock was too out of it. Michael saw the board where nurses write notes of what meds he got and when he got them but couldn't decipher it. He tried to take a picture. Not enough light. Still didn't stop him. He wrote it all down. Later we checked and it looked like they had him on super strong tranquilizers."

"Wouldn't it make sense to give him sedatives to calm him down and ease the hallucinations?"

"Possibly, but he could be getting something not listed on the board. No way to be sure without access to his records."

"His medical records from the center?"

"Yep. The ones they lock up tighter than a gnat's ass. Shit! I did it again. I spend most of my time with a bunch of geezers who cuss like the drunken soldiers they are. I don't have a lot of contact with nice girls like you."

"You know what they say about nice girls, don't you? It's about good girls, but close enough." I tossed my hair in what I hoped was a recognizable imitation of the woman who influenced my development of Garnet, then in my sexiest voice said, "Good girls go to heaven, bad girls go everywhere."

He laughed. "Where'd a young thing like you come across Mae West?"

"From old black and white movies in the middle of the night. Back to those records."

"I guess Sister Mary Alice didn't see confidentiality the same as her bosses did. She gave Michael access to everything: Aftershock's records, all medication logouts, financial stuff. Wouldn't let him take them out of the office but let him have enough time to copy the files onto a flash drive."

"What happened to it?"

"Nobody knows. I thought he might have left a clue somewhere. I did a little surveillance where he worked, but it looked like somebody had cleared out everything. Then I got worried you might have found something there or at home and not know what you had."

I didn't tell him it was Andy who cleaned out whatever had been left after Michael's coworkers at the tech firm took anything related to business. He had packed away a few desk photos and a half dead potted plant. And I kept quiet about the box Andy found, the one marked *For K's Eyes Only*. I hadn't been able to bring myself to open it and had asked him to put it in the guest bedroom closet. Later, I shoved it as far back as possible. It sat there, untouched since then.

"I wish I could help, but I haven't come across anything." His face dissolved into a picture of despair, so I added, "I could take another look, though, just to be sure. But you're right. I'm not sure I'd recognize what it was if I did find it."

"That's what worries me. Because you and I know that, but the people who killed your husband don't. In fact, they might think you have the incriminating evidence and are unaware of exactly what it is. That makes you a problem. The same kind Michael was—until he wasn't."

Chapter 22

After dropping the bombshell about there being people who might want to kill me, Clive gave me a series of unnecessary warnings: always be aware of my surroundings, keep my pepper spray handy and my doors locked. And he promised to check in.

I wanted to ask if he was the one smoking on the edge of my property but thought better of it. Clive's personal aromatic signature didn't include the stink of cigarettes. Plus, he sat at my house for over two hours. The kind of smoker willing to take the risk of starting a forest fire or being observed while he observed me wouldn't be able to resist lighting up for that long.

He refused my offer of a sandwich to go, but accepted the Oreos, thanked me, and left through the garage. The sight of him slinking along the side of the house and darting behind Ira's bushes added to my growing discomfort.

As I walked by the powder room, I detected the heavy scent of lilac and disinfectant. Clive must have sprayed the area after retrieving his jacket. The mental picture of him holding the deodorizer in his crooked fingers, misting the air until it was thick with faux floral, brought on an avalanche of remorse about not following through on Michael's project.

That reminded me of the third person involved in the collaboration. It still puzzled me that my husband had never mentioned Lucas. If Clive was right, Michael could have held back information to protect me. Had I been too trusting when I'd accepted the reporter's account of what happened between the two of them? He'd seemed so sincere and…

Hot enough to melt your mascara?

"As usual, your timing sucks." Uncertain whether I delivered my retort aloud, I was sure of one thing. Instead of depending on other people for information, I concluded that if Michael had left something behind that might shed light on his murder, I would find it. But not now.

Tonight, I had to come up with plans for Tuesday's class. I tried to rub away the tension gathering in the spot between my brows but was too exhausted to do more than drag myself to the den where I hoped a little mindless TV would clear my head.

Alex Trebek was asking which character had appeared the most times in horror movies.

"Who is Dracula?" I shouted over a housewife from Des Moines. "Jeez, lady. Frankenstein? What a moron."

My outburst sapped what remaining energy I had, and I fell asleep as a statistician from Poughkeepsie was choosing Mathematical Symbols for four hundred.

When I woke, the room was dark and quiet. Although I was still reclining, there was too much support for me to be on the sofa. I recognized the cool, smooth fabric as the silk comforter on the bed Michael and I had shared.

I closed my eyes, desperate to determine how I ended up in the spot I'd been so diligently avoiding. That was when I heard it: the unmistakable snuffling snorts my husband made when he snored. The immediate certainty that my husband had returned pulled me toward his side of the bed. Reality hit me mid-roll, freezing me with the knowledge that whoever or whatever lay beside me was not Michael.

I can't guess how long I stayed like that, waiting for his breath to tickle across the back of my neck. It never came, and neither did any more of the sleep sounds, the sniffs and clicks that had both annoyed and comforted me. After an indeterminate amount of time, I inched to the edge of the bed, eased my way off, and bolted from the room.

It was only a little after ten, but I could barely keep my eyes open. I brushed my teeth and took a swipe at my makeup. After shaking the pills into my palm, I remembered the new bottle in my purse. Adding it to the others, I popped them in my mouth and downed them with tap water.

As I waited for the drugs to take effect, I dismissed my waking nightmare as the result of not yet adjusting to the mix of medications and the trauma of my earlier other-worldly encounter. Then I reviewed my visit with Dr. Riley, hoping to discover what had spiraled me into conjuring Michael.

An unrealized thought tugged at my strings of consciousness—some question the doctor posed toward the abrupt conclusion of our session. Words that seemed out of place coming from his mouth. Whatever he said continued to elude me, and I drifted into sleep. But it wasn't the sedative-induced blackness I'd grown accustomed to. No. It was a horror show with no beginning, no end.

I was in the master bedroom, motionless on the bed. My stillness was involuntary. I was in a state of paralysis, every sense heightened. Sinking into the plush material, I wondered if this was what people experienced when the anesthesia didn't work, and they woke up mid-surgery, helpless as scalpels sliced into their exposed organs.

I heard night birds calling to one another, harsh and discordant. The chirping of the cicadas was both symphony and solo, as I discovered I could distinguish the individual melodies of each insect before they blended into their combined cacophony.

The scent of pine and jasmine, strong enough to taste, flooded the room. It was followed by a cloying stench of decay that permeated my pores and emanated from my body. I lay there for what seemed an eternity, thinking please, dear God, don't let this be what death is like. This terrifying awareness of everything and nothing at the same time.

The strident buzzing of my alarm filled me with dread at the prospect that I wouldn't remember how to stop the shrill sound, would be forever trapped in my own body. I began testing my mobility. First, by wiggling my toes, then stretching my arms and legs, and finally sitting upright in my own bed.

Eager to wash away the night and its terrors, I sprinted to the shower. A whiff of something both sweet and rank wafted over me, as if someone had sprayed air freshener over a piece of rotting meat. I slammed the bathroom door, then tucked a towel in the space between it and the floor, determined to escape all remnants of my evening.

●   ●   ●

Coffee in hand, I surveyed my backyard, pleased at how green and peaceful it was in the daytime. I longed to return to a world where imaginary characters remained on the pages of a book and the dead stayed dead. I wasn't sure if last night's horror meant I was crazy or that I'd become a spiritual medium able to bridge not only the gap between literary land and reality but also between life and death.

The worst part was I had no one I was comfortable talking to about my mental collapse. Andy wasn't my only friend, but he was the only person I stayed in close contact with after Michael and I started dating. My love for my husband had been so all-consuming that from the very beginning I wanted to spend as much time by his side as possible, and he felt the same way. At first my girlfriends teased me about becoming that girl, the overly dependent female who loses herself in a man. But I hadn't lost myself in Michael; I'd found myself with him. My friends stopped inviting me for dinner or drinks. They still sent text updates, and as far as I could tell, none unfriended me on Facebook.

I could talk to Andy about my fears concerning my sanity. But although he would try to hide it, the subject was sensitive for him. His own mother had suffered from what was probably undiagnosed bi-polar disorder. His father called her a psycho and left twelve-year-old Andy to sort out the differences. After her husband's abrupt departure, she began self-medicating with booze and valium and ended up wrapping her car around a telephone pole a few months before Andy turned twenty.

The authorities ruled her death accidental, but he was determined to take the blame. If he'd been a better son, he would have found a way to get her into treatment. If he'd gone to a local college, he wouldn't have let her drive that night. And a host of other self-recriminations. I witnessed the following years of struggle and knew first-hand how hard it was to work through the pain and guilt. I wasn't about to be the one to destroy his progress by sucking him into my special world of crazy.

That left Wanda, Barb, and Dad. Wanda would give it her best shot, but I imagined her advice would be to suggest I incorporate my insanity into another Garnet story. Barb would start drawing up commitment papers. As for my father, I had no idea what his reaction might be but knew if he sided with my stepmother, our relationship wouldn't survive.

I was down to the person I should have thought about in the first place: Dr. Riley. But when I pictured him sitting at his desk with Michael behind him, warning me to stay silent, I couldn't bring myself to call him. No, I'd tough it out until our next session, when I would decide what to reveal and what to hide.

Thinking of that adage about idle hands being the devil's playthings, I determined focusing on work was the only way to get through the week.

Finally, something we agree on. Active hands are much more fun and if you're with the right player—they sure as hell can bring out the devil in any man.

I started to tell Garnet mine had been idle in that department too long to remember how to do anything of a titillating nature but chose to ignore a voice that couldn't be real.

After pouring a second cup of coffee, I sat down with my laptop and checked Twitter to see if there were more nasty tweets about me.

Other than quite a few positive responses about Garnet being in bed with the sexy detective, it seemed my fans had given up on me. The lack of interest on my blog was similar, but three people did ask specific questions about the upcoming sex scenes.

I should have been relieved, happy even, that my online tormentors appeared to have lost interest in me. Oddly, I felt let down. I never believed the saying that being ignored was worse than having folks say bad things about you. Now I wasn't so sure. I spent the next thirty minutes drafting possibilities for my nonexistent book. A hot-meet scene would stimulate both discussion and libido, but I rejected the classic approach, where eyes caress bodies or fingertips ignite flame and went with a different sensory encounter.

> She heard his voice before she saw him. It was liquid silk flowing in the breeze, making it impossible for her to catch her breath. The thought of that cool, smooth fabric reminded her of the sheets on her bed. If he looked half as good as he sounded, the two of them could be destined to end up gasping for air together.

I posted it and sent a tweet hinting at even more titillating peeks into Garnet's sex life. A twinge of culpability about hyping a book I might not write nagged at me, but I shook it off. While I didn't adhere to the belief that all was always fair in love, I subscribed to a no-holds barred approach in a fight against Twitter trolls.

Chapter 23

From behind my desk, fluorescent bulbs cast a glaring light over the classroom. After my evening of horror, I welcomed their harsh reality.

I began class by canvassing to see if anyone was having problems developing plot and character. Several students expressed concern about creating realistic dialogue. I asked for volunteers to share snippets of conversation that were causing them the most trouble, and we discussed how to make characters sound more authentic.

"Is there anything else you'd like to talk about?"

Howard raised his hand. "Unfortunately, in my line of work, I learned a lot about the awful things people do to each other. Most of the time, when someone murders another person, there's an obvious reason as to why they did it. But there were some cases I could never understand. They were most likely to end up unsolved. I guess I'm still trying to make sense of the ones that got away. Some writers say there are basically four motives for murder: love, hate, money, and power. Would you agree with that, or do you think they left something out?"

"Great question," I said on my way to the board, where I posted the list. "Can you name a mystery you've read or one you're writing with a motivation that doesn't seem to fit with these categories?"

The overweight man who temporarily blocked my view of Garnet spoke first. "How about *Silence of the Lambs*? That dude didn't have a motive; he had an eating disorder."

When the laughter subsided, several other students called out the titles of books where the killer was too twisted to understand. The list included novels like *The Alienist* and *Jack the Ripper*.

"But those killers were crazed maniacs. Psychos don't need a motive," Madame Defarge offered, without dropping a stitch.

"What if they have a reason that only makes sense to them?" Betty's childlike voice startled me with its dramatic contrast to the subject matter.

"That's an excellent point. We should add it to our list, but I'm not sure what to call it."

"How about 'insanity'?" Louisa suggested.

"Yes." I wrote it on the board. "But does it fit with Betty's suggestion? Is hers more about personal justification?" I looked at her, she nodded, and I added it. "Have we missed anything?"

"What about Garnet?" Nina asked. "What motivation does she have? Money isn't important to her, and she couldn't care less about love. She doesn't even hate the people she kills. She only gets involved when the system fails the victim. When justice isn't served. What is it she says?" She paused. "Oh, yeah. 'Revenge may be a dish best served cold, but justice is better when it's—'"

"Delivered hot and bloody." We finished the quote together.

She smiled and nodded. "Yes 'hot and bloody.' Isn't wanting to right wrongs the purest motive of all? Isn't that what drives Garnet, makes her who she is? Someone with the courage of her convictions—a woman who doesn't let laws stand in the way of living by her own moral code."

I agreed with most of what she said but feared validating her thoughts. It was true I created my heroine to serve as an avenger outside the law. But if I admitted it, I could be giving the young girl permission to follow in my character's footsteps. I could be facilitating the murder of the man she considered responsible for her mother's death.

Betty saved me from coming up with a response. "But how can anyone be certain what true justice is? Don't get me wrong. Garnet's a great character, and I love your writing. I'm just not sure how realistic it is for a person to determine who's guilty or innocent. Wouldn't that require the ability to see what's in other people's hearts?"

"First, thank you for reading my books. Second, you're exactly right. It isn't possible for someone to run around administering justice, at least not without experiencing personal consequences. And Garnet does occasionally suffer from doubt, guilt even. In each story, she becomes a little more troubled, more human and vulnerable. She hasn't completely evolved, but I'm hoping that in my next book she will."

Until I said it, I'd had no such hope. It was one thing to make a promise to a faceless online audience, quite another to deliver it to a roomful of writers. Now I would have to search for depth in a character I purposely created without it.

"But Nina's right," I continued, hoping a quick change of subject might distract some of the group from what I'd said about plans for my heroine in the next novel. "So, we'll include 'the quest for justice' on the list."

When I stepped back from the whiteboard, I noticed the time.

"Wow! How did it get this late? I planned to begin individual conferences to talk about your work. We should be able to squeeze in a few before the end of class. And I'm happy to stay later, so feel free to keep working."

My lady of the needles and yarn asked if she could have the first conference to discuss her mystery. I expected something comfortably predictable, like a cozy. When her opening paragraph began with a meeting of a small-town knitting club, I assumed I guessed correctly. I was taken aback when she introduced the group as The Happy Hookers and even more so to discover the name was no accident, nor was the category the least bit cozy. Apparently, I underestimated Bernadine's creative aspirations and what I quickly realized was a wicked sense of humor.

Only three other students were ready to discuss their progress, but several groups, including Nina's, stayed behind. Some wrote on their own, others shared and discussed their material. They seemed to be self-sufficient, so I answered a few emails. Then I remembered my vow to finish, or at least start, Michael's project.

I googled veterans and PTSD and came across a series of articles about the effectiveness of using synthetic oxytocin to treat sleep disorders and nightmares in men suffering from the syndrome. It was way over my head, but I understood enough to imagine it was something doctors at the center would have tried. I noted it, then leaned back in my chair and stretched my neck. It was almost 12:30, and only Howard and Louisa remained.

He approached my desk. "I know you're a busy woman, what with working on your next book and this class, but we would like to take you to lunch. Someplace with a little privacy."

"I'm not all that busy." I could have added I had been unable to work on Garnet's story before I spouted off about how she was evolving as a character, but I kept that to myself. I also didn't admit the reason I was happy to join them had nothing to do with my schedule. I agreed because I was afraid to go home.

•   •   •

If the crowded lot was any indication, the Village Tavern was a popular spot. The red wooden doors suggested a bustling pub atmosphere, where everybody had to shout to be heard. Not a place to talk about sensitive issues.

Larger than I expected, the restaurant teemed with people. Business types in dark suits sat at orderly tables; more casually attired clientele paired up at the bar; a rowdy group of women filled one of the high-tops. Before I could speak to the hostess, Howard appeared and guided me through the main dining area where brass chandeliers hung below exposed wood beams to a quieter room where Louisa waited in a booth.

She scooted over, and I slid in beside her. Without her glasses and rigid posture, she was much less intimidating, but something about her continued to set off a tiny bell in my brain. Not an alarm, more like a Google alert.

He spoke first. "Thanks for coming."

"Thank you for inviting me."

"Now that we've established what an appreciative group we are, let's order our drinks," Louisa added.

Normally, I would have prickled at her bossy behavior, but it was hard to be annoyed when alcohol was involved. Our waitress came and Howard ordered a draught with a name I'd never heard. Louisa asked for a PBR. Somewhat of a connoisseur, Michael had turned me on to the intricacies of craft beers. The only time I had one after his death, though, it had tasted stale, flat, and I hadn't had another since then. Today, beer sounded good. I glanced at the selection and randomly landed on a German-sounding lager.

"I'll try this." I held up the menu and pointed.

"Good choice." The waitress nodded her approval, and I felt a disproportionate sense of validation.

"Wouldn't have taken you for a beer drinker," Louisa said.

Still pleased with myself for pleasing the waitress, I took her remark as a compliment, possibly a backhanded one, but better than the alternative.

"I'm full of surprises."

"Hmm," she murmured.

"I guess you're wondering what we needed to talk to you about," Howard began.

"Let's hold up until the drinks come, then order. That way we won't keep getting interrupted."

Her suggestion made sense.

"If you like burgers, you gotta try one of theirs. They're all good, but my favorite's the cheeseburger, medium rare. Louisa likes the fancy types. Right, sweetheart? The one that's got bacon jam, whatever that is, and pimento cheese. Real low-cal. But she doesn't have to worry about that."

He touched her fingertips with his and let them linger a moment. She lowered her eyes and smiled. Talk about being full of surprises. These two were way more than critique partners. They were sweethearts. I prided myself in my ability to sense attraction between people. So, how had I missed something this obvious?

Our drinks arrived, and we all ordered burgers.

He raised his glass. "To writing our troubles away." We clinked glasses and drank. My beer was crisp with no lingering, bitter taste. Michael would have approved.

"Several of us have belonged to the critique group for a good while. Louisa and I met about five years ago. Two years ago, we joined the Crime Family. Betty had been a member a year or so before, but she took a break. We had a lot in common, so we stuck together. We didn't really get to know Nina until your class. Louisa was less than thrilled about having her in our foursome."

"You make it sound as if I didn't like her." She smacked his hand, not too hard but not exactly playful. "I just thought she was too young, that we wouldn't relate to each other. But I was wrong." She looked toward one of the heavily paned windows and sighed.

"That's right. She fit right in. Which isn't that great for her. The three of us have what you might call a pessimistic bent with not a lot of happy endings."

"But we're old enough to understand how temporary happiness can be." Louisa added. "Good times come and go, just like unhappy ones. Nina doesn't get that yet, and I'm afraid she never will."

Our waitress and a younger server, both loaded down with enormous plates of burgers and fries, came to the table and distributed the food.

My Old-Fashion burger was too big to hold, so I began sawing it in half. Then I realized it was too thick to fit in my mouth and tried squishing it down with my palm. A trickle of red oozed from the patty, reminding me of how Garnet and Nina thought justice should be delivered: "Hot and bloody."

"What do you mean you're afraid she never will?" I took a break from the burger and gave her my full attention. Although I had a suspicion what she was getting at, I couldn't tell if Nina was haunted by her failure to save her mother or driven by determination to avenge the woman's death.

"I'm assuming you know her story?" Howard asked.

"Some, not all." I wanted to see if Andy's information omitted any important details about the girl's past.

Howard recounted how she had been away when her stepfather fell asleep while smoking a cigarette, burning down the house and killing her mother. The specifics about his trial and sentencing matched my friend's account with one update. The man could be up for parole as soon as early next year.

"We're worried about her," she added.

"You don't mean she might hurt someone, do you?"

"Like commit murder?" She turned to Howard.

He shrugged. "Nina doesn't strike me as the violent type. If you're looking for the killer instinct, you should—"

"Howard," she interrupted. "That's not our story to tell. Let's stick to Nina. He's right. I doubt she would go after that son of a bitch who burned the house down. No, she's not waiting around for him to get out so she can gun him down. I'm scared because when I look at her, there's no light, only darkness. As if somebody snuffed it out. I've seen that expression before and it's never good."

"I don't understand. If you aren't afraid she wants to kill the stepfather, who…"

Then I got it. Hamlet. Nina had been determined to avoid his inability to act. But when the time had come to deliver her own justice, she, too, had failed. I was so shocked by her referral to Garnet's philosophy about following her own instincts, I mistook the closing lines of her story as a vow to follow through on her plan for revenge.

Now my fear wasn't that her writing reflected vengeful determination. I feared that, like Hamlet in his "to be or not to be" soliloquy, she was questioning the value of her own life.

Louisa and Howard seemed to expect me to speak, but I didn't know what to say. I dipped a fry in ketchup, then dropped it back on my plate. Finally, I asked, "Has she said anything about, uh, about…"

"About killing herself? Not directly. But her work is taking a dark turn. When she finishes it, the story might not be the only thing she ends."

I wasn't proud of the irritation I felt at being drawn into another's trauma when I hadn't dealt with my own. But I suppressed it and responded with genuine concern.

"I completely misread everything about Nina. And I want to help. I really do, but I've never known anyone depressed enough to consider suicide."

"You probably have but didn't realize it. You shouldn't feel bad, though. Most people, even those unfortunate enough to have experience in the area, haven't a clue what to do." She lifted her glass but set it down without taking a drink.

Howard put his hand over hers. This time he left it there. "We didn't want to bother you with Nina's problem. Betty wasn't totally on board with involving you. Said you had enough on your plate. But she agreed that with the way Nina feels about you, it made sense. She couldn't be here but asked us to tell you she's sorry to add to your burden."

"The way she feels about me?" Other than admiration for the blood-thirsty nature of my main character, she had expressed nothing but mild disdain for me.

"It's hard to determine with a girl who's been through what she has, but Howard's right. She thinks you're the greatest thing since sliced bread."

"If you say so. What can I do?"

"We wanted to stage one of those interceptions," he said.

"Interventions, honey, interventions. We could get together for dinner at my place. Our schedule is flexible, but in this case, sooner is better."

I took out my phone and studied my calendar. frowning as if I were having trouble finding time for Nina's surprise party. After a few seconds, I told them I could rearrange some things and make tomorrow night work unless it was too short notice for the guest of honor.

"Are you kidding? There's no way she'd miss it if she knows you'll be there." A brilliant smile transformed her stern face. "I'll text her later." She reached into her purse and removed several thin booklets. "I was hoping you'd agree to join us, so I brought some brochures on the signs of suicidal ideation and how to talk about it."

I hesitated a second before accepting them, and she added, "We don't expect you to say much. Just having you there will help."

"I hope you're right."

Louisa and I picked at our food while Howard finished his burger and half of hers. At first, I considered his overly zealous appetite somewhat insensitive considering the severity of our discussion. Then I remembered his background in homicide. If he'd gotten off his feed after every difficult case, he could have wasted away.

That reminded me of my new four-legged friend, and I asked the waitress to pack up the rest of my lunch.

We said goodbye outside, and I watched as they crossed the parking lot, holding hands. I waited for the familiar pang of jealousy mixed with melancholy, but it never came. Instead, I recalled what Howard's remark about Nina not being the violent group member and the way Louisa shushed him.

If Nina didn't have the killer instinct he had referred to, which one of my students did?

Chapter 24

Still contemplating the possibility someone in my workshop had homicidal tendencies, I almost ran off the road when a kamikaze crow zeroed in on my windshield. He came from nowhere, jolting me out of that familiar lapse in consciousness where people reach their destinations without being able to recall the journey. What should have been a lightening-like attack played out in slow motion, bringing me eye to eye with the bird's bright white iris and black marble pupil. I slammed on the brakes and squeezed my eyes shut, waiting for the inevitable thud.

It didn't come. I forced myself to look at the windshield, expecting streaks of blood and gore. But the glass was clean; no broken body lay on the hood. There was nothing at all.

My impulse was to floor it and get the hell home, but I had to find out what happened to that damn bird. I got out and made a full circle around the vehicle, stopping every few feet to check underneath. I expanded the perimeter of my search to include the nearby bushes and yards. Still no sign of crow carnage.

I climbed back in the car and reviewed the moments before and after the appearance of the bird, frame by frame. Physics was not my thing. All I remembered was when an irresistible force meets an immovable object…okay, I was clueless. But I understood it was impossible for my black bird to have disappeared into thin air. Unless he'd never been there.

An image of the avoid-alcohol label came to me. Could one beer be enough to conjure death-seeking fowls? Had all those glasses of wine stayed dormant, waiting for just the right moment to wreak havoc with my meds? Or had I been sabotaging my efforts to get better, holding onto my pain until it erupted into horrifying hallucinations?

Gripping the steering wheel in a strangle-hold, I crawled along at least ten miles under the speed limit. By the time I pulled into the garage, I had almost convinced myself the bird hadn't been a drug and alcohol induced hallucination, rather the manifestation of the stress I was under. Students capable of violence. Clive's information about Michael's murder and the possibility I might be next on the killer's agenda. Guilt over my failures as a wife. Sessions with a doctor who was more concerned about how I measured my writing progress and projections about the release of my non-existent book than he was about my mental stability.

That was it. All those questions about "my process" and those incongruous comments that eluded me after my session with Dr. Riley. The way he expressed his very specific interest in the launch date for my next Garnet adventure.

During our first meeting, he encouraged me to throw myself into my writing but steered me away from working on Michael's project, as it could be too taxing. I dismissed his tone as condescending. Now it seemed likely he might have had another reason for discouraging me from getting acquainted with men like Clive and encouraging me to continue producing titillating Garnet escapades. I hadn't pegged him as a secret fan, desperate for more naughtiness from my sexy heroine. I still didn't. But he had discouraged me from pursuing the veterans' stories. The last time I saw him, the subject never came up.

It was possible he assumed I'd dropped it at his recommendation. His ego was over-inflated enough for him to think I was so impressed with his expertise I would accept anything he suggested. But why would he care what I wrote?

My inability to pinpoint the doctor's intent left me restless and irritated. I needed to do something that would give me the illusion of being in control. I needed to write. Unfortunately, that didn't immediately translate into action.

Even before I lost Michael, I lacked the discipline it took to sit for hours at a time struggling to come up with two or three pages of quality material. Rather than commit, I would succumb to any distraction. I would wash a half-load of clothes, mop the already-clean kitchen floor, water plants—anything to avoid the difficult task of telling a story people would want to read.

Today, I was determined not to procrastinate. But first, I had to get something cool to drink. How could I be creative if I didn't stay hydrated? While standing at the sink, I glanced toward Rex's yard and saw him lying on his back steps, looking very lonely. I remembered the doggy bag.

He and I spent the next ten minutes reenacting our previous meat-sharing scene. Rex reacted with his usual enthusiasm, whirling in circles while I broke the burger into smaller pieces. No longer fearful of losing a finger, I was much more relaxed.

After running out of food and conversation topics, I trudged inside to the sunroom, intent on getting down to business. I sat at the desk and got as far as opening my laptop before I noticed my cell phone and decided I absolutely had to check for missed calls. There weren't any, but my email and Twitter accounts were probably full of comments from readers about Garnet.

My in-box was overloaded, mostly with invitations to conferences or political diatribes. I began deleting, stopping on one from Wanda: "Just checking on what's up with our heroine." Since no response was required, I went to the next message. It was from Todd.

I sincerely hope I did not offend you by overstepping my role. I can assure you it was only out of genuine concern. Please forgive me.

His boss must have read the poor guy the riot act when she found out about his suggestion I contact him directly if I needed help. I was trying to come up with an answer when another subject line caught my attention: *An Intimate Look at K.E. Conroy.*

Instead of a message, there was only a link. I knew better than to click on unknown addresses—that I should hit delete—but the heading made it impossible to dismiss.

The video opened on my book jacket photo. The caption beneath it repeated the subject of the email. A quick dissolve revealed selected scenes from my supermarket adventure, complete with the disturbing audio of me shrieking and cursing while I wreaked havoc in the cereal aisle and terrorized everyone around me. Nothing the world hadn't seen before.

The videographer, however, had just begun. He had edited my first encounter with Rex to make it seem as if I were taunting the dog by offering food I never delivered. He added what sounded like angry German opera and followed up with various vignettes of me coming and going from my house, leaving the rec center, and sitting with Lucas in the restaurant.

The music shifted to some depressing instrumental I recognized from *Les Misérables* as the video continued with long shots of me sipping wine on the deck and a tight shot of empty bottles in my trash can. The final close-up, taken from outside my window, was of me staring at a blank computer screen.

I gripped the edge of my desk, fighting against the impulse to run inside and pour myself a vodka. This demonstration of my vulnerability should have terrified me, and it was frightening. But what I felt was rage at the continued attempts to manipulate me through fear. The vitriolic tweets and comments. The dead flowers. And now this nasty portrayal of me as some out-of-control, washed-up writer.

Andy had been right. I should have called the police when I got that stupid bouquet. Possibly, it wasn't too late. The evidence, or whatever it was, might be tainted, but it was worth a try. I walked to the laundry room only to find that the box was no longer on the shelf where I left it. Although it was unlikely, I hoisted myself onto the dryer to see if there was any way it had fallen. There was nothing there. If I hadn't shown those crumbling flowers to him, my word would be the only proof of their existence.

•   •   •

"Please don't say I told you so," I begged as soon as I opened the door.

"Nice seeing you, too." Andy stepped in, kissed me on the cheek, and headed straight to the kitchen.

"I'm sorry," I said, following him down the hall. "I should have called the police like you wanted me to. I was just so tired."

I pointed to the laundry room. "I put the box in there right after you left, and now it's gone." I looked away, trying to push down the hysteria threatening to overcome me. When I faced him, he seemed calm. If he thought I had slipped over the edge, he gave no indication of it.

"Is there any way you could have taken the flowers out and accidentally tossed the box? Or maybe you put them in one of those giant zip-lock bags to keep them from disintegrating? Did you check the freezer?"

He was rummaging around in it before I could answer.

"God, Kara. Do you even know what's in those casseroles?"

"Who gives a shit about casseroles?"

Delivered by women I had never met, the dishes were offerings from my stepmother's tennis friends or people from her church. Hopefully, Barb had forgotten my promise to keep track of and return the containers.

"You're right." He shut the door. "Let's see the latest in the ongoing campaign to terrorize my favorite author."

I led him to the den, and he sat beside me on the sofa, waiting for my inbox to appear on the screen. When it did, I scrolled past a few new messages, then stopped where the email with the video should have been. Only it wasn't.

Desperate, I checked every folder: trash, spam, Wanda. No sign of *An Intimate Look at K.E. Conroy*.

Tears welled in my eyes, and I took an angry swipe at them. "I know it was there."

But did I? I had been certain Garnet was sitting in the last row of my class, and that Michael stood behind Riley's back, and that I'd been involved in a hit and run with a crow.

He scooted the computer from my lap to his and began clicking on icons. A few seconds later, he shut the laptop.

"This is ridiculous," he said.

"Please, Andy. You've got to believe me. That video—"

"Honey, I believe you." He put his arm around me. "I'm the one being ridiculous, pretending I know anything about hacking software or hardware or whatever. But if my hunch is right, I think someone may have installed a keylogger."

"A key what?"

"Keylogger. I don't understand exactly how they work, but Greg should be able to help us."

"Greg?"

"You remember. The guy who was fixing my computer when you stopped by for lunch? Tall, thin, looks like he's about sixteen?"

"The one with the extreme buzz and the *All my friends have FBI files* t-shirt? Isn't he a little, uh, shady?"

"Please. What kid hasn't had a least one or two run-ins with the Feds?" He brushed back a strand of hair from my cheek. "Does Old Blue still work?"

Old Blue was the desktop computer on which I created my first Garnet novel. He was clumsy and outdated, but the two of us had spent so much time together, I hadn't been able to part with him. He was currently residing on the desk in what Michael and I had designated as our someday-nursery.

"I haven't used him since I got my laptop, but he was still functional. Just took a little longer to get up."

"Don't we all?"

I ignored the quip. "Why are you asking about Blue?"

"Because a keylogger lets the person monitoring you in on every single one of your keystrokes. Your searches and those naughty novels. Who and what you're emailing. And they have your passwords—all of them. Greg can clean it up for you. I'm guessing it will take a few days."

I wasn't a predator or a purveyor of pornography, but being a writer lends itself to having a colorful online history, especially when your main character prides herself in diverse sexual antics. Add Garnet's love of firearms, the bigger the better, and her fondness for inflicting pain into the mix, and I could easily be mistaken for, at best, a slightly kinky type, at worst, a perverted felon.

But if Andy was right, I had a lot more to worry about than what the sites I frequented said about my character.

"Why would someone want to track me with a key-what's-it?"

"Logger, but the more pressing question isn't why, but who. Have there been any strangers in the house recently? Repairman? Delivery boys?"

I thought of Clive and realized Andy had no idea who he was, so I summarized his visit, omitting the part when the veteran had scared the hell out of me in the garage. I assured him the man hadn't been near my computer.

"Besides, he doesn't strike me as a high-tech guy. Anyway. He said Michael had been collecting more than background stories. He'd been gathering data about some accounting discrepancies at the shelter and copies of patient files on a flash drive, but nobody knows where it is."

"Sounds like Clive thinks he's some kind of septarian James Bond."

"Maybe, but Lucas said pretty much the same thing. Did you come across anything unusual when you packed up Michael's office?"

"Not really. But I didn't touch the box marked *For K's Eyes Only.* Your attorney had all the paperwork he needed, so we stuck it in your closet. I'd be happy to go through it for you."

"Thanks, but it's something I need to do for myself."

"Sure, but if you change your mind, call me. Now back to the homeless guy you had tea with."

"It was lunch, and I'm telling you it was no big deal. There was one thing a little troubling," I said, hoping to downplay Clive's warning. "He seemed to think I might be in danger. He was worried that Michael's killer could suspect I knew something that I don't."

"A little troubling, my ass. Are you saying this homeless guy thinks someone murdered Michael because of that flash drive? No shit you might be in danger. And you're just now telling me about it?"

"I didn't think it was important."

He snorted and said, "I'm not leaving until we go through all of Michael's things."

"Please, not tonight. If the flash drive was that important, he would have put it in a really secure spot. I promise I'll look tomorrow, right after class."

He sighed. "All right, but at the very least, we need to change your passwords. Let's see if we can fire Blue up."

Inside the nursery that would never be, I brought the trusty old computer back to life. Then we spent an hour logging into every online platform I could remember using, going through the tedious process of coming up with different passwords for each one. I compiled a handwritten list of them and promised I would store them in a place safe, like my underwear drawer.

"You mean your granny panty drawer. Definitely safe." Satisfied at last, he stood and stretched.

"I'll drop off the laptop on the way to work in the morning and check in for a progress report on your search through Michael's stuff. In the meantime—"

"Make sure the doors are locked and the system is armed." I finished for him.

"Right, and no more dining with old men dressed in camouflage and spouting conspiracy theories."

We hugged goodbye, and I the closed door, then leaned against it, wishing I believed Clive's warnings were the ramblings of an addled senior citizen. I rechecked my locks, then trudged up the stairs.

After taking my pills, I turned on the TV and made the mistake of watching a rerun of an old Hitchcock movie, where nothing is what it seems. It struck me my own life had become an ongoing series of events that weren't as they appeared. The most troubling of my musings was the question of what would happen if I reached the point I could no longer make the distinction between reality and illusion?

Chapter 25

I woke to the drumming of my old buddy Woody after 8:30. I must have shut off my alarm when it sounded at 6:00 and returned to a blissfully dreamless sleep. I jumped from the bed, took a quick shower, and threw my hair into a ponytail. While I waited for the coffeemaker to heat up, I picked up a protein bar to eat on the way.

I caught every red light, which wasn't all bad since it gave me time to slap on mascara, blush, and lipstick at the stops. It was 9:40 when I scrambled into the classroom, where most of the students were already writing.

"Sorry I'm running a little behind," I said, tossing my bag on the desk. "It was one of those mornings."

"Too much nightlife?" a young man whose name escaped me asked.

"I wish. You all look like you've gotten a head start on me, so just keep going while I settle in. Then we'll pick back up on individual conferences."

Once seated, I scanned the list, still trying to match names to faces, when Louisa walked toward me.

"Nina can come, so we're on for tonight, my place at 7:00. I told her 7:30, so we could talk before she gets there." She dropped a piece of paper on my desk. "In case you haven't had a chance to check."

It was a copy of an email she had sent late last night, complete with directions to her house.

"Thank you. I'm looking forward to it."

Sure, you are. Like a root canal.

For better or worse, Garnet's intrusions no longer startled me. Besides, she was right. I *so* wasn't looking forward to it.

The conferences went well with no one taking offense at my suggestions for improvement or bursting into tears over what I intended as constructive criticism. Despite the frantic rush of the morning and my dread of the intervention party, I was in a decent mood.

It was so good that on the way home, I didn't mind stopping at the grocery to pick up a few essentials. Not a big deal. Not as if I were going back to the scene of my encounter with craziness to face down boxes of GoldieO's, which I couldn't have done if I'd wanted to since I wasn't allowed within a thousand feet of the store. And it wasn't a Rex moment, where I conquered a long-held fear. It was a normal shopping trip. But anytime I could use the world normal to describe my life was a good day.

The rest of my ride was bird-free, and I made it home in time to put away the groceries and make a sandwich before turning to the task I'd been avoiding for months.

Armed with a box cutter, I headed to the guest room, turned on the light, and opened the closet door. I pushed past the winter coats until I could see it lurking like a sleeping beast in the shadows.

Wedged between suitcases and a shoe rack, it was difficult to dislodge. I gripped the sides and tugged. When I tried to pick it up, I discovered it was more awkward than heavy, so I braced my back against the wall and shoved with both feet until it was in the middle of the closet. From there, I pushed it to the foot of the bed, and retrieved the box-cutter.

Before I could change my mind, I tore into the cardboard. The amount of double-strength, high quality mailing tape was typical of Michael. My husband was big on security measures. Fearful of slicing off a finger, I sawed slowly back and forth through multiple layers of adhesive only to find another one criss-crossing in the opposite direction.

I pried open the top flap with more force than intended, sending some of the plastic bubble-wrap flying. Then I rested on my heels before unwrapping a cylindrical object covered in brown paper. It was an oddly shaped trophy, a rectangle marked with what looked like a lightening symbol. Inscribed in gold on the black base was Michael's name with the words *Winner of the Prestigious Bolt Award for Innovation in Software Development.* The date was March 12, a year before we met.

Never one to tout his accomplishments, Michael had never mentioned he received a Bolt trophy, and even though I had no idea what the honor meant, it bothered me I knew nothing about it.

For God's sake. It's not like he won best actor in an adult film.

Garnet's lack of reverence would have pissed me off if the mental picture of my extremely modest husband bringing home a prestigious porn award hadn't cracked me up. I set the trophy aside and continued unwrapping.

There was a smooth wooden letter opener with the letters MJD carved on the handle. I recognized them as his father's initials. I never met the man, but Michael spoke of him with love and respect. He said his dad enjoyed working with his hands. When he'd gotten too old for major building projects, he took up woodworking. The letter opener must have been one of his later creations.

Next, I discovered a misshapen piece of pottery, an ashtray or possibly a soup bowl. The childlike scratching on the back read *Happy Mother's Day, love Michael.* When I met his mother, she'd been in the early stages of dementia. She confused me with her dead sister, not her favorite one, and died a month before our wedding.

Underneath the distorted pottery, I discovered a zip-lock plastic baggy with three ragged dog collars inside. Even though the bag was filmed with age, I could read the names carefully printed on each one: Roxie, Sport, and Sprinter. I knew the trio were beloved Golden Retrievers from his childhood.

All these mementos made me feel like an uninvited guest to the party that had been my husband's life. Everyone from his family to a bunch of computer geeks had known him longer, probably even better.

Tears clouded my eyes, then pooled and trickled down as I wrapped my arms around myself and rocked back and forth. I should have taken Andy up on his offer to help me sort through this minefield of memories.

All that remained in the box was a bound packet of elementary school report cards. I thumbed through them, not surprised Michael had excelled in academics. He even topped out on the conduct side. Instead of the kind of comments my teachers had written—talks too much or daydreams during science class—his had praised his careful attention to detail and superior ability to work with others. Too bad none of those attributes had kept him safe.

In the middle of possessions that had meant enough for my husband to take such pains to preserve them, I was at a loss as to how I should proceed. The Bolt award was the only piece of memorabilia worth displaying, but if he hadn't done it himself, would he want me to? The letter opener with its finely polished wood was cool and smooth in my hand, and although I rarely wrote or received letters, it would add a touch of class to my desk. The dog collars were probably a health hazard. But the bowl worked for me. I wouldn't be crushing a cigarette in it or eating chicken soup out of it, but I liked it was something Michael had made. And that it wasn't perfect.

I transferred the school records along with the retriever memorials to a shoe box. In deference to my husband's need for meticulous packing procedures, I picked up the bubble-wrap, planning to use it to secure the contents. The plastic was still partially attached to the top, and when I pulled it loose, an envelope dropped to the floor. Not bound in with the rest of his things, it had gotten stuck between the wrapping material and the lid, possibly an afterthought, although afterthoughts were rare for my husband.

It wasn't just the placement that set it apart. It was also its condition. Unlike the brown paper and report cards, there were no smudges of mildew or musty odor. Despite its relatively pristine state, I handled it as if it were fragile—as if doing so might preserve my husband's touch. I ran my fingernail under the sealed flap, then removed a small packet, where I discovered folded pieces of paper, inside more folded pieces of paper, Russian nesting-doll style. I found the note at the next to the last level.

> *Kara,*
> *Never forget that I love you even if we didn't get the chance to change our corner of the world. Maybe you still can.*
> *As always, you make my heart healthy.*
> *Michael*

My eyes burned at the sweet familiarity of the final line. When I had teased him about his inordinate love affair with GoldieOs, he responded by telling me how much I had in common with his favorite cereal, that we both made his heart healthy. I touched the note to my lips, then unfolded the last layer. In the center of the creased pages was a reminder of both his love and my role in his death: a tiny golden 'o.'

If not for the buzzing from my pocket, my cell phone reminding me of a calendar event, I don't know how long I might have stared at Michael's last gift to me, rereading the note, and puzzling over the circle of cereal before carefully rewrapping everything.

It was then I remembered the event I dreaded: Louisa's confrontation dinner.

Chapter 26

After dealing with the uncertainty of Michael's message, I appreciated the fact that Louisa's directions were as precise as the corners of her newly mown lawn. Her ranch-style home was a combination of wood and stone set in a neighborhood of contemporary houses that had been popular in the seventies. Closely trimmed azaleas flanked the entrance, their pink blooms providing a splash of color against the austere gray of the exterior.

What I guessed might be Howard's dark brown Ford Explorer was parked near the garage door. Rather than risk getting blocked in, I stopped at the curb, behind a silver Camry with a paw print-shaped bumper sticker that read *Rescued is my favorite breed*.

Although I was more than reluctant to accept Howard and Louisa's request to join this little exorcism, I had to admit it had come at a convenient time. Without something to take my mind off Michael's note, I would most likely still have been sitting in my bedroom staring at it the way I'd done for a good part of the afternoon.

Louisa opened the door before I had a chance to ring the bell. Her hair was brushed away from her face, and she was wearing a silky top that flowed gracefully over tailored jeans.

"You're right on time," she announced as she ushered me in. Windows that stretched to the ceiling overlooked a wooded back lot dotted with islands of pine straw. The fading sunlight across the beige carpet dappled it like a forest floor. On the opposite wall, Howard and Betty sat next to each other on a navy sofa. He stood when he saw me.

"We're real glad you could make it."

I took his extended hand and smiled.

Betty remained seated but echoed the sentiment in her soft voice.

"Sit anywhere you like," Louisa said. "I'll just be a minute."

"I'd take the recliner if I was you. Best seat in the house. I'm going to see if she needs some help."

I took his advice and sank into the plush fabric. "Wow, this is comfortable," I said, trying to think of something non-furniture related to say. Before the silence grew awkward, Louisa bustled back into the room, carrying a pitcher and a glass of ice. Howard was close behind, with the hors d'oeuvres.

"We decided tonight will go better if we avoid alcohol. I hope tea's okay?"

I thought a little liquor would make it a hell of a lot easier for me to get through the evening. But I said, "Yes, please."

We spent the next few minutes piling veggies and dip onto small plates. When everyone had scarfed down a few carrots and celery stalks, Louisa began.

"We'll eat first, then have coffee and dessert in the den. After that, we should probably get right into it, just rip off the band-aid."

Despite Louisa's assurances Nina wasn't the violent type, I was pretty sure I didn't want to be around for any band-aid ripping. I nodded approval I didn't feel and ate another carrot.

"I'll start by telling her we're worried because we care about her. And we can tell from her writing she's sad, maybe even hopeless. What we say after that will depend on how she reacts."

After reading the brochures Louisa had given me, I could see signs of depression, but not necessarily in Nina's actions or attitude. The way she affected lack of interest, then threw herself into the assignment, her dark sense of fashion, her initial aversion to working with a group—all these were not atypical behavior for someone her age.

Her writing was another story. She created characters who were isolated, depressed. But they were fictional. Their desperation and hopelessness didn't definitively reflect her outlook on life. I wasn't certain if the voice of the girl who didn't want to make the same mistakes as Hamlet was Nina's. But the pamphlet warned suicidal thinking might not be obvious.

Our guest of honor didn't show until 7:45. Dressed in her signature color, Nina had gone with a slightly more formal look. She had pushed her black hair away from her face and wore a black hoodie over leggings the same shade.

"Sorry, I'm late. My car wouldn't start, so I hitched a ride."

"When you say *hitched*," I began, trying to rearrange my face into something other than horror stricken.

She cut me off. "It means I got a friend to give me a lift. You didn't think I meant hitchhiked like in the olden days?"

I was embarrassed but relieved. Relief morphed into doubt when I remembered Nina was a fiction writer. She might have edited the truth into a version that better fit her audience.

Howard wasn't satisfied with Nina's response either. "Unfortunately, it's still around, and even more dangerous. Aside from getting picked up by some crazed psycho, hitchhikers stand a good chance of getting run over. When I was on the force—"

"Howard," Louisa interrupted, "Nina might like something to drink."

He took the hint. "How about some sweet tea?"

Louisa was an excellent cook, but I was too busy trying to keep my balance on an emotional high wire to enjoy the food. I teetered between nervous laughter and napkin twisting, and I wasn't the only one exhibiting signs of acute nervousness.

Betty kept swirling pasta, which dangled then dropped from her fork before making it to her mouth. Louisa busied herself refreshing drinks, heating bread, checking on dessert. Every few minutes, Howard cleared his throat as if he were about to speak. Only he didn't. Instead, he drained his water glass, giving Louisa an excuse for another trip to the kitchen.

When we finished, our hostess began by telling Nina how worried we were about her, and Betty seconded the emotion, her voice stronger than usual. Then both women turned to me. I murmured agreement, desperately wishing I'd stuck a flask in my purse.

The young girl stared at a spot on the wall.

Betty added, "We're worried you might be depressed."

I wanted to help but felt like a fraud. Yes, I was an expert on depression—not so much in how to get undepressed.

Come on, woman. Do what you do best. Write your way out of it.

Garnet had a point, only not about *me*. "Nina, you're a great writer, but your work has a darkness to it. And I can't tell if it's coming from your narrator or you."

She remained silent, and I wondered if my hopelessness would seep into my work, if I ever returned to it.

Louisa took a more direct approach. "Have you talked to a therapist?"

She shook her head.

I kept waiting for Louisa to spit it out, but it was Betty who stepped up.

"The reason we asked you to come tonight is because we're afraid you've been considering giving up—on your stories, yourself, life in general. That you don't see in yourself what other people do: a kind, beautiful, and talented young woman."

Her words elicited the first change of expression I'd seen from Nina. Her eyes widened and her mouth dropped open. She slouched back in her chair for several seconds, then raised her head and sat ramrod straight.

"You think I'm kind and beautiful? You barely know me."

"True, but it doesn't take that long to discover the kind of person you are, the way you really listen when we read and the questions you ask. You say something positive about everyone's work, and you never judge. Then there's *your* writing. In many ways, it's so beyond your years we forget how young you are." Betty had found her voice.

"What about the darkness?" She looked directly at me.

"It's a beautiful darkness. Like a deep lake on a moonless night, but I'm afraid you might drown in it." Was I talking to Nina or to myself? And did it matter?

There was a moment of quiet, as if everyone was waiting for me to continue, but I had nothing else.

Betty saved me. "Kara's right. You have so much life ahead of you. So many lovely, terrifying decisions to make. That's what we want for you: the chance to make those choices, good and bad, to celebrate your successes and learn from your mistakes. But, Nina, please trust me when I tell you there are some choices that lead you down awful paths to places you can't come back from."

No one spoke. Then Nina stood. "Thank you. For dinner, for caring, all of it. But it's getting late, and I have an early shift at the diner. And, please, don't worry about me. I'm fine."

Howard intercepted her on his return from the bathroom. "Hold on a minute, and I'll take you home."

"That's okay. I can call my—"

"There's no need for that. And it might be a little out of your way, Howard." Betty smiled at Louisa, and from the look that passed between them, I got the impression Louisa approved of Betty's offer.

Nina offered more protests, but Betty, in her quiet unassuming manner, persisted until she gave in.

I didn't have the energy to stay and rehash the evening. As soon as Betty and Nina left, I thanked our hostess and sprinted for the door.

•　　•　　•

Without the glow of the low-hanging moon, I might have driven right by my own home. I never forget to leave on lots of lights—at least one interior, the front flood lights, and both porch lights. I did it by rote, the same way I unplugged my curling iron or turned off the water in the tub. But I must have forgotten because the house, inside and out, was completely dark.

I pressed the garage door opener and was immediately rewarded with the illumination from the overhead light. I took comfort in the knowledge that it would stay on for five full minutes after I shut off the engine.

I surveyed the corners for any unexpected drop-ins. After concluding I was alone, I darted from the car. On my way through the house, I flipped switches as if I were dropping breadcrumbs. Kitchen, hall, den, dining room, porch—I turned on every single one, creating a trail for my return trip. That was when I noticed the television screen was as dark as the house had been. I tried to remember not leaving it on. What is it they say on courtroom dramas about how hard it is to prove a negative? In this case it was certainly true. There was no way I could prove I hadn't turned my TV on.

I also gave up on my resolution to avoid alcohol. Even without finding Michael's message, swearing off liquor prior to Nina's disastrous intervention had been foolhardy.

Propped up in bed, drinking vodka and watching television with the sound down, I thought about Nina's response and how strange it had been when she unwittingly echoed my "I'm fine" line. Saying it hadn't made it so, but I had never entertained thoughts about hurting myself.

Nina was different. While we had both experienced devastating loss and the guilt associated with it, because of her age she was more vulnerable and more isolated. Whereas I insisted I was fine to placate people who cared about me— Andy, Dad, even Barb— she didn't seem to have any support system other than the group and now me. Betty might have been right about longevity not always being necessary in a relationship but having a history mattered.

Oddly, though, I felt as if Nina and I shared a history. Whether it was from the intimacy of her writing or our similar loses, she had quickly become more to me than a passing acquaintance. They all had. And like the others, I had an overwhelming need to help her.

Before I could be of any use to her, however, I would have to take care of myself. I would have to strap on own oxygen mask before assisting Nina with hers.

Chapter 27

The whispery voice that woke me had an urgency to it, a dramatic undertone similar to that of the detectives on the crime show I'd been watching when my meds kicked in.

Kara! Wake up before it's too late.

Louder and more forceful, a shadowy figure on the other side of the room issued the frantic warning. Dressed in black from ball cap to high-heeled boots, the intruder stood at the window, staring out into the night. Even with her raven hair hidden, I knew it was Garnet.

"You are not real. You are the result of an unfortunate pharmaceutical mix," I croaked and tried to clear my drug-dried throat.

This is not the time to sweat the details. Can't you hear it? Grab the goddamn pepper spray and get your ass up.

Footsteps sounded from below. I scrambled for the canister I kept in my bedside table drawer, eased my legs over the side of the bed, and listened.

"I don't hear it now." But when I turned toward the spot where Garnet stood, she had vanished. "Really? What kind of super heroine are you anyway?" I hissed, then answered my own question. "The useless kind who wakes me up, so I'll be totally conscious while being raped and murdered, then runs off—probably to get her nails sharpened."

Anger coupled with terror worked well to clear my head, enough that I made a bold choice. I would not sit around waiting for my attacker to burst in on me. I would act. So, pepper spray at the ready, I tiptoed to the door and pressed my ear against it. Outside was quiet, and I began to doubt whether those footsteps had been real.

I eased into the hall. With my back against the wall, I inched toward the stairs. When I reached the top, I clutched the rail and slow-walked down, one foot at a time like an elderly aunt.

Light from the porch flooded the foyer, turning me into a silhouette, a perfect target. I crouched low and scurried to the unlit area. The thumping of my heart was now the only sound. Ducking into the den, I dropped behind the recliner and waited, scanning the room for a potential weapon. My fireplace was gas, so no heavy pokers or sharp-edged shovels. I'd seen one too many movies with silly-ass girls who thought they'd be able to land a lucky blow with a paper weight, and Michael's letter opener was too dull to serve as a back-up for my pepper spray. I needed something with the power to incapacitate or at least inflict serious injury.

From the bookcase, my husband's copy of *A Game of Thrones* caught my eye. I slipped it from the shelf. If used correctly, it was heavy enough to do the trick. Some of its savagery might even rub off on me.

I tucked the book under my left arm and held the pepper spray in front of me with my right hand, then marched forward. Ira's flood lights shot a wide beam across the tile but failed to penetrate shadowy corners. I stood frozen in the doorway, where I rethought my aggressive strategy. A creaking hinge, followed by the sound of cans crashing on the floor, startled me into motion. Instead of taking the reasonable course of action, running out the front of the house, I moved toward the noise.

A dark figure bolted from the pantry and out the back. Without thinking, I rushed for him, but he was too fast. When I made it outside, he was already leaping down the steps, two and three at a time.

"Hey, asshole!" I shouted. He paused long enough for me to take aim at his head. "Winter's coming." I hurled the book with its six hundred plus pages flapping as it flew. Although there was a satisfying thud before the epic novel careened off the rail, my intruder kept running into the darkness below.

The blow had little impact, but our encounter elicited howls from within Ira's house. He appeared and released Rex, who ran to the fence, snarling and growling. His owner followed.

From my perch on the deck, I could see Ira carried the shotgun he kept over his mantel. He joined the guard dog and the two stood there staring in the direction my burglar, if that's what he was, had fled.

"Is that you, Kara?" Ira called out. "Stay put. I'm coming over."

•   •   •

It was almost dawn when the police finished completing their report. I didn't want to disturb Andy, and, thanks to my good neighbors, hadn't needed to. Rex had trotted alongside us while we searched for what wasn't there. As if sensing my anxiety, the dog stayed by me throughout the evening.

Until Michael's death, I had no experience with police at my door. When I was a kid, I saw them appear at our next-door neighbors' house. Dad made light of the frequency of their visits, but despite his attempts to play off the seriousness of those appearances, even then I knew the sight of uniformed men at the door was never a good thing.

I had fallen asleep on the sofa the night of Michael's murder. The repeated ringing of the doorbell woke me. I remember shivering as I tunneled out of deep sleep. I blamed the chill on our faulty thermostat. Through the peephole, I saw a policeman, more a boy, with his smooth face and slender neck, and determined my reaction came from a much colder place.

The sight of him standing there in his uniform wasn't frightening at first. Certainly, the authorities would never have sent this man-child to deliver terrible news. When I opened the door and he began shifting from one foot to the other, I knew I was wrong. He had come to destroy my world.

The police who came to investigate the intruder I slammed with a hardback medieval epic, however, had no such power. Dressed in nondescript suits, they introduced themselves as detectives Graves and Davis. They walked outside to check for breaches in the security while we waited inside.

When we rendezvoused in the kitchen, Detective Davis said, "There are no signs somebody physically tampered with your alarm."

"Well, I'm positive I armed it."

"Oh, no, ma'am. We're not suggesting you didn't set it. Popular wireless systems like yours rely on radio signals, which means someone could have jammed the frequency."

"Jammed it? So, what good is even having an alarm? I might as well hire Rex." The dog's ears perked up.

"I'm not sure who that is, but the equipment to disable a system like yours isn't cheap. It's not out of reach for a sophisticated burglary ring, but those guys go after neighborhoods where the houses run a million plus. The pros won't risk breaking in if they suspect the owner's home, and they would have cleaned you out."

"Then what kind of burglar did I have?"

"I can't give you the categories, Ms. Dolan." Graves stepped in. "But it is possible you interrupted him before he got whatever it was he came for. It might not be the first time he's been here."

"Not the first time he was here?" My knees weakened, and I fell into the nearest chair.

"The way nothing seems to have been disturbed could indicate he was familiar with the layout of the house." He paused, then asked, "And you, Mr. Weinstein? You said you came outside because your dog was barking, but didn't actually see the intruder?"

"That's right. If I'd been a little quicker, I might have caught the guy."

Neither of us referenced the shotgun Ira had stored underneath my sofa.

The officer turned back to me. "Have you had any run-ins with someone you work with or maybe somebody from your past holding a grudge against you?"

I had the irrational urge to justify myself as a nice person, the kind who got along with everyone. Fear won out over my desire to be one of the popular kids, though, and I came clean about my online stalker, who might or might not have escalated into the real-time creep who sent me the disappearing dead flowers.

In addition to their professional manner, they were patient. They didn't scold me for not calling sooner or not being able to describe my invader. Graves smiled and nodded as he recorded my irresponsible behavior on his phone while Davis scribbled in a notebook. When I got to the part about Michael and Saint Cecilia and the story Clive had told, however, they exchanged quick glances, and I wondered if they still believed me.

"I think that's all we need for tonight," Davis said. "We'll be in touch if we learn anything new."

Panic surged over me, and I tugged at his sleeve. "What if he comes back? I mean if they messed with my alarm once, what's stopping him from doing it again?"

"I'm afraid there's no way to be sure your intruder won't return, but it's unlikely. Even if he didn't get what he came for, hitting the same house twice is risky."

He smiled. If I were casting good cop, bad cop, Davis would have been my first choice for good cop. But years of experience with crime dramas and real life had taught me life roles could be interchangeable.

"We'll have a car patrol the neighborhood," Graves added. "And don't hesitate to call if you see something unusual. Anything at all."

Definitely interchangeable.

As I walked them to the door, I noticed a flutter of white curtain across the street. No surprise. I expected most of my closer neighbors had been stealing more than a peek or two as they speculated on what was going on inside the poor widow's house.

Ira and Rex stood beside me as the police drove away.

"If you hadn't come outside when you did, I don't know what might have happened."

"You seemed to have a handle on the situation. If you had more time to aim, I bet you would have taken him out."

With my recent history of seeing and hearing people who weren't there, I couldn't be sure my would-be thief was even real.

"Do you ever think you might be losing it, Ira?"

"Honey, at eighty-eight years old, I know I'm losing it. But you listen to me. You've been through hell and back, and you're one tough cookie. Don't start doubting yourself. And if you need us, me and Rex can be here in a flash."

At his age, "in a flash" was a relative term, but I appreciated the sentiment.

"You're sure you don't want to hang on to my security blanket?" He held out his shotgun, and I shook my head.

"I'm not really a gun person." Proximity to firearms made me jumpy, sometimes even queasy. Michael's death hadn't helped. The thought of bullets penetrating the body I knew so well, of the fiery agony before he went cold, had done nothing to change my mind.

Pink and orange streaks spread across the gray sky, promising more color to come, but I was too tired to enjoy the approaching sunrise. After double checking my security system, I trudged up the stairs and climbed under my rumpled covers. My energy drained with my adrenaline, and I fell asleep.

Chapter 28

I woke to sunlight warming my face. A choir of birds outside my window serenaded me with their relentless chirping. Then the grinding whine of the garbage truck reminded me it was after eight, and I was about to be late for the second day in a row.

The fact no one commented on my appearance when I rushed in at 9:35 underscored how bad I looked. I had pulled my unwashed hair into a tight ponytail but not taut enough to lift the skin around my swollen eyes.

"I'm so sorry. Things got a little crazy last night about two in the morning, and I didn't get to bed until dawn."

I hadn't expected giggles from the group, then realized the source of their amusement. "Not that kind of crazy," I clarified and paused, not sure if I should reveal the events of the previous evening.

Although I had almost ruled out the possibility any of my students wanted to hurt me, if I was wrong and it was one of them, the culprit might exhibit some sign of guilt during my account. I would be on the lookout for stiff shoulders and evasive behavior.

"Seems someone broke into my house."

There were gasps and a few expletive outbursts.

"Not to worry. I wasn't about to be one of those ditzy heroines, cowering in the closet. I kept my cool and applied my best literary strategies." I studied their faces as I continued my story, glossing over my terror at waking to the sounds of someone rumbling around below me and omitting my heroine's role, one that might have saved my life. Instead, I emphasized the plucky way I banished my would-be thief by hurling George R.R. Martin at him.

Appropriately concerned, students began asking questions: Did I have any likely suspects for who might have broken into my home? Did I have a gun? Should I think about getting one? Did I watch *Game of Thrones*?

I told them I had no idea who the intruder could have been. And no, I didn't own a gun as I would be the kind of person who would get shot by her own weapon. And yes, not only did I never miss an episode of the blood-thirsty saga, but I had also read the books. Only after I assured them I wasn't worried because the police were on it, did everyone settle down.

Despite the re-establishment of our routine, I felt nothing like normal. Apparently, neither did Louisa and her group, who huddled together talking softly. I took a break between conferences and approached them.

"Sorry I wasn't more helpful last night." I nodded toward Nina's empty desk. "I hoped we got through to her, but I guess not. Did she say anything on the way home?"

"Nothing very revealing," Betty replied. "She thanked me for the ride and for caring about her and repeated how fine she was. As she was getting out of the car, I said I'd see her tomorrow. She didn't answer, just shut the door like she didn't hear me."

"Howard and I are going to stop by her place later," Louisa offered.

"Good. Let me know what you find out, please."

When class ended and everyone had gone, I remained behind the heavy old desk that had started as a barricade between me and the students. Even with all the drama, teaching this course had provided a stabilizing challenge for me, one I hadn't realized how much I needed. It had given me a purpose, a reason to get out of bed, once I'd stopped dreading it, and it had been fun. While I wasn't sure I wanted to teach another soon, I wanted to get to know Louisa's gang better. I might even start a writing group and invite them to join.

I was considering what that might look like when my phone rang.

"Hey, it's me, Lucas." As if I wouldn't recognize that voice. "I know this is kind of last minute, but I wanted to run something by you. Are you up for a quick cup of coffee?"

Although I dreaded returning to the scene of the break-in, I hesitated. I'd been dealing with quite a bit of unwelcome debris slipping from the depths of my subconscious lately, and I wasn't excited about digging for more. I was curious to know if Clive had been in touch with him after our encounter, so I agreed to meet him at Scooters Coffee in half an hour.

I drove slowly, took my time parking, and did a makeup check before I got out of the car. The dark circles under my eyes had developed an immunity to my concealer. Lipstick and blush failed to provide much improvement.

"What difference does it make?" I asked my reflection in the rearview mirror. "This is strictly business." I thought of Andy's advice about not shutting myself off. What he didn't realize was that in my heart I was still a married woman, and I didn't want that to change.

Lucas was seated when I arrived. "Thanks for coming on such short notice," he said, then asked what I wanted to drink. I watched as he disarmed the teenage barista with the same smile he gave me during our first meeting, and I wondered if his charm was innate or calculated.

The possibility it was the latter made me get straight to the point. "So, what did you need to run by me?"

If my businesslike approach surprised him, he hid it well. "It's Clive. He called to tell me about how he waited for you in your garage, so *they* wouldn't see him. When I asked him who he thought *they* were, he clammed up. Said he had some things to take care of and would be in touch. Frankly, I'm concerned about him."

"What is it that bothers you?"

"How paranoid he is. He takes some heavy anti-psychotics. If he's off his meds, I'm not sure what he might do."

"He didn't act like somebody who was out of it." It said a lot about me that I accepted hiding in a garage rather than ringing a doorbell as conventional behavior.

"That's good, but the truth is we can't be certain the clinic has him on the right prescriptions because with PTSD you never know."

"What do you mean, *you never know*? Are you saying he's dangerous?"

"More like delusional. I wouldn't put too much faith in anything he says. If he stops by again, call me and don't let him in without me there. Do you have a friend or family member you could stay with until I can get Clive to see a doctor? I could hang out at your house. Make sure no one breaks in." He paused and touched my fingertips with his.

I slid my hands away and placed them in my lap. I knew Andy and Paul would be happy to put me up for a few weeks, and there was always—God help me—Dad and Barb. Yet wasn't leaving the house Michael and I had turned into a home a form of betrayal? Because if I left, I might never work up the courage to return. But it was the eager way Lucas looked when his hand brushed against mine that was the most disturbing.

Now I was the one being paranoid. Unless I wasn't. What if he only wanted me to think Clive was the problem?

Or make you look like a hysterical female because it's a hell of a lot easier to discount a crazy woman than it is to deal with a strong one.

"Good point."

My remark had been intended for Garnet, but it was Lucas who responded: "So, you'll stay with someone?"

"I'll think about it."

"Please, do. And I meant what I said about keeping an eye on your place while you're gone. If something bad happened to you, I'd never forgive myself."

"That's really nice of you." I glanced at my watch. "I didn't realize it was so late." I stood abruptly and knocked my knee against the table. He started scrambling to his feet, but I motioned for him to sit back down.

"Please, promise you'll call when you decide where to stay."

"I promise." But I had made my decision. I wouldn't be leaving my home and had no intention of reporting back to him. Paranoid or not, both his offer to take care of me and the implied intimacy of his touch were troubling.

It wasn't until I was halfway home that it came to me. I hadn't told him anything about the intruder. So, why had he specifically offered to make sure no one broke in while I was away?

·   ·   ·

"Hey, Rex." I tossed him a treat, which he caught mid-air before wolfing it down. I fed him another, then knelt to scratch behind his ears. He groaned his appreciation.

"Thanks for the backup last night." I froze for a few seconds as the image of my intruder running from my deck flashed through my mind. He nudged my hand. "Sorry, buddy. I'd rather hang out with you, but I've got to go inside and obsess over my new friend Clive, who might not really be a friend, but has definitely disappeared." I didn't share my suspicions about Lucas; after all, there was only so much a dog could take.

He whined as I walked toward my steps. There had been no surprises waiting for me when I got home from my meeting with Lucas—no muffled footsteps above, no unwelcome gifts, no strangers darting from my pantry—so I wasn't nervous about re-entering the house. I would have been more relaxed, however, having the good boy by my side. Maybe Ira would rent him out on an as-needed basis.

From the den, the sound of a local talk show host droning on and on comforted me. Tomorrow's class required no preparation. I would give students the option of reading another excerpt from their work or continuing with their writing. That left me with time to check my blog. Because I'd blocked GarNetted and anyone named after characters from my books and a few others because they were asses, I wasn't too concerned about discovering hostile comments. And I was right. There were only more questions about her relationship with the detective and several requests for more non-existent excerpts.

In my previous novels, my heroine frequently got tangled up in the sheets, but she avoided any emotional entanglements. If I followed through on the reckless promises to my fans, that was about to change.

"So, Garnet," I said. "I think it's time you put more than skin in the game. How about a little piece of your heart?"

Of course, when I wanted to hear from the unrepentant hussy, she was nowhere to be found. My failure to view the lack of auditory hallucinations as a good thing spoke volumes about my state of mind.

I began reading the two chapters I'd written before the shooting. My heroine was relaxing on a beach in the Dominican Republic, mentally reviewing her exploits from the previous book. In the rough outline I started, I planned for a beautiful, young woman who worked at the resort to be accused of murdering one of the guests. Garnet, the only one convinced of the girl's innocence, would be drawn into the investigation.

Although I intended for her to get cozy with the lead detective on the case, I had no intention of her falling for him. Spurred on by the excitement of my fans, I decided to play around with the idea while she played around with the hot guy.

For the first time in months, I lost myself in a world I created, where women had the power.

Garnet ached to feel Jean Pierre's smooth chocolate skin against her pale ivory breasts.

My heroine remained silent, but I sensed her approval as I developed the relationship between the two over the next ten pages. The scene ended with Garnet lying beside her sleeping lover, considering, then rejecting, the possibility of letting herself go from attraction to attachment. After hitting save, I leaned back and was surprised to see that while I'd been writing, the afternoon sun had faded.

I was hungry and not the kind that can be satisfied with cheese and crackers. I wanted real food—a full-on meal with meat and potatoes and buttered rolls. I craved the kind of food Garnet ate after an afternoon of steamy sex. The kind of sex I just finished writing about.

Damn it! That floozy had given me her voracious sexual appetite, minus the sex.

Chapter 29

All I could scrounge up to satisfy my non-post coital appetite was plain spaghetti topped with butter and some questionable parmesan cheese, but it was the best boring pasta I'd ever eaten. After two platefuls, I poured myself a glass of wine and relocated to the den. Reclining on the sofa, I surfed through the channels, finally settling on a *Seinfeld* marathon. One rerun became four, and if not for the interruption of an especially irritating commercial on the importance of having a home security system, I might have continued watching them until dawn.

The annoying ad reminded me to double-check my windows and doors. And even though it was potentially useless, I made sure my not-so-secure system was armed. The thought of a sophisticated network of thieves busily jamming my alarm gave me chills, so I poured another glass of wine to warm me up.

As usual, I avoided looking directly at the cluster of Michael-and-me photos. But today, I sensed a change. Instead of hanging crookedly, the frames were perfectly aligned. The precision of the arrangement was of the caliber I once insisted on. I stepped back and leaned against the banister as I took in each grouping along the stairwell. Someone had gone to the trouble of straightening every one of them. I closed my eyes, hoping that when I opened them, I would find the smiling faces returned to the chaotic state I left them in.

After several seconds, I summoned the courage to reassess the situation and bile rose in my throat. Although the frames had been placed at perfect right angles, the pictures themselves were wrong. Each one was upended. I dragged myself up the stairs, shrinking as far away from those images as possible. It was terrifying to speculate on why someone had gone to the trouble of restoring order to my memories, only to rehang them in such a bizarre way. Despite my horror, I was struck by just how ridiculous Michael and I appeared in row after row of standing-on-our-head shots.

I choked on laughter I knew would quickly roll into giggling hysteria and focused on how perfectly this visual captured my new reality. Only a few steps from the top of the stairs, I stopped in bewilderment. I expected to see my favorite photo, where we're beaming into the camera unaware of what lay ahead of us, mocking me topsy-turvy style. But there was only a faint outline on the wall. The picture that, when I touched it, sent a current of energy I foolishly hoped was Michael trying to communicate with me, was gone.

•   •   •

The hours between the moment I discovered the newly arranged photos and a little after two in the morning became lost time. I had no recollection of stepping onto the upstairs landing or of lying down on the bed in the guest bedroom. When I came back to myself, the furniture was cast in silhouette, brightened only by a shaft of light from the bathroom. Other than taking a few quick shallow breaths, I remained immobile, fearful that my previous paralysis might have returned. I flexed my fingers, then my toes, relieved at their mobility.

But just because I could move didn't necessarily mean I should. Whoever rearranged the photos might still be in the house. It was even possible that person had carried me from the staircase to the bedroom while I was in the same fugue state I experienced in Riley's office. Only this time, Michael wasn't hovering over me. Like my favorite picture, he had disappeared.

I stayed put, giving my eyes and mind a chance to adjust. I concluded if someone had gone to the trouble to carry or lead me up the stairs to my bed, he hadn't planned to hurt me, not physically anyway. More likely, I walked away on my own, too shocked by my discovery for the rational part of my brain to tell the difference between twisted fantasy and harsh reality.

Further evidence no one had man-handled me was the condition of the clothes I wore. My shirt was in place, my pants covered my ankles with no folds or crinkles, and my shoes were neatly placed on the floor beside me.

It was too late to call Andy or Ira, even though both men had promised they'd come running if I needed them. But what exactly did I need them for? It wasn't as if getting my photos back to their original positions qualified as an emergency. And I was becoming more confident that whoever had rearranged the pictures was no longer in the house.

I squeezed my eyes shut, visualizing the stairwell as it was when I'd been scurrying around, trying not to be too late to class. Often what a person expects to see, something that's been there day after day for what seems like forever, is exactly what she sees. The mind tricks us into the complacency of expectation. The way I continued to expect Michael to come home from work or to be sitting across from me at the breakfast table.

The more I thought about it, the more certain I was. I wouldn't have missed the repositioning of the frames. Even though I trained myself not to look at our happy faces—hadn't been able to straighten them—I would have noticed they were different. And then there were the police and Ira. Surely one of them would have seen the photos were upside down. Of course, they might have written it off as crazy-widow syndrome and been afraid to point it out, but I didn't think so.

Despite my belief no one was in the house, I remained reluctant to get up. I was that child terrified the monster under the bed would snatch her by the ankles the second her feet hit the ground. But I was painfully aware staying put offered a false sense of safety. My bladder made the call for me. I hopped from the bed and dashed for the bathroom, locking the door behind me.

The row of bottles by the sink reminded me I needed to take my meds. I shook out the correct dosage and swallowed, immediately questioning the possibility I might have taken them during my walking blackout. Ignorant of what overdosing on happy pills could be, I doubted it would be worse than ramming my finger down my throat to induce vomiting.

I reset my alarm to 7:30, crawled into bed, and pledged to text Andy in the morning about setting up security cameras as soon as possible. And I would take a picture of the wall as proof of the events of the previous night. Then I would put the photos into their proper order before I left for the rec center. Except for our honeymoon shot, the missing piece of the puzzle.

Seconds before the medication took effect, a troubling thought came to me. If I didn't remember the period between discovering the rearranged photos and waking up in my bed, were there other moments in time I misplaced? Could I have forgotten repositioning each frame to represent the way my life had been turned upside down? Did I take the honeymoon picture and hide it from myself?

Although I couldn't imagine being unable to recall something that significant, I planned to come straight home from class and search for my favorite photo.

When the alarm sounded, I woke from the disconnected sleep modern pharmaceuticals provided. I stumbled to the shower, threw on a form-fitting dress that—thanks to my loss of appetite no longer was—and started toward the stairs. Recalling my plan to document the photographic arrangement, I reached for my phone on the bedside table where I always put it, but it wasn't there.

After surveying the room and checking the bathroom counter, I saw that I'd left my purse on the floor, close to the bedroom door—also puzzling, since I normally left it on the kitchen table. I wrote off my break from routine as a result of the whirlwind of unexplained events surrounding me, then fished around in my bag where I found the phone with a notification there was a voicemail waiting from Dr. Riley.

I got your message would like to see you as soon as possible. Until then, increase your anti-anxiety medication to once every twelve hours. If your hallucinations worsen, call me immediately. Regardless, call my receptionist tomorrow to get that appointment scheduled.

My immediate impression was that it was Dr. Riley, not me, having the hallucinations because I hadn't called him. More likely, he had me mixed up with another patient. If so, not only was he freaking me out, but also there was a crazy woman out there who was distraught over being ignored by the good doctor. The idea Riley might be that disorganized wasn't particularly believable. From my observations of his office, he seemed like the kind of guy who organized his underwear by style and color.

Hoping I was wrong about his compulsions and he was mistaken about my lack of sanity, I conducted a quick check of my call history to solve the mystery. And there it was: confirmation I was on the verge of completely losing it. Last night at 10:22 I had placed a call lasting thirty-two seconds to Dr. Riley.

My stomach lurched, and I made it to the toilet with no time to spare. I sat on the cool tile, head against the wall, until the nausea passed, then stood at the sink where I splashed cold water on my face, and finally stumbled to my bed. I lay there trembling, trying to make sense of the recent developments on this timeline of encroaching insanity.

"Calm down," I told myself, fearful if I didn't take hold of my emotions, I might spiral out of control. I took deep breaths in through my nose and out through my mouth, uncertain if I was taking a page from Garnet or from a Pilates class I'd dropped out of. Whichever it was, it worked, and I returned to rational thought.

The easiest and least frightening explanation was that the lapses in memory, throbbing headaches, and growing paranoia were a result of Riley's medication. If true, weaning myself off the meds should reverse the damage. But I wasn't taking anything when Garnet whispered in my ear at the bookstore parking lot and had only begun my prescriptions when she showed up in class. Michael's appearance could be attributed to a side effect from a bad combination of drugs, but he seemed so solid. Yes, seeing his face, feeling his touch had been terrifying. In a strange way, though, it provided comfort, as if he were still trying to take care of me, to warn me. But what was warning me about?

I couldn't be sure, but suspected it had to involve the man galloping down my steps. I was certain he had been real and hadn't randomly wandered into my home. He came for a reason and as irrational as it sounded, maybe it had been to scramble both my photos and my mind—to gaslight me the way husbands did in old black and white movies. I remembered my intention to document my intruder's actions with photographic evidence and propped up on my elbows. I tested my stability before sitting up, then dropped my feet, one at a time, to the floor.

You've got this, I said to myself. Only I wished Garnet would echo the sentiment. But she was either irritated with me for having her fall in love or still wrapped around Jean Pierre because she refused to speak. Once again, I drew on images from my novels. I threw back my shoulders, thrust out my chest, and strode down the hallway.

I paused to capture the scene from several angles before I repositioned the pictures. But someone had beaten me to it. Each was restored to an upright position. The only indication I hadn't imagined the entire incident was the orderly manner each photo had been returned to. It was the missing honeymoon picture that derailed me. Instead of the empty space from last night, Michael and I were beaming from our proper place at the top of the stairs.

Chapter 30

In the drive-through at Starbuck's, both hands on the steering wheel to steady myself, I tried to make sense of the photo phenomena. There were several possible explanations, none of them good.

One scenario had me imagining the entire incident, which indicated I was losing my mind. Another suggested I could have switched the pictures, which meant I'd already lost my mind. Less threatening to my sanity, but not my safety, was the theory my burglar mixed up the photos, and I failed to notice the change. That premise offered no positive explanation for everything being upright and in its proper place this morning. If I set them right and didn't remember, I was back to the option I was a few fries short of a happy meal. There was also the possibility I was wrong about being alone in the house, which made me want to go with the missing french fry theory.

The girl in the takeout window brought me out of my reverie with a steaming hot cream and sugar trenta, a thirty-one-ounce blast of caffeine. I needed both hands to get it in the car and then fumbled around fitting it in my cup holder. By the time I reached the center, it had cooled enough for me to sip it.

Despite the morning setbacks, I was fifteen minutes early. Usually, the custodian unlocked the classroom before I arrived, but today it was locked, and I had to rummage my purse for the key. Inside, it was dark and seemingly empty. A soft rustling came from behind the teacher's desk. I scuttled backward as if I were a crab fighting the tide, then switched on the lights, sending a fluorescent glow across the room.

"Surprise!" Students popped up like the little rodents from whack-a-mole, and I emitted a short but extremely high-pitched squeal.

Sporadic gusts of air conditioning rippled through multi-colored streamers dangling from the ceiling. An enormous cake covered most of my desk, and student desks were covered with a bright pink tablecloth laden with snacks.

"What's all this about? Today's not my birthday."

Louisa stepped forward. "This is our way of thanking you for the workshop. For encouraging us to develop our projects, working with everyone individually, staying late to help—all that is beyond what we expected."

"I, uh, I don't know what to say."

"You don't have to say anything," a guy wearing a Georgia cap shouted. "But we'd appreciate it if you cut that cake."

Several students echoed the request, and Betty took over, insisting I sit down and eat the first piece. Nina leaned against the wall, apart from the group.

The chatter died down as everyone began eating. One layer was white with a hint of almond flavoring; the second, a rich, dark chocolate. Topped with a thick cream cheese icing, it was tooth-achingly sweet. I washed it down with a gulp of coffee and watched as class members, many of whom had met for the first time during the course, talked and laughed like classmates at a reunion.

Howard stood, holding an index card in one hand and a plastic spoon in the other. He rapped the spoon against a red Solo cup. "If I could have your attention, please," he said in an official detective voice.

When the noise subsided and everyone stared at him, Howard stiffened like a possum caught in headlights. His hands shook, and his face turned a deep shade of crimson. For a moment, I was afraid he was having a mini stroke, but he gripped the edge of the desk, took a breath, and powered on.

"Writing was something I did for myself, a way to make sense of the crap I had to deal with at work. When my wife came down with cancer, getting all my fear and anger down on paper helped get me navigate the hell of watching her die. It made it a little easier to consider a life without the person I'd woken up beside for over forty years. I never shared what I wrote. Why would I? Then a special friend asked—demanded, I should say—to see it. When she liked it, a light popped up in my brain. Not so much because I expected to be the next Faulkner. Because someone I trusted found value in what I had to say. Said it expressed a truth folks going through the same experience might take comfort from."

He paused and looked at Louisa. She nodded her encouragement, only a slight trembling of her lips suggesting the depths of her emotions.

"And if it hadn't been for her, I would have hightailed it out of here when Ms. Dolan said we'd be reading our work out loud."

Murmurs of agreement and laughter followed his statement. I was relieved his three-alarm facial color had faded to pink, and that his hold on the desk was less of a death grip.

"But I'm real glad I didn't. I'm not sure I'm any good, but I don't mind making people suffer through my readings."

I smiled at the vulnerability of this hardcore cop.

He continued, "Like Louisa said, Ms. Dolan went beyond what we expected. She gave us ways to make our writing better. More important for me and for most of you, the way she demonstrated how to listen to what other people have to say and to care about that, got us started on becoming better people."

Complete silence filled the room before a smattering applause grew louder and louder. When it died, Howard looked at me and I was afraid he expected me to speak. But he wasn't finished.

"Ms. Dolan, Kara, we have a token of our appreciation, a little something to remember us by."

He handed me a small box. Inside was a leather sleeve engraved with my initials in the center and, in smaller print below it, RCF.

"From the Roswell Crime Family." Howard explained.

I slipped the brass pen from its cover. It was exactly like the one Michael had given me.

"We wanted to get you one of those Montblancs, but it was a bit over our budget. So, we put one on hold for when one of us hits the bestseller list."

Howard kept talking, but all I could hear was the sound of Michael's voice promising to upgrade me to a Montblanc.

•   •   •

At home on my sofa, I flipped through the TV channels, looking for mindless entertainment. I settled on a rerun of *Friends*. Halfway through my second episode, my stomach rumbled. Other than a piece of my thank-you cake, I hadn't eaten today. I found a can of tomato soup and ate it with cheese toast. Then I poured a glass of wine and took it with me to the den where I'd left my laptop.

The lyrics of "Popular" from *Wicked* blasted from my purse. Barb's ringtone—just what I didn't need.

"Hey, Barb."

Instead of returning my greeting, she asked, "You still take the paper, don't you? Check out the third page of the sports section. I'll hold."

I read the news online, but Michael insisted it wasn't the same as a print copy, and I had been unable to make myself cancel our subscription. Every day I would automatically bring in the paper and add it to the heap on the dining room table. When the pile began to topple, I would take it to the recycle bin. Sighing, I got up and retrieved today's edition from the top, then pulled out the sports section and turned to the specified page.

Although the photo was black and white, Barb's light helmet of hair immediately caught my eye. The caption read *Regional ALTA Champions*. A tall brunette standing next to my stepmother held a giant plate over her head. Like Barb, she had an ecstatic grin on her face.

"Wow! That's fantastic." I hoped my voice registered the enthusiasm I didn't feel. No matter how hard I tried, I couldn't wrap my mind around a bunch of adults salivating over a trophy. "I know how important that, uh, that plate is to you." I began pacing the dining room, trying to come up with a reason to end the call, which was going to be difficult, as she gave no indication she had plans to stop talking long enough for me to speak.

"I can honestly say it was one of the best, if not the best, day of my life."

Sorry, Dad, I thought, as Barb began babbling on about how close her doubles match had been and how they'd snatched victory from the valley of defeat. *Jaws, you mean jaws of defeat,* but I didn't bother correcting her. That was when I noticed the woman kneeling in the front row of the photo.

Of all the women, she was apparently the only one who hadn't been frozen in place staring at the camera when the photographer snapped the shot. Even though her face was blurry, she managed to exude her trademark irritation. It was Dr. Riley's chronically annoyed receptionist.

"Kara, are you still there?"

Barb must have stopped talking.

"I'm sorry. I got lost looking at the team picture. You all look so happy and fit."

"We do, don't we?" She was practically purring now.

"Well, most of you anyway. What's going on with that lady on the front row, the one who looks pissed off?" I squinted, finally lining up a name with her face: Tiffany Elliott.

"I'm not looking at the picture right this minute."

"That's okay. She's Tiffany Elliott, the one who recommended Dr. Riley."

"Oh, her. She hasn't been on the team that long. I barely know her." Barb sounded a little defensive.

"It sounded like she was about to become your best friend. And isn't that unusual? I mean for someone to start playing late in the season?"

"Not really and who cares anyway? We won. I'm calling to invite you to the club tomorrow to celebrate. We're having heavy appetizers and cocktails at 6:30. I know you're not crazy about—"

"Don't be silly. I wouldn't miss it."

She paused, then said, "That's great. Oh, dear. I didn't realize how late it's getting. I've got to run."

She hung up before I could say goodbye, giving me the impression she wanted to avoid any additional discussion concerning Miss Elliott.

I began searching for information on Dr. Riley's receptionist. There were several Tiffany Elliotts on Facebook: one was looking for people to invest in her beauty salon, another was a grandmother in Des Moines, and the third was an aspiring swimsuit model. They weren't the only ones, but none of the profiles matched my Tiffany Elliott. I had no better luck with Google or LinkedIn.

I attributed the return of my headache to the three glasses of wine I had and gave up on finding the elusive Tiffany. I would have to squeeze out whatever Barb was hiding when I saw her at the party. I began my nightly ritual of looking for boogeymen and double-checking locks. I had avoided the stairwell and wondered what surprise awaited me. Would my pictures be in the orderly fashion from this morning or back to the disorder of the previous evening? Or had they vanished?

The rush of relief I felt upon finding them aligned in the same positions they'd been when I left for class was short-lived. Just because no one, including me, I supposed, had messed with my pictorial arrangement didn't mean no one would. Because if I wasn't going completely crazy, someone was entering and exiting at will.

I shoved a chair under the knob of my bedroom door and slipped the canister of pepper spray under my pillow. Tomorrow, I would plan a long vacation. Somewhere without happy couple photos on the wall. Maybe I would never come back. I'd sell the house with everything in it and start over where no one knew me.

I made sure the chair was positioned firmly, then set my vanity stool behind it. Satisfied my barricade would at least slow down any intruder, I reached for my medication.

Is that really such a good idea? I don't trust that condescending asshole doctor of yours. And I haven't seen any evidence those pills are working. It's not as if you've been dancing in the streets.

Garnet wasn't telling me anything I hadn't already considered about the effects of my prescriptions. And Riley was a condescending asshole.

"You could be right," I said. "But I've heard it's never a good idea to quit antidepressants cold turkey."

The real reason I couldn't give them up had more to do with the months of insomnia I experienced after Michael's death. Night after night I stared at the ceiling, picturing his murder–his face when he saw the gun, his body jerking as he fell to the ground, the blood pooling around him.

I shook out the pills and dry-swallowed them before Garnet could continue with more rational arguments. Then I hurried to the bathroom for a glass of water.

In bed, I thought of my writing class and how much I'd enjoyed it. Not enough to rush into another one, but enough to give me a warm feeling of accomplishment, a combination of elated and content, similar to my emotions after a good day of writing.

My familiar drowsiness signaled the approach of thick amnesiac sleep, and I sunk deeper into the covers. Just as the drugs began to suck me under, I heard a soft rustle to my right and rolled toward the sound. An evening breeze rippled through the sheer curtains. Nothing to worry about.

Are you sure?

I was too tired to spar with Garnet. She reminded me it was allergy season, a time when I kept my windows shut tight. But the warning slipped away as I surrendered to the darkness.

Chapter 31

I awoke groggy to the unmistakable smell of fresh-brewed coffee. With closed eyes, I listened for the sound of Michael walking up the stairs, expecting that when I opened them, I would see him carefully place a hot cup on the bedside table.

But there were no footsteps, no steaming coffee, and no husband. I couldn't remember the last time I touched the confusing array of buttons on the elaborate machine Michael insisted we needed. After leaping from the bed, I yanked my phone from its charger and called Ira.

"Come on, come on," I urged, as the ringing went on and on. I was about to give up and call Andy when my neighbor picked up.

"It's Kara. I hate to bother you, but could you come over? I'm probably overreacting, but I think someone may have been in the house and could still be here. Ring the bell and make a lot of noise, then let Rex sniff around. If you hear or see anything out of the ordinary, call the police."

"Got it. Might be a good idea to call 911, just in case."

"Please, not until you come over. I'm ninety-eight percent sure whoever was here is gone now. And if I'm right, the police won't be able to tell he was ever here."

I hated to acknowledge the possibility I had been alone in the house. That I was messing with my own mind.

I also didn't add my fear that the police might decide I was an attention-seeking lunatic who sent herself make-believe bouquets of dead flowers, manufactured cigarette-smoking stalkers, and got freaked out by her coffee maker. All those false alarms might slow their response when I really needed them. Like when I ran out of heavy literary works to throw.

"Okay. It'll just take a minute to put on my shoes and get Rex's leash. Where are you now?"

I explained I was locked in the bedroom, and he told me to stay there.

"Don't hang up. I'm gonna stick my phone in my pocket and walk you through along with me. And holler if anything changes."

I started to tell him how to put me on speaker, but then he'd have to get his reading glasses and try to figure out which one was the icon, which he probably wouldn't be able to do.

•   •   •

After his step-by-step narrative of his actions from the time he reached my porch, to his careful surveillance of the perimeter of the grounds, and the back deck, Ira determined it was safe for me to let him in. The three of us spent at least an hour walking through every room. Rex sniffed and whined as we went, but there were no signs of an intruder. I appreciated that Ira didn't look at me as if I were crazy.

After we finished our search of the house, I invited him to join me on the deck. With Rex curled up between us, we floated possibilities of who would risk being charged with breaking and entering for the sole purpose of making me coffee. I suggested it could be my angry fan trying to make me think I was losing it, or possibly Todd lurking around. Neither theory made sense, but during the past two weeks, nothing much had.

"I know you've got one of those new-fangled alarm systems, but when I was traveling and my wife was home by herself, we didn't have stuff like that. I bought a basic kit from the hardware store and set it up. It fritzed out on us during a storm, but I was retired by then. Never did get around to replacing it. Having a low-tech one for back-up couldn't hurt. I bet Home Depot's got something. Mind if I look around, maybe pick up two of them?"

"That's a great idea," I said, tearing up a little at his kindness.

Then he surprised me. Never one to talk about himself, he began sharing how lonely and lost he was after the death of his wife. How he and Rex wandered through the neighbor in the middle of the night. He confessed to pretending he wasn't there when well-meaning friends stopped by. Worse, he admitted there were times when he wanted to end the relentless pain.

"I might have done it, too, if it hadn't for my good boy Rex." At the mention of his name, the dog thumped his tail. Ira explained how the all-consuming force that could have destroyed him eventually lost its hold. Then he stood and announced it was time to get going.

"I can't tell you how much your showing up and believing I'm not a nutcase means to me." Stepping around Rex, I hugged him. The dog thrust his muzzle between us, and I knelt to acknowledge him. "You, too, buddy." I patted his broad back, and he licked my hand.

After they were gone, I thought about the isolating selfishness of grief. It had never occurred to me that other people could sink into the same depths of despair I had. Sure, others experienced loss, but not as soul-destroying as mine. Ira and his wife had been together over fifty years. If I became half a person over losing Michael after less than two years, how much deeper had my neighbor descended? But he had returned to the surface.

Still buoyed by the flicker of optimism Ira's resilience provided, I put in extra effort with my appearance for Barb's celebration. I showered and brought out the expensive conditioner for my hair. Instead of letting it air dry and allowing the curls to fall haphazardly, I dried and straightened each strand. Then I painted both finger and toenails a shade of hot pink guaranteed to make my stepmother cringe. Normally, I don't wear a lot of makeup, so it took several tries to get the right amount of foundation and blush. I gave up on eyeliner but hit the mascara hard.

I selected my favorite little black dress, one I hadn't worn in ages. Then I rummaged through the drawer where I kept my good underwear, located the only pushup bra I owned, and fastened myself in. There were gaps in the cups, but when I tightened the straps, the technology kicked in, squeezing my boobs together to create the illusion of cleavage. It was looser at the waist and hips and the neckline plunged deeper, but when I twirled around in front of the mirror, the former Kara whirled with me.

•　　•　　•

"Kara!" Situated at a table near the bar with my father beside her, Barb waved and motioned me over. The party room at the club with its heavy oak or mahogany or outlawed Brazilian rain forest paneling, dark wooden blinds, and thick green carpet had more of the ambience of a good old boy man-cave than a place for watery drinks and superficial chatter. Normally, I would have avoided it and my tennis-maven stepmom, but tonight I was on a mission. I excused my way through the crowd and joined them.

Dad stood, kissed me on the cheek, and held out the only empty chair for me. "Glad you could come, honey," he said before returning to his seat.

"I think most of you know our daughter Kara."

Shit. I hated when she did that— introduced me as her daughter.

I looked at my father, but he was totally engrossed in the intricate pattern on the tablecloth. After pasting a smile on my face, I nodded at each of the three couples, hoping I wouldn't be expected to remember names.

"We've heard a lot about you," a tight-faced woman with silvery white hair said.

From the corner of my eye, I could have sworn Barb flinched. I wondered if she told them how sad, lonely, and mildly psychotic plummeting into widowhood had made me.

"It's as if we already know you," the lady to her right elaborated. Light from the wall sconce highlighted the sparkle of her enormous diamond earrings.

A hush fell over the table, and the women turned toward me. The rules of conversation required me to respond with some quip like "I hope it's not all bad" or "What has my lovely stepmother been saying?" or "Hey, bartender, another round for my girls." But what I wanted to say was "I don't really give a shit." Since I knew that was a violation of the girl-talk code, I kept quiet and smiled.

Barb, who never met an awkward silence she couldn't make worse, said, "I've told them what a wonderful writer you are."

One of the them—I wasn't sure which because, despite their varying degrees of hairspray and surgical enhancements, they'd become the same entity to me— said, "A wonderful writer. That's exactly what she said."

Group compliments about books I doubted they had read were hurled at me until the waiter appeared. I listened as the wives ordered wine and the husbands requested manly drinks like scotch and soda or bourbon neat.

"And you, ma'am? Will you be having white or red?"

Whether it was that matronly "ma'am" or his assumption I was one of the wimpy wine ladies, I said, "Neither. I'd like a vodka over ice with a slice of lemon."

Barb's nose twitched, and Silver Hair pursed her bright orange lips.

The waiter was jotting down my order when I pushed back from the table and stood. "Never mind. You've got your hands full with this crowd. I'll pop over and get it myself." I bolted for the bar.

I repeated my request to the bartender, who didn't look old enough to drink. "On second thought, make it a double, please."

I moved to the side to accommodate the people lining up after me and stared at the hunting scene on the wall: a reddish-brown fox, chased by snarling dogs and dwarfed by men on horses, was frozen in desperation. Also captured forever is the look of glee on the face of the lead hunter as he looks down at the poor creature who by now must have realized the race was fixed.

Struck by how much I identified with that doomed fox, I barely noticed when the person behind me thrust out a hairy fist and slammed his empty glass onto the counter.

"What's takin' so long?" he growled, then added, "What kinda bartenduh are you?"

There was no need to turn. That rumbling, consonant-dropping voice was unmistakable. He was the guy from the drugstore, the one who helped put my prescriptions back into my purse.

I inched farther toward the edge of the bar, facing away from him, then tossed my hair so that it covered half of my face. When the bartender set my drink down, my furry-knuckled friend reached for it.

"Sorry, sir," the bartender said, dislodging the glass from his grip. "Yours will be up in a minute. This belongs to the lady." He slid it toward me. The man from the drugstore mumbled something under his breath.

My hands shook as I took it. I stuck a few dollars in the tip jar, then hurried to the table, where I downed more vodka before sitting. I pulled out my compact and pretended to check my make up, so I could watch him as he double stepped through the crowded room. When he turned into the hallway leading to the restrooms, I lost sight of him.

My attempt at subterfuge was interrupted by the sound of someone calling my name, at first fuzzy and far away, then sharper, closer.

"Kara!" It was Barb.

I lowered my mirror and tried to get a read on the table. The men had disappeared, probably for the ritual cigar smoking. Now it was just us girls. My stepmother was a deep shade of plum. The other three women were staring at me, their faces registering varying degrees of shock.

"What?" Had I broken some rule of etiquette forbidding freshening up in public? I snapped my compact shut and dropped it into my purse.

"Your dress, honey," Diamond Stud whispered, then touched her breastbone.

I mimicked the gesture and felt way more flesh than expected. Apparently, in my rush to play secret agent, I hadn't noticed both straps had slipped off my shoulders. I was more embarrassed at how little I had to expose than at the exposure itself. I yanked the dress back in place.

"Sorry, ladies. I usually insist on getting dinner before I flash my date."

Silver Hair's upper lip twitched, but her lack of facial mobility made it impossible to tell if she was going for a sneer or a smile.

I took another healthy sip of my drink, distracted by the heat of the icy vodka as it slithered down my throat. Barb was glaring at me.

"Now might be a good time for me to take a trip to the ladies' room." The table tilted when I stood.

Or maybe I was the one who tilted. I held onto to the edge for a moment, then began weaving through what was fast becoming a rowdy crowd. I hoped to catch my target coming out of the restroom. Along the way, it hit me I had no real plan other than to see who had accompanied my mystery man to the party and realized I'd been distracted from my original motivation for attending in the first place: to confront Tiffany. My heel caught on the carpet, and I stumbled, steadying myself on the back of an empty chair.

After regaining my balance, I tried to take another step, but my legs wouldn't cooperate. The floor roiled under me as if I were cruising on a stormy sea. Faces around me blurred, then sharpened. I closed my eyes and when I opened them, I was more stable. And that was when I saw her—Tiffany, standing at the entrance to the same hallway where Jersey boy had vanished.

I wobbled to my feet and immediately bumped my hip against a waiter, carrying a tray loaded with full salad plates. Behind me, someone shrieked. The sound cut through my head, leaving a smear of pain in its wake. The room erupted into a discordant symphony: high-pitched giggling and deep-bellied guffaws combined with clanking silverware and rumbling conversation.

Tiffany was still there, but she seemed farther away than before. I managed a few staggering steps toward her when another wave of vertigo crashed over me.

"Let me help you, Kara." Despite the subdued tone, the priestly voice penetrated the noise. Before I could turn to identify its source, someone gripped my elbow and began steering me toward the tennis-playing receptionist, who continued to stare in my direction, a widening grin on her thin scarlet lips.

I shut my eyes. When I opened them, I saw the dark-haired woman behind Tiffany. Resplendent in a shimmery gold lamé dress that clung to her curves, Garnet wore an expression I didn't recognize at first. Her tightly drawn brows created worry wrinkles I hadn't given her, and she was biting her full lower lip. My fearless heroine's trademark not giving-a-fuck vibe had morphed into something that was at best grave apprehension, at worst, mild terror. She extended her arms and held out her hand, palms turned toward me in warning.

I couldn't have stopped if I wanted to. The man with the unearthly voice had transferred his grip from my elbow to my upper arm. With his other hand, he applied pressure on the small of my back as he maneuvered me through the crowd. Soon I was close enough to see the smear of Tiffany's lipstick on her sharp incisors. Garnet had vanished.

Chapter 32

I floated back to consciousness on a cloud of Chanel No. Barb. My initial attempt to open my eyes failed, and they remained stuck together as if an overly enthusiastic kindergartener had slopped on too much Elmer's glue. I desperately wanted to rub at the crusty globs, but my arms refused to cooperate. If not for the tingling sensation rippling from my hand to my elbow, reassuring me I wasn't trapped in a vegetative state, I might have succumbed to my rising panic.

I slowed my shallow breathing and tried to concentrate on a conversation between Dad and Barb—one in which I was the subject, but not an active participant. It was the same distanced reaction I had while going through Michael's unfamiliar memories, as if someone had thrown a party in my honor but hadn't invited me.

"This has to stop." Barb's hiss coiled and hovered over me. I pictured my father as a mouse hypnotized beneath her.

"You do realize her drinking has become a serious issue." Soft and sibilant, her voice lulled him further into his trance.

I tried to shout a warning: *Quick, back away before she strikes.* But, like my eyelids, my tongue refused to come unglued.

"And the way she spends most of her time stumbling around in that empty house. Now she's humiliated us in front of the entire club. All that screaming and shouting and running and—"

"That's enough." He spoke in a muted tone with a curious lack of inflection, but the mouse had roared. Although part of me wanted him to let Barb continue with her account of my behavior, since I had no memory of it, I was pleased she had lost her hold on him.

I, too, was freed and begin to awaken, Sleeping Beauty without the lip action. When I blinked, the dangling crystals from Barb's ornate chandelier sent sharp slivers of light through my brain. I forced myself not to sink into my previous oblivion.

Through squinted eyes, I saw Barb and my father, too intent on one another to notice the princess was back. Before I could break through my fog, the doorbell rang, and my stepmother scurried out, leaving Dad to stare vacantly at the floor.

I wanted to reach out to him, to say I was all right, not crazy at all. But the sound of footsteps stopped me.

I suggest lying low.

This time, Garnet and I were in complete agreement.

"I can't tell you how much we appreciate your coming," Barb said.

"Please, it's no problem. None at all. I was afraid this would happen. That Kara would take on more that she could handle and not be able to cope."

A blast of angry adrenaline shot through me. Why in the hell had they summoned my psychiatrist? Nothing he'd done had brought about any positive change in my life. And he was still harping about me not taxing myself. In different circumstances, I might have asked him exactly how I was supposed to avoid *taxing myself* when people kept harassing me, both online and in the real world.

And how could anyone expect me to cope with intruders who messed with my stuff and my mind, or a stalker who turned me into a YouTube phenome? Of course, no one in the room was aware of the poison pen messages or the flowers or me chasing someone out of my house. Barb knew about the supermarket fiasco, but I was the only one who'd seen the disappearing video.

Riley's musky odor made it hard for me to control my breathing. And it was even harder not to pull away when he slipped his cold fingers around my wrist and announced, "Pulse is a bit rapid."

When he put his hand on my forehead, I held my breath and willed myself not to flinch.

"Warm, possibly feverish, but not unusual for someone experiencing this kind of psychotic break."

Seriously, psychotic break?

"Shouldn't she be regaining consciousness by now?"

Comforted by my father's question, I also felt guilty about making him worry. But my thoughts were still a little too fuzzy around the edges to join the conversation.

"The sedative I gave her at the club is a strong one, especially for someone Kara's size. And frankly, rest is the best thing for her. If she wakes up too soon, the hallucinations and violent behavior could return."

The image of a wolfish grin and bloodstained teeth flashed in front of me. Not blood, though. Lipstick. And not a wolf, Tiffany with Garnet behind her. Although my heroine seemed as real as her companion, she was an illusion. So, could that mean I imagined Tiffany as well?

I struggled to place the voice of the man who guided me into the hallway. But the only sounds I recalled were those terrified shrieks—screams I now understood came from me. Had I given a repeat performance of my behavior at the grocery store? But there, on some level, I was cognizant of my actions. Even as I rammed my cart into the cereal display and the store employees, I'd been conscious of my craziness. Why was I unable to focus on the scene I'd made at the clubhouse?

Somebody slipped you a Mickey, that's why.

Annoyed at Garnet's ridiculous phrase—nobody says "slipped you a Mickey" anymore, and I certainly wouldn't have put such cheesy words in my heroine's mouth—I had to agree with the premise. I mentally retraced the steps that landed me in that hallway with Tiffany, rewinding the images in slow motion. Staggering through the country club crowd, flashing Barb's tennis ladies, ordering a vodka and tonic. Wait, that was it. The bartender must have drugged my drink. No, that wasn't right. But if not him, who?

Riley interrupted my thoughts before I could extract that final detail.

"I think the best course of action is to admit Kara to the clinic. That way I can monitor her progress while keeping her from hurting herself or others."

"That seems extreme to me." My father's voice of reason helped calm me.

"Please, honey," Barb whined. "You saw how she was—flailing about, screaming when the security guard tried to stop her. It's not unreasonable to think she might hurt herself."

"I'm afraid your wife is right. Of course, I am bound by my oath not to share details with you, but your daughter has been exhibiting some troubling symptoms, not unlike someone with suicidal ideation. At the clinic, we will keep a close watch over her."

Cheap shot playing the suicide card. Yes, I'd been depressed, but I'd been too intent on finding out who killed Michael to consider doing myself in.

"I don't know." Dad's tone indicated his resolve was fading. "How long a stay are we talking about?"

"Until she stabilizes, and we adjust her medication. A week or two at the most, barring anything unexpected. I'll call for the emergency van, and we'll have her in a quiet room before midnight. Until then, it would be best to keep her sedated. I can administer her another shot—"

"No. No more shots. We can give her a pill if she gets agitated, but I don't like her being out this long."

"Mr. Conway, I understand how you feel, but—"

"That's good because if you don't, I'll bring in someone who does."

I willed myself to stay dry-eyed in case unconscious people were incapable of shedding tears. If Riley realized I was coming around, no telling what kind of horse tranquilizer he might give me.

"All right, then." The doctor sounded resigned, but I hoped Dad wouldn't leave me alone with him. "I'll contact the clinic and have someone here in less than—"

"No. We'll keep her here tonight and see how she is in the morning."

Riley sighed. "You must know I'm not comfortable with this arrangement. At least let me stop by early tomorrow to assess her condition."

"Excellent plan, Doctor," Barb chimed in. "That way we can all be sure what the best course of action is. Right, dear?"

Dad grunted in response.

I thought everyone had gone, but I counted to sixty twice before opening my eyes. I peeked under the blanket and discovered my little black dress had been traded for one of Barb's overpriced warm-up suits. After scootching up on my elbows, I waited for the room to stop spinning. When it did, I planted my feet on the floor and sat up. I needed a plan, something to make sure I didn't get locked up in the looney bin. The problem was the drugs were making it hard for me to concentrate.

I held onto the bedside table, stood, and surveyed the room. My purse sat on top of the dresser. My legs shook, but I made it. I fished out my phone, and called Andy.

"Come on," I repeated with each ring. I was trying to piece together a message that might make sense when he answered.

"I'm stuck at Dad's and have to get out." I wondered if my words sounded as slurred to him as they did to me. "And no, I'm not drunk. But I am in trouble." The clicking of heels coming down the hallway meant Barb was closing in on me.

"Park on the street and go around the house under the back bedroom."

"The street behind your dad's?"

"Yes, and hurry."

"Okay, but is the back bedroom the one with that tacky little balcony that looks like a New Orleans whorehouse? I don't know what Barb was thinking with all the wrought iron."

I stumbled onto the bed as the doorknob began to turn. Cowering under the covers, I whispered, "Andy, please. It's pineapple time."

•   •   •

I had no idea how long I lay there listening to my stepmother open and shut drawers before she breezed past the bed toward the master bath.

"No, Barb," I thought and concentrated on sending a telepathic command. "You do not want to take a bubble bath with your crazy stepdaughter in the next room."

Whether it was my mind message or Barb's own aversion to being that close to me, she spent only a few minutes in the bathroom before walking through the bedroom and out the door.

I tiptoed across to the closet, where I located a pair of white tennis shoes. They were too big, but I didn't plan to wear them for long. Then I rummaged around until I found Barb's belt rack and removed four sturdy-looking leather belts. From the window, I looped three together and tied the fourth around my waist, loose enough that I could undo it, but hopefully tight enough I wouldn't slide through and hang myself.

Then I eased the sliding door open and stepped onto the narrow balcony, crouched low, and waited. Within minutes, a shaft of light flickered over me. It happened so quickly, I wasn't certain if it came from a passing car or my friend.

"But soft." A stage whisper drifted up, confirming Andy had arrived. "What light through yonder window—"

"Cut it out," I hissed.

"Ah, it is the east and Juliet is the sun."

I leaned over the railing and saw Andy standing there with a flashlight shining under his chin.

"You are an idiot. Stop talking and get ready to catch me." I threaded the sturdiest-looking belt through one of the posts and began climbing over.

"Holy Mother of God, woman, don't do it! You'll kill us both."

But I had already begun my descent. Conjuring images of climbers rappelling down a mountain, I tried planting my feet against the bricks as I tested the stability of Barb's fashion accessories. The belts held, but the tennis shoes slipped. Before I could say Geronimo, I was hanging from the side of the house.

"I've got you." He grabbed my legs and held on tight while I fumbled with the belt. When I undid it, I dropped to the ground, taking him with me.

Chapter 33

"Barb is going to be pissed when she sees what you've done to her lucky tennis shoes," Andy remarked. "You know what they say: Red clay on white, that just ain't right."

Still giddy from our wild escape, I laughed and tossed a sofa pillow toward the recliner where he lounged. Instead of hitting him, it smacked into the floor lamp, which teetered but didn't fall.

"Another example of violent behavior."

"Too soon." I frowned. "They're probably warming up the electric shock paddles as we speak."

"You don't have the height to carry off a straight-jacket. But I can see you in a nice padded cell."

"Seriously, Andy. It wouldn't surprise me if there's an Amber alert with my name on it."

"You're too old to be an Amber and not old enough to qualify for Silver. And despite the occasional irrational reaction, you're not demented enough to be committed. Almost, but not quite."

"Thanks a lot." I paused to look at my unlikely hero. "I mean it. I don't know what I would have done without you."

"Any time, pal. But I'm still confused. Could you go over it again from the beginning?"

I didn't blame him for not understanding. After hopping into his car and urging him to speed away, I hadn't been too coherent. Part of my lack of communication skills was from terror at the prospect of being locked up, but the medication in my system hadn't made it any easier to fill Andy in on the details of my performance at the club.

Before I began, I checked my phone: four missed calls and three text messages from Dad, all begging me to come back home. I answered the last one.

I'm spending the night at a hotel. Will call when I've had time to sort everything out.

I shut down the phone and started the story of my wild evening, beginning with meeting the couples at Barb's table and ending with seeing Tiffany in the hallway. I didn't mention Garnet.

"At first, I wasn't sure she was real, but the more I think about it, the more certain I am. Not only that I saw her, but that's she's Riley's receptionist. And I'm absolutely positive the man at the bar was the same one I collided with at the drugstore."

I waited for him to suggest that I had too much to drink or that the mix of drugs and alcohol could have caused me to imagine the whole thing. But if he was skeptical, his expression didn't reflect it.

"Hold on." He got up and walked from the room. His departure was so abrupt I was afraid I'd misread him, that not only did he not believe my story but was also terrified to be in the same house as me. Before I had time to make yet another escape plan, he returned with his laptop.

"It's Simon Riley, right?" I nodded, and after a few long moments, he shouted, "Holy shit."

"What? What did you find?" I bolted from the sofa and stood behind him.

"Did your doctor mention the name of the clinic he wanted to take you to?"

"I can't remember, but I was pretty out of it. Why?"

He turned the screen toward me and pointed to a grainy picture of four men standing in front of a rambling Victorian house. "Look familiar?"

"That's St. Cecilia's shelter in the background."

He zoomed in on the men's faces. "How about this guy?"

The silver-streaked hair was shorter, and he was thinner, but there was no question about the identity of the man standing directly above the caption *Investors Expand Program for Veterans*. It was my psychiatrist, Dr. Simon Riley.

"When I mentioned working on Michael's story about the men at the shelter, he never said a word about his involvement. In fact, he discouraged me from picking up where Michael left off."

And that was when he began pushing me for information on my progress with Garnet's next adventure. It was becoming obvious he hadn't wanted me to pursue my husband's project. But why?

Andy kept scrolling through the article. "Says he's on the board, but doesn't show that he's active in the day-to-day operations."

"But if he is associated with the clinic, wouldn't he have to be registered there to have medical standing?"

He held up an index finger. "Didn't you tell me Riley was a priest before he became a psychiatrist?"

"That's what Barb said."

Andy resumed his search. After a minute or so, he sighed and looked away from the laptop.

"Nothing?" I asked.

"Thousands of Simon Rileys. Consultants, filmmakers, Simon 'Ghost' Riley—"

"Did you say ghost?"

"You know, from *Call of Duty*?" he coaxed. "The video game? You are seriously pop-culture impaired. Anyway, the point is none of them appear to be a psychiatrist who was once a priest."

"That doesn't make any sense."

"Actually, it kind of does if he was asked to leave the priesthood."

"Maybe he's not even a doctor. Maybe he's a big fat fake." I thought about all the pills he prescribed, and my stomach flipped.

"Before we start coming to any hard conclusions, I need access to the database we use at the office, and there could be something on the dark web. Greg should be able to help with that. Let me get you settled in the guestroom while I give him a call."

"I don't want to be any more of a bother to you and Paul than I already have. I'll be fine at home."

"First, you're no more annoying than usual. Second, Paul's visiting his family in Texas. And third, have you completely lost your mind? I didn't spend the last two hours rescuing you from the diabolical doctor—if he is a doctor—to take you someplace where you're bound to get kidnapped or murdered the minute I leave."

"Seriously. I don't want to put you in danger. What if they come here looking for me?"

"Oh, please. Your dad's too laid back to be a threat, and some aging shrink impersonator doesn't frighten me at all. Truth be told, Barb does scare me a little, but, for you, I'm up to the challenge."

He bullied me into taking a hot shower while he called Greg. After I changed into a pair of his pajamas, I went to the kitchen, where I found him standing at the stove.

"Look." He pointed to the pot he was stirring. "I made canned homemade soup for us. Tomato with milk, just the way you like it."

He filled our bowls while I removed two beers from the refrigerator.

"You look much better. Not so, you know, Looneytunes."

"I feel better. Mostly thanks to you, but also because knowing Riley isn't exactly who or what he claimed means I may not be crazy. I never really trusted him and being right—even though it could mean he's nuttier than I'm supposed to be—validates my judgment. And my sanity." I picked at the beer label with my fingernail. "Did you reach Greg?"

"Left a message. He's good about getting back to me. Gratitude for keeping him on the outside. Why don't you get some rest?"

I didn't tell him I was too keyed up to sleep. Instead, I agreed and headed to the guestroom, taking his laptop with me.

I slid under the pale blue comforter, sat up, and propped the computer on my knees. The dove-gray walls covered with watercolors of ocean scenes should have been soothing. And being here with Andy standing guard was. But nothing could rid me of the dull sense of dread that had been steadily building since waking up in my father's house with no memory of anything after seeing Garnet and Tiffany. Lying there helpless while people talked over me had been more unnerving than I realized, and I still couldn't understand how I'd gone from relative clarity to frightening oblivion so quickly.

It could have been a build-up of my prescription drugs, but it felt more intense than that. As if someone really had slipped me that Mickey. While I could see any one of Barb's tennis buddies popping Xanax on a regular basis, I seriously doubted they would waste one on me. Besides, I didn't even have a drink until I—

To the bar. That was it. Earlier I'd ruled out the unlikely possibility it had been the bartender who had drugged me. But when the guy behind me, the one from the drugstore, made a grab for my drink, he had plenty of time to drop something in it. Not a happy tranquilizer, though. It was something strong enough to send me spiraling into a kind of madness.

If it had been him, however, I was out of luck since I had no idea who he was or even a clear recollection of what he looked like.

Then I remembered a conversation I had with a friend about a week after I met Michael. She suggested he sounded too good to be true and recommended I check him out on the criminal records site she used on a regular basis, assuring me it would uncover any dark secrets lurking in Michael's past and compile them in an extensive report. By then I was in too deep to care.

I might not be able to get that kind of information on my unnamed Jersey boy, but maybe I could turn up something useful on Tiffany. My search for her on social media had yielded nothing, and I didn't have the advantage of Andy's private database or a Greg, who understood the intricacies of the dark web. But uncovering secrets in her past might not be as difficult as I thought.

I went to the address my friend gave me, entered her name, and narrowed the search by adding Atlanta. In seconds, a list of five possible Tiffanys and ten or so relatives came up. I discovered I would have to pay $19.99 to review the full report. That modest fee would give me one month to run background checks on as many people as I wanted. I had to admit the idea of having access to dirt on everyone in my life who had annoyed me, starting with Barb and her entire tennis team, was appealing. And since I needed more information to determine if any of them was the one I was looking for, the expenditure was totally justified.

As I was about to enter my credit card information, I noticed the relative column of the third Tiffany where Antonio Russo appeared as husband. The name initiated one of those unscratchable brain itches. I closed my eyes, trying to retrieve whatever it was about Antonio Russo that was bothering me.

"Russo, Russo, Russo." Repeating it out loud didn't help, so I tried calling out each letter separately, like some participant in a weird spelling bee.

"R . . . u . . . s . . ." I paused, then began again. "R . . . u . . . That's it!" The itching stopped. This time when I closed my eyes, I saw furry knuckles belonging to the man who picked up my prescription bag. It had happened quickly, but I remembered seeing the first two letters on his bag: Ru.

I logged into Facebook and typed in Antonio Russo. He had no page of his own, but a Gina Russo did, and she was obviously very proud of her son Antonio. Proud enough to make her background picture a photo of him at the altar kissing his not-so-blushing bride.

Antonio Russo and Tiffany Elliott were husband and wife.

A shiver went up my spine. She worked for Riley, and both were at the clubhouse when I had my latest break with reality. Antonio had to be the one who drugged me, which suggested he might also be in my doctor's employment or at least helping his wife make me seem as if I was certifiable. The question was why they would want to discredit me. It had to have something to do with Michael's involvement with the homeless shelter and the clinic. I spent the next hour looking for anything remotely connected to St. Cecilia's.

My search revealed nothing I didn't already know. Frustrated, I got distracted by Cecilia herself. There was a trove of information—most of it unverifiable—on this Roman noblewoman who was forced to marry a pagan despite her pledge to retain her virginity. Said husband wasn't buying it until he saw an intrusive angel keeping watch over his honeymoon bed, or something like that. The marriage remained unconsecrated, and Roman soldiers killed them both.

I couldn't decide if the story was an argument for or against celibacy.

Chapter 34

Wanda's ringtone startled me out of what might have been two to three hours of real sleep.

"Have you heard from Todd?" she asked by way of a greeting.

"I haven't checked my email, so I'm—"

"Not that. I mean have you *heard* from him. More important, have you seen him?"

"Seen him?" Things had been hectic, but I couldn't imagine forgetting a visit from Todd. "Was I supposed to meet with him? Because—"

"Look, Kara. Todd's gone off the rails. That virus I had? My doctor worried when it kept coming back—nausea, dizziness, throwing up my guts. He ran some tests and turns out it wasn't viral. That little bastard was poisoning me. Seems like he got the impression he was getting a promotion, that I'd be turning over some major accounts to him. I guess when he realized it was never going to happen, he took matters into his own hands."

"But how do you know it was Todd?" I was still groggy, too sleep-deprived to process the idea Todd might be diabolical enough to plan a murder, especially not one with such strictly literary motivation.

"Moron left a trail on his computer: poisonous mushrooms, symptoms of mushroom poisoning, most deadly, least deadly. Looks like he landed on fly agaric which, praise God, isn't in the most-deadly category. I'm going to assume he didn't really want to kill me—just make me sick enough to miss work. I guess he thought if I started to neglect my clients, he could swoop in and steal them."

"My God." I was fully awake now.

"Apparently, he intercepted a message from my doctor about me coming in for more tests. He must have realized it was only a matter of time before I figured out what he'd done, so he disappeared."

"That's awful." And it was, but, in a way, I understood his actions. Not the poisoning part; that was unbelievably terrible. More about how it was possible to want something bad enough to lose sight of yourself. So badly you would do anything to get it. Because that was how I'd come to feel about finding Michael's killer.

"That's not the worst of it. Well, I guess it's the worst of it for me." She cleared her throat. Wanda's uncharacteristic trouble expressing herself made me nervous.

"Who is it the worst for?" I asked although I was pretty sure of the answer. I just couldn't imagine what Todd's homicidal tendencies and subsequent disappearance had to do with me.

"Queries about how to kill someone with mushrooms weren't the only disturbing stuff we found on his computer. There were two Twitter accounts. One for agency work, the other under the handle GarNetted."

"Todd is GarNetted?"

"I'm afraid so." She sounded tired, and I suspected those mushrooms continued having a negative effect on her health.

"No way! All those posts were written by one person. We underestimated Todd's talent."

"Who gives a rat's ass about his talent. Stay focused, girl."

"You're right. I just can't understand why he would want to do this to me."

"Hard to say. My theory is that he somehow thought you would be one of the accounts I was going to hand over to him. That's why his posts were so pushy about how you needed to get started with the next Garnet book. Regardless, I'm worried about what is going on in that tiny reptilian brain of his. New York state police are looking for him, and they've notified the Atlanta cops since he might be headed your way."

"But that doesn't make sense. He knows he won't be getting any accounts now. What possible reason would he have to come here?"

"Maybe none, but we also found what looks like a journal. More like a list of people he thinks did him wrong. No surprise I'm on the top of that list along with a host of publishers who rejected that damn novel he's been working on since the beginning of time. But, well, you're on it, too."

"Me? What the hell did I do to Todd?" I was fast losing empathy for Wanda's whiny assistant.

"Nothing, except be a better and more successful writer. That seems to be enough for a self-serving, jealous asshole like Todd."

No longer ambiguous about my feelings, I agreed with Wanda. We discussed how I might remain safe. Rather, I spent the next few minutes listening to Wanda tell me how to keep safe. I promised to stay vigilant and call the police the moment Todd showed up, assuming he would.

Despite the diabolical turn he'd taken, it was hard to imagine being in any physical danger from her scrawny assistant. Yes, I could envision him chopping up mushrooms and slipping them into Wanda's soup. But coming to do me bodily harm seemed too up close and personal for a man with Todd's delicate sensibilities.

But what did I really know about him? I had no idea how long his resentment had been festering or how painful it was for him to see others excel in the area he couldn't. And if he was capable of the kind of cold-blooded planning that had gone into poisoning Wanda, what else might he do to get even with the people he thought had caused his ongoing humiliation?

After ending the call, I lay in bed staring up at the ceiling, trying to make sense of what my beleaguered agent had told me. Despite my fears about Todd showing up for revenge, I was relieved all those nasty comments hadn't been from one of my fans. It was even more reassuring to know none of my students held me in such contempt.

Less comforting was the knowledge my online harasser and the person responsible for messing with my mind were two different people. I understood Todd's twisted reason for wanting to intimidate me. But why would someone want to make me and the people who knew me question my sanity?

I thought of all the outlandish situations I created for Garnet. I'd dangled her over a raging river, brought her face-to-face with diabolical villains, tied her up, surrounded her with hissing snakes. But I always let her win because that's what readers wanted—what they demanded. Only this was the real world, and I had no benevolent author to save *me*.

I would have to do it myself by recognizing that I had been and would still be—if Wanda was right about Todd coming after me—fighting battles on two fronts. This truth sapped what little energy I had after my restless night. A ten-pound weight held me down, and I was unable to fight the thick darkness that descended over me.

• • •

The high-pitched peal of raucous laughter rose in a crescendo as Riley's voice cut through the noise.

"There's no need for agitation."

What should have been soothing words fell flat, and the female cackling peaked, joined by a rumbling guffaw. A burst of cold air shocked me with its intensity. I crossed my arms over my chest and received another surprise when I touched bare skin. A quick glance revealed an even greater expanse of nudity. I crossed my legs and wished there was a way to stop the hideous noise surrounding me.

"Many patients suffering from your form of psychosis prefer baring more than their souls. It's only right that I observe the same protocol." Riley stood and began unbuttoning his shirt. When he stepped away from the desk, I saw he'd already removed both his pants and underwear. Thankfully, the body of my psychiatrist had been switched for the one of the Pillsbury Dough Boy.

This ridiculous twist should have made me want to join the chorus that continued to chortle. But it only added to my horror—horror that was heightened when I discovered the source of the laughter. From the corner of the room, Tiffany and Antonio stepped forward, and I began falling from my chair, landing, wide-awake, in my bed.

Outside my window, sunlight streamed through the trees, suggesting several hours had passed since my conversation with Wanda. I had fallen into a sleep deep enough for nightmares.

I replayed the dream, then recalled my last visit with Riley, the one when he appeared at his door disheveled and irritated, insisting I was early. I had the distinct impression he had hustled someone out through the backdoor of his office. At the time, I attributed his frustration to over-scheduling. Now I wondered if it had something to do with Tiffany.

I bet you interrupted the doc and Miss Congeniality during a little dictation session. Get it? Dick-tation?

"Come on, Garnet," I responded, while slipping out of my pajamas and into a pair of jeans. "Isn't that a pretty big leap? And you know she's married."

Sometimes I wonder how someone like you can write someone like me.

I had often wondered the same thing. But I didn't have time to discuss my writing strengths or personal weaknesses. I checked my phone and found there were no more texts from Dad, but there were three from Barb and two from Andy, plus a voicemail from an unknown number. I almost deleted my stepmother's messages, but decided I needed to know what was going on in the let's-commit-Kara campaign.

> *Your father is worried sick. So is Dr. Riley. He's not sure if you fully comprehend the seriousness of stopping your meds cold turkey.*
> *Call me back.*

I considered the possibility she might be genuinely concerned about my mental health. I tried to picture the two of us sitting down together, having a conversation about our feelings but couldn't get there, not while she was on Team Riley. Her next message was similar, more campaigning for me to open my eyes and see the light and stop being the cause of my father's elevating blood pressure. The last was different.

> *Send your address and we'll come get you and help you get the rest you need to recover.*

The tone of this text set off an alarm. Not one of those emergency ones that make you want to run screaming into the street. More like the ping of an email notification, amplified about ten times and never-ending. I think it was the "need to recover" part. My stepmother had a thing about sickness. Unless a person had a documented terminal disease or a fever above 103, she considered being laid up with an illness a character flaw. And while she might be worried, she cared a lot more about what people were saying about me and, by association, her.

The "come get you part" reminded me of Riley. I envisioned a team of mental health ninjas in white jackets kicking in my door. I put that thought on hold and read Andy's message.

> *Don't freak out. I was headed to pick up donuts and noticed a black SUV parked on the street. Probably nothing but might be someone hoping I'll lead them to you, which means they aren't sure where you are. The house*

is locked, and the security system is much better than yours, so sit tight while I take my new buddy on a test drive.

"Shit, Andy," I said to my screen. "Who the hell doesn't freak out the second someone tells them not to?" I didn't like the idea of sitting tight, but what was the alternative?

My heart raced, and sweat pooled in my armpits. Was excessive perspiration one of the symptoms of withdrawal? A cool shower while I waited might help.

Great idea. The perfect B-movie plot. Naked and alone with water cascading down your back and the killer standing outside the door wielding a hatchet.

"A little over the top, don't you think?"

But Garnet was right. I needed to finish dressing and make a plan. The phone rang before I began.

"You're still at the house, aren't you? Because my friend has been tailing me for the past hour. Grocery store, dry cleaners, Home Depot. Picked up a lug-nut wrench. No idea what it is but liked the sound of it."

I smiled at the thought of Andy cruising the aisles of Home Depot.

"I'm here, but I am starting to freak out."

"I've run out of imaginary errands, but I don't want to lead him back to you, so I called a cop friend of mine. Former police officer, I should say. But that's another story. Anyway, he should be sitting across the street in a green van. I'm going to the office for a few hours. Hopefully, our SUV driver will get tired of waiting for me. When he leaves, I'll switch cars with my secretary and come home."

I peeked out the window and just like he said, the van was there. Somewhat reassured, I clicked on the voicemail from that unknown number, expecting a political recording or an offer for carpet cleaning. Instead, it was Lucas.

Hey, Kara. I wouldn't bother you so early, but I wondered if you'd heard from Clive. He called a few hours ago, sounded like he was in bad shape. Kept mumbling about Aftershock and being sorry about all the stuff he's done. About betraying his friends. He mentioned Michael. If you hear from him, please give me a call at this number. Had to switch phones. I'll explain that when I see you. Which, by the way, I hope is soon.

I stood and the room spun, more withdrawal symptoms or the result of not having eaten in forever. I needed caffeine and whatever I could find in Andy's kitchen before I tried to make sense of Lucas's voicemail.

The refrigerator was filled with greasy cartons of Chinese takeout, foul-smelling milk, and suspicious-looking cheese. I checked the pantry and found a box of protein bars. I washed one down with coffee, then replayed Lucas's message.

My cell rang before I decided if I should return his call. Another unknown number.

"Are you alone?" It was Clive, his raspy voice barely above a whisper.

"Yes, there's no one but me here. Are you all right? Lucas said—"

"Forget Montgomery. I'm at the shelter in the basement. May have hit the motherlode, but I need your help. Can you come now? Better alone since I'm not exactly supposed to be here. Gotta go."

I knew meeting Clive in a dark basement might not be a great idea. If Lucas had been telling the truth about the veteran's state of mind, it was probably a terrible idea. Except my instincts told me I could trust Clive. The next question was whether I could trust myself.

Chapter 35

Ira didn't hesitate when I called to see if he would pick me up.

"Did I catch you at a bad time?" I asked, as I hopped in beside him.

"Not at all. I was stuck on nineteen down in my crossword. Everything okay?"

"Things are a little complicated." I gave him an edited version of the events, leading him to believe I left my car at the club. When we were a few blocks from his house, I asked for another favor.

"Would it be okay if I borrow your car? A friend of mine is having some issues, and I need to check in with him right away. It's probably nothing serious, but you never know."

"Happy to help. Wasn't going anywhere anyway." He paused. "That's it! An eight-letter word for a dangerous situation: jeopardy."

•   •   •

My plan was to drive to the shelter and find Clive. I couldn't imagine what he had uncovered, but there was no way I would let it go.

At the stop sign on my street, I caught a glimpse of myself in the rearview mirror. With my hair tucked under one of Andy's old baseball caps, my cheekbones seemed more pronounced, the hollows below them deeper. The hat was too large, partially obscuring my eyes. They could have been any color: pale blue, my true color; light brown; or emerald green, Garnet's color.

Garnet pulled the cap low, shading her cat-like eyes. From a distance, there was nothing threatening about her. But if the man stalking her was unfortunate enough to get closer, he would discover what a terrible mistake he had made.

For a second, I lost myself in the narrative I created in my first book when Garnet's transformation from victim to vigilante began. The blast of a horn returned me to the present, but not all the way back to myself.

As I merged into traffic, I steadied my shaking hands by grasping the steering wheel hard enough to make my veins pop. A stabbing sensation in my temples brought tears to my eyes, and I strained to stay focused on the road. I massaged my aching head until the pressure lessened. I started to relax when a birdlike apparition appeared a few feet ahead of me. Fearful my suicidal raven was dive bombing again, I braced for the impact, but it was only a cloud shadow.

I saw my exit and signaled a lane change. But the tractor-trailer in front of me was moving too slowly for me to maneuver around it. Cars and trucks flew by with cartoon-like speed. My chest tightened and I struggled to breathe. After several terrifying seconds, I managed to inhale. I counted to five before exhaling, then repeated the process three or four times. I never had a panic-attack, had never understood they were a real thing. But I couldn't dismiss whatever had highjacked my ability for rational thought.

By now the truck had sped up. I veered off the expressway and turned onto the first side street I came to, stopped, rolled down the windows, and leaned my head back. A light breeze drifted through the car, bringing with it a sense of urgency I didn't understand. I returned to the main road. The closer I got to the shelter, the more pressing my need to reach Clive became. But it wasn't the only thing weighing on me. It was all the "what ifs" surrounding Michael's death that crushed me.

Most survivors are haunted by those nagging little questions that can never be answered. Parents ask what if we'd said no when Junior wanted to borrow the car. Wives agonize over not insisting hubby have that colonoscopy. These are terrible remnants of grief that grip people in the middle of the night and refuse to let go. No one can deny how excruciating they are or expect them to disappear. Eventually, however, their power lessens. Instead of waking its victims, it slips in and out of their dreams, whispering occasionally, but rarely screaming.

For those who survive the loss of someone they love from an act of violence, the "what-ifs" are different. Whether delivered randomly by a stranger or the premeditated action of a murderer, the questions from acts of brutality are more pointed, more sharp-edged. What if I had been there? What if I'd gone to the store? What if I hadn't forgotten the goddamn cereal?

Instead of keeping a person awake in the middle of the night, these questions annihilate sleep. They leave gaping wounds that appear to heal, but only scab over and rupture time and time again. They keep screaming.

The shelter was only a block away when I began to understand why finding Clive was so important. If he had uncovered the reason my husband had been killed, that knowledge might put an end to my what-ifs—might silence the screaming.

•   •   •

The sprawling home in the cul-de-sac bore little resemblance to the picture on the pamphlet I received in the mail. In the shiny brochure, both house and wrap-around porch were peachy-pink with white gingerbread trim. The tower with its turret crown jutted proudly above the entrance and the front lawn was a deep, even green. The winding drive was lined with purple flowers.

In reality, the peachy pink was a dull, faded rose with pock marks where sheets of paint had lost their hold. The scrolling brackets and arches of the trim were grayish white, with fist-sized chunks missing every three or four feet. Overgrown grass, thick with weeds, dotted the lawn in uneven shades of brown and yellow. The cracks and potholes played havoc with my alignment, and there wasn't a purple flower in sight.

Michael told me the place needed work. His plan was to let the men in the program help with repairs, give them a sense of purpose and ownership. It appeared his death had ended that initiative. The parking lot was deserted, but I assumed it was for visitors with a separate area for employees.

I sat in the car, questioning my impulse to retrieve Clive by myself.

Since when have you been by yourself?

It seemed Garnet's ego knew no bounds. Of course, that was the way I created her, and it was true I barely remembered a time after I began writing the series when she hadn't been with me in one form or another.

"I meant physically alone, and you know it."

I shut off the engine and stepped from the car. Along the narrow path to the front of the building, I could see it wasn't just neglect that contributed to its dilapidation. It was a dark aura of defeat and abandonment. Despite the warm spring air, goosebumps rippled over my arms as I reached the steps. Rickety wooden rocking chairs were clumped too close together, suggesting they had been empty for quite a while. That, or their former inhabitants had been spirited away after putting up quite a fight.

Unlike the rest of the façade, the door had been freshly painted a shiny black. Instead of improving the overall appearance, it emphasized the shabbiness surrounding it. Someone had hung an oversized wooden cross a few inches above a sign that read "Visitors must register at the front desk. No exceptions."

I rang the bell, waited, and rang again, this time pushing the button several times. Still no response. I tried knocking, then pounding, but no one answered.

Was it possible I misunderstood Clive, or he'd been confused? Had he fallen off the wagon and had no idea where he was?

Sounds like you're stalling. At least try the door. It could be unlocked.

Although highly irritating, Garnet was right. The problem wasn't that I thought Clive had been in a drunken stupor. The problem was I didn't want to go inside this spooky old house, and I most assuredly did not want to check out the basement.

"Shit, shit, shit," I muttered, then grabbed the doorknob and twisted. Locked. I backed away from the door, turned, and took the steps two at a time. On my way around the house, I noticed a window near the base of the structure.

"Please be locked." I repeated several times while approaching it.

Squatting on my heels, I peered through the filthy glass. I could see what appeared to be bulky pieces of furniture shrouded in sheets but no sign of Clive. It was impossible to determine what might be waiting for me in that darkened room.

I moved into a kneeling position and examined the window. Locked or not, there was no way I could squeeze through it. And even if I could, the drop was so steep I might break or at least sprain an ankle.

After brushing dirt off Barb's tracksuit, I stood and walked toward the backyard. It was more overgrown than the front. Something rustled in the ivy, and I skittered from the sound. The back entrance was more modest than its counterpart. A tattered awning shadowed the postage stamp-sized porch and door. There were slim rectangular openings on both sides, but the thick glass was covered with cobwebs and dust, providing no view of the interior.

I reached for the doorbell but stopped before ringing. It had been about ten minutes since I'd begun announcing my presence. If anyone was home, he or she had shown no interest in letting me in.

"Maybe I should give Andy a call and wait till he comes."

That wimp? You know he'll insist on calling the cops. What if you get that poor old guy arrested or worse?

"Andy's not a—" I gave up defending my friend because it was a waste of time, and he was a bit of a wimp.

"Fine," I said and grasped the tarnished bronze doorknob. When it turned easily, I withdrew my hand as if from a hot stove. Normally, an unlocked door indicated the owner had nothing to hide. In this case, I suspected it was something more sinister. Regardless, I was compelled to open it.

After a few seconds, my eyes adjusted to the gloom. To my right, a long, low bench ran alongside the wall. Empty shelves lined the opposite side. Whether it had been used as a place to store muddy shoes or extra supplies, it no longer filled either need.

A short hallway opened to a kitchen that spanned the width of the house. Pots, pans, and other utensils were scattered on Formica countertops. Cabinet doors had been flung wide and the pantry was bare, as if their occupants had staged a prison break. I saw no sign of a basement entry point. Fearful of what a closer inspection might reveal, I walked quickly through and into a large dining room. This must have been where Michael had sat with the men at dinner, honoring them by listening to their stories. Thinking of them reminded me of my reason for breaking and entering. I kept moving, looking for a way to get to Clive. When I stopped at the doorway and surveyed the area, shafts of sunshine striped the walls and thickened the air with row after row of floating dust motes.

Facing a wide staircase covered with threadbare carpet of an indeterminate color and pattern, I detected a small door to the left. Most likely a closet. Probably nothing more than mothballs and mouse poop, but I had to check. With each step, I felt more and more like some doe-eyed damsel in a horror movie. The audience screams warnings, but she keeps getting closer and closer to her imminent and bloody demise. Now that I was some poor fool caught between courage and survival, I had a better understanding of the poor girl's dilemma.

Yes, it was highly likely there was a knife-wielding madman behind door number one. But what if it wasn't a slice-and-dicer? What if that passageway led to rescue and redemption? I studied the scuffed wood and grimy knob. Resigned to the reality I would have to see what lay beyond, I came up with a variation on my recurring movie scenario. I might have to open it, but I didn't have to fling it toward me and watch for the downward arc of a freshly sharpened axe. I could open it and use it as a partial shield—not a great plan, but it would have to do. I flew into action, yanked the door open, and stepped behind it.

No monster glared down at me. There was only the musty smell of things people leave behind and darkness. A closer look revealed shades of blacks and grays. I'd found the basement; I flipped the light switch, but nothing happened.

The thin beam from my flashlight app revealed a steep staircase with a loose-hanging handrail. I stared into the abyss, toying with the idea of fleeing the scene. And most likely, that's what I would have done. If not for the sound of the front door opening.

Chapter 36

I crouched on the narrow basement steps until my legs cramped. A mixture of sweat and mascara trickled into my eyes. Half lame and partially blinded, I doubted I could move fast enough to make it to the back door undetected.

Listen up and get your ass in gear.

Garnet heard the voices before I did. I took her advice literally and began a slow butt slide from step to step until I reached the bottom. The window cast a shaft of light across the room and its shrouded contents. Before I had time to take a better look, a broad beam flooded the area. Someone had opened the door. I ducked into the open space under the staircase, brushing away what I hoped were cobwebs, and held my breath.

"I could'a sworn something was moving around down there." I recognized the voice; it was Antonio. "Shouldn't I go down and check it—"

"We don't have time for that." Tiffany cut him off, then continued in a less strident tone. "He was unconscious when you tied him up, right? Even if he comes to and gets loose, we've got him locked up tight. You stay here while I pick up the van. When we're finished loading everything, we'll take care of that nosey old bastard."

"Okay, but hurry. This whole house gives me the creeps. And that shithole down there is the worst."

The door shut before I could get an idea of how long Tiffany would be gone or where Antonio might hang out while waiting. What I did know for sure was that Clive was somewhere in this shithole basement, and he most likely wasn't in the best of shape.

An eerie quiet blanketed the area, making the air even more dense and dank. I eased out from under the stairs and moved toward one of the many sheeted objects scattered throughout the long rectangular room. My cell flashlight guided me through a conglomeration of partially hidden junk: chairs, a table, boxes, and two large metal machines that looked as if they belonged in an operating room. Antonio was right about the creep factor. The dirty white sheets were sepulchers in a graveyard where I'd been charged with finding a specific plot. Only I wasn't looking for the dead; I was trying to save the living.

Don't lose your cool, honey, or you're the one who'll be in the market for a gravestone—something in marble with your name on it.

Although unsought, both the timing and the warning were welcome. And so was the company. With Garnet by my side, I wasn't alone.

"What now?" Instead of an answer from my heroine, a soft, other-worldly moaning rose. I suppressed a shriek and was in the process of planning a quick exit when I heard another groan, more substantial, coming from the middle of the room.

"Clive," I whispered. "Is that you?"

The response was muffled but helped me pinpoint its source. The sheet on top of what could have been a small sofa or loveseat rippled erratically. I rushed to it and snatched it off. There with his hands, feet, and mouth duct-taped, Clive blinked up at me.

"Thank God. Are you okay?"

He mumbled.

"Sorry." I peeled the tape, wincing along with him. When it was off, he gulped in deep breaths. I eased him into a sitting position.

"Stay here while I—"

What do expect him to do? Chew his way out?

"Not the time for sarcasm," I said. *Shit.* But if Clive heard the retort to my invisible associate, he didn't react.

"I need something sharp to cut through that tape. I'll be right back."

I tossed sheets and searched corners until my stepmother's tennis shoe landed on a shard of glass from a broken windowpane.

Remember how we turned those diamonds into weapons?

"*Hidden Jewels!*" In my first book, Garnet used the jagged edge of a diamond to scratch the eyes of her abductor.

I squatted down to check out the scattered pieces and carefully moved them around until I found a decent sized fragment. My hands shook as I picked it up.

"No way I'll be able to use this without slicing me or Clive or both of us."

Come on, MacGyver. Think!

"I am thinking, dammit, and I don't see anything that will—"

Running a fingertip over what could have been a small file case, I noticed the sheet had several tears in it.

"The sheet!" I half-shouted, then began shredding it into strips.

I returned to Clive and wound the cloth around the glass until only the pointed end protruded, using that edge to cut through the tape on his wrists. While he wriggled his hands free, I sawed through the binding around his ankles.

"Are you okay?" Stupid question.

"Head hurts, but I'm good."

"Can you stand up?"

He nodded, and pushed himself up, wobbling when upright. Fearful he might not be able to walk, I wrapped my arm around his waist, and we slow-stepped it to the bottom of the stairs.

"Sit here while I see if their goon is on the other side." He slumped onto a step, gray-faced and breathing heavily. I began to question the wisdom of trying to sneak past Antonio and make a run for the car. Unfortunately, I couldn't think of an alternate plan.

When I reached the top, I pressed my ear to the door and heard nothing. I turned the knob, cringing as it squeaked in protest. At every twist of my wrist, I stopped to listen for the clump of Antonio's boots. The hinges groaned as I peeked out. There was no one lurking. I opened it another inch or so, thinking someone could be on the staircase. It was empty. Slightly encouraged by my good luck, I stepped into the foyer. Although I was walking on tiptoe, the sagging floorboards creaked and whined. I froze outside the kitchen, certain the noise was loud enough to alert our captor.

Don't worry about Big Tony. That moron couldn't find his ass with a flashlight and a map.

I nodded in agreement and was ready to proceed when laughter from another room sent me scurrying toward the basement. Familiar music stopped me. It was the theme song for *The Price is Right,* indicating I'd only been in the house less than an hour. It also meant Antonio and I had the same taste in game shows.

I called softly to Clive. "Can you make it?"

Several long seconds passed and just as I was about to return for him, slow but steady footsteps sounded on the stairs. When he reached the top, he leaned against the doorframe and wiped his forehead. His color wasn't any better, but his breathing was less labored.

"I'm pretty sure the guy on guard duty is in the back with the TV on. If we hurry, we should be able to go out through the kitchen. Are you up for it?"

He nodded, and we began moving toward the hallway.

Late afternoon sun filtered through one of the grimy windows, creating shadows where none had been earlier. I glanced over my shoulder to check on Clive. His lips were set in a grim line as he moved forward.

"Once we get outside, we'll have to move fast." I took my keys from my pocket. "I'm going to count to three, then follow me, okay?"

"Got it." His voice was dead calm, like someone who'd come through more dangerous circumstances. Like the veteran he was.

I took a deep breath and hoped his steady courage would rub off on me. Before I reached the door, it flung open, leaving me face to face with Lucas Montgomery.

"Kara."

My heart raced with relief. I raised my arms, ready to throw them around his neck and cling to him. And I would have if Clive hadn't taken hold of my shoulder. I was ready to shake him loose when a woman spoke.

"If it isn't Miss Buttinski herself. Always showing up where she's not wanted."

"Lucas?" I searched his face for an answer to a question I didn't know how to ask. But he refused to look me in the eye and stepped aside. Behind him like an unwelcome spirit, stood Tiffany Russo—armed with a chilling smile and a very large gun.

Chapter 37

The combination of shock from seeing Lucas with Tiffany, the size of her gun, and the drugs, reluctantly leaving my system, enveloped me in a thick haze. When it lifted, Clive was calling my name and gently shaking me by the shoulders.

"Ms. Dolan, you okay?"

I nodded, and he released me.

"Thank the good Lord." He relaxed and sighed.

"Where are we?"

"Right back where we started—in the goddamn basement."

We were, indeed, sitting on the floor of the basement, huddled beside some of the larger boxes. I tried moving my hands and legs and was surprised when I discovered them unbound.

I almost asked him why they hadn't taken such an obvious precaution, but there was no need. I knew why. They didn't think we were a threat, and most likely weren't planning on keeping us around for long.

Instead, I asked, "What happened?"

Clive explained that after seeing the two of them together, I zoned out. Tiffany pointed her gun at him, and they marched us down the stairs.

"I told them they wouldn't get away with it. That bitch just laughed, and Montgomery never said a word. I thought about going for the gun. The way she kept sticking it out in front of her was strictly amateur hour. But then that tub of lard showed up and decreased my odds."

"You must have come across something they didn't want found."

"Lots of somethings. Those boxes are loaded with everything from antibiotics to anti-psychotics. Stuff meant to help the men the clinic was supposed to be treating."

"But wouldn't the guys know they weren't working?"

"My guess is they started them out on the right medication, then gradually substituted placebos. That's why Aftershock got better then worse and worse. The bastards had to be selling the good shit to the highest bidder."

He rubbed his eyes and continued.

"Michael got to the truth. He realized something funny was going on with the books, put two and two together—"

"And they shot him." I finished the hard part for him, then sat quietly trying to determine which of the three had pulled the trigger. Riley, with his cool analytical approach, seemed the most capable of developing the plan; Antonio the most likely to carry it out with Tiffany to spur him on like a rabid cheerleader. Before I could ask for Clive's input, the door opened and a beam from what must have been a high-powered flashlight flooded the room. I shielded my eyes, wondering if we were Antonio's next project.

But it wasn't Riley's thug slowly shedding light in and out of the corners. It was Lucas.

"Kara? I'm going to get you out of here, but we've got to hurry."

Clive and I exchanged confused looks. Moments ago, he had been standing next to Tiffany, and he hadn't looked like an unwilling captive. He could have only been pretending to be on her side to win her confidence and get the evidence we needed to convict Michael's murderer. Or was he pretending now?

Either way, Clive and I weren't in a position to demand answers. We apparently reached this conclusion at the same time. He shrugged, I nodded, and we stood.

Lucas stepped toward me. "Are you all right?"

He took my hand, and I stiffened at his touch.

Ignoring my lack of enthusiasm, he turned to Clive. "How you doing, buddy?"

"Not your buddy, asshole."

Lucas grinned the same grin that had once given me a warm, fuzzy feeling and addressed Clive.

"I don't blame you for being pissed, but I can explain—after we get the hell out of here." He released my hand but moved a few steps closer. "Please, Kara, you have to believe me. I'd never do anything to hurt you."

I turned to Clive for guidance, but he was lasered in on Lucas, so I made the call.

"Let's go."

He led us through the kitchen to his car. I sat up front, and Clive stumbled into the back. When we sped away, the tires dug into the driveway, sending gravel spewing. I was certain the racket would bring Tiffany and Antonio outside, but when I looked over my shoulder, no one was coming for us.

"Now's a good time for that explanation you promised. You know, the reason we should trust you."

"Right. Riley caught me snooping around his office, so I told them I wanted in on the game, that I had a list of buyers, contacts I'd made during investigations. He bought it, then let it slip they had Clive at the center. I volunteered to go with Tiffany, thinking I'd catch her at a weak moment. I thought Antonio would be off picking up the van, so Clive and I could make a run for it. I had no idea you were there."

When I looked at Clive to gauge his reaction to the story, I was alarmed by his grayish hue.

"You okay back there?" I asked and had to lean over the seat to hear his answer.

"I'm fine, just a little tired, that's all."

He looked more than a little tired, with his sallow skin and abnormal breathing. Were victims of head injuries supposed to sleep or stay awake?

Lucas put his hand on my forearm. "Don't worry. He'll be good once we get him some settled in."

I pulled away. "And where would that be?"

"Not my apartment; that'd be the first spot they'd look. And your house is out. A friend of mine's out of town for a month, and he gave me a key. We can crash there until we decide what to do."

"Shouldn't we just go to the police?"

"And tell them what? I mean, technically, you and Clive were trespassing."

"That doesn't give them the right to hit Clive on the head and keep us prisoners."

"Maybe not, but Georgia's a stand-your-ground state. Who's to say they didn't consider Clive a threat? And what would your justification for breaking and entering be?"

He had a point. We hadn't gone through the records Clive found. That could be the reason Tiffany and Antonio didn't come after us. They'd been busy getting rid of the evidence and hiding the drugs. Too discouraged to answer, I leaned my head against the window and closed my eyes.

"And don't forget about Riley," Lucas continued. "He's the guy in charge, which means he's directly responsible for your husband's death. We don't have anything that would implicate him unless you located the missing flash drive. Or discovered something else in Michael's things."

Although I suspected Riley, I wondered how Lucas was so confidant the doctor was the one behind Michael's murder. Also curious was the intensity of his inquiry about what I had uncovered among my husband's belongings. Before I could question him, Clive groaned.

"What's wrong?" I asked. Previously a faded gun-metal gray, his complexion had taken a turn toward olive green.

"Could you roll down the window? I'm feeling a little pukish."

He hit the button for Clive's window, and I did the same with mine.

"How about some water?" Lucas offered. "There should be some in the glove compartment."

I opened it at the same time the car in front of us stopped short. Lucas hit the brakes hard, sending the bottle rolling to the floor. I had to strain against my seatbelt to retrieve it. As I sat up, I hit my head on the edge of the compartment door.

"Shit," I murmured. I tried to punish the offending object by slamming it shut, but something kept it from closing. It was a gray-striped cigarette pack with a green band at the top. The same green band, complete with identical lettering and coat of arms, that was on the butt in my backyard.

Chapter 38

After riding in silence for a little over half an hour, Lucas turned onto the drive of an apartment complex like the ones that had been the rage in the late eighties when people relied on clubhouses and pools to find romance. Although clean and well-maintained, the grounds, with dry fountains and a squat building attached to a covered pool, hadn't been updated in some time. The apartment itself was sparsely furnished: a gray sofa, mismatched fake leather chairs, cheap coffee table. Most notable was the lack of any personal touch. No pictures, knick-knacks, silly salt and pepper shakers—nothing to provide a clue about the inhabitants.

Screw some guy's lousy taste. What about the fact Mr. Smooth's the one who's been spying on you?

Like Garnet, I couldn't come up with another explanation for my stalker's cigarettes being in Lucas's car. That meant this was no escape and rescue mission. It was something darker. And I had no idea how to get out of it.

Well, get one. Because if you go, I go, and I'm not ready to be permanently shelved.

The good news was Clive had perked up since we reached our destination. Lucas served him chicken noodle soup, the only staple in the pantry other than off-brand chocolate chip cookies and a can of SqueezyCheese. I declined the soup and while they ate pretended to search the cabinets for coffee. My real goal was to find something I might use to defend us against the man I had so foolishly trusted. The cabinets were empty. I joined them, wondering how to arrange a moment alone with Clive. They'd just finished slurping down the main course when Lucas's phone rang.

"It's my editor," he explained. "Why don't you guys get more comfortable in the living room?"

I doubted the call was from his boss and suspected he simply didn't want us to hear, but I went along with it.

Clive's coloring had greatly improved, and he was surprisingly steady on his feet; me, not so much. I swayed against the table and held on until the room stopped spinning. He put his arm around my shoulders.

"Easy there," he said. "Let me help."

I leaned against him and together we made it to the sofa.

"How long's it been since you ate something?" he asked while opening the cookies.

"I might be a little hungry." I sank deeper into the couch.

After two stale cookies, I said, "Much better." There was no need to tell Clive my light-headedness was probably the result of going off my meds. I scooted closer and whispered, "I don't trust Lucas."

"Me, neither. And I sure as hell don't buy that crap about him planning on grabbing that bitch's gun. You ask me, those two have got something going on."

Clive was right. There was a vibe between them. I wondered if Antonio was too thick or too into Tiffany to pick up on it. Probably a little of both.

"Whatever they have, we need to get out of here, but—" The sound of Lucas's approaching voice silenced me.

"Right. Whatever you say, boss." He was louder now, probably still trying to sell us on the idea he'd been talking to his editor.

"Follow my lead," Clive said as Lucas entered the room and sat in one of the cheap chairs.

"The man is a royal pain, always nagging about deadlines. But I told him my next installment would be worth the wait." He sat and propped his feet on the coffee table.

"So, you've been working on Michael's story?" I asked.

"Not exactly. I—"

"Hate to interrupt, but I really gotta pee." Clive hopped to his feet with a look of desperation on his face.

Lucas stood. "I'll show you the way."

"Not necessary. Just point me in the direction. You two keep on talking. I could be in there awhile. Damned prostrate."

Lucas hesitated but didn't stop him. Then he looked at me as if he'd forgotten what we were talking about.

"Not exactly," I coaxed. "I asked if you were working on Michael's story, and you said *not exactly*."

"It's complicated," he began. The sound of a key turning startled us both. "Dammit!" He hurried to the entry way, then turned to me. "Keep quiet and stay put." There was a moment of confusion while the person on the other side kept fiddling with the lock.

"Hold on a second." Lucas opened the door, and Dr. Riley stumbled into the room.

"What's going on? I was in the middle of dinner with Father—" He saw me and stopped mid-tirade. "Why the hell is she here?"

Annoyed with his dismissive attitude, I spoke with a confidence I didn't feel. "*She* is here because *he* freed me from your flunkies. What the hell are *you* doing here?"

"Let's all take a breath, okay?" Lucas motioned Riley toward the living room.

"I don't have time for this," Riley muttered. He was just settling in on the chair across from me when the door burst open again.

"Isn't this lovely?" Tiffany exclaimed. "Look, honey. It's a surprise party, and we're the guests of honor."

Antonio stumbled in behind her, carrying a black canvas bag. "Party? What party? I thought you said—"

"Forget it," she snapped. Her husband's face twisted in an expression somewhere between hurt and bewilderment. With a face like his, he wasn't an easy read.

"Tiffany?" Dr. Riley rose. "I don't understand. Aren't you supposed to be at the clinic?" He cut his eyes toward me. "Taking care of those *business* arrangements."

"You don't have to be coy, dear. Our little Kara's been snooping around, and I'm afraid she's learned a bit more than she bargained for." She turned and spoke directly to Lucas. "Did she give you the flash drive?"

"No, but I still think we should take another look for it ourselves. We might have—"

"It doesn't really matter now, though, does it?" She snapped before showing her teeth to me. "We really didn't want it to turn out this way. I hoped your viral video would put you out of play. But no. You couldn't let it go."

"You're the one who filmed me at the grocery store? And the disappearing stalker video? I suppose you made that one, too?"

"I have to give Lucas credit for that one. He's much more tech savvy than I am." When she looked at him, her smile morphed into a frown. "Hey! Where's the old fart? Don't tell me you lost him."

"Of course, I didn't lose him." It seemed clear to me that—overcome by Tiffany's presence—he had forgotten about Clive. "He's in the bathroom. Should be out in a minute. But I'll go check."

She fluffed her hair and directed her attention to Riley, who had halfway risen from his seat. "Where do you think you're going? Sit back down; we need to talk."

"We have nothing to talk about. This is your mess, and I expect you to clean it up." He stood and stepped away from his chair. Antonio dropped the bag, whipped around his wife, and waved a gun in the doctor's face.

"She said *sit down*, motherfucker."

The motherfucker sat, and I wondered if Antonio was brandishing the same weapon she had pulled on me and Clive or if they were a two-gun family.

"First, we need to decide what to do with Miss Snoopy Pants."

This bitch is getting on my last nerve.

"Me, too," I mumbled.

Lucas bounded into the room. "He's gone."

"What do you mean *gone*? Goddammit! Do I have to do everything around here?" She grabbed the bag, unzipped it, and rummaged around for a second before pulling out another gun identical to the one her husband held.

Definitely a His-and-Her Glock family.

I didn't know the difference between a Glock or a whatever the hell other guns there were. But I was glad Garnet did.

"I'm sorry, Tiff." Lucas's voice drifted from the hallway.

"Did you hear that?" I gave Antonio what I hoped passed for a sympathetic look and shook my head. "It's *Tiff* now."

"Huh?" He raised an eyebrow.

"I thought you were cool with it—you know, *Tiff* and Lucas."

"What the fuck are you talking about?" Without waiting for an answer, he turned to Riley. "What the fuck is she talking about?"

"I doubt if *he* knows. Or maybe he doesn't want to admit things didn't work out for him and Tiffany."

Antonio waved the gun at the doctor, who sputtered, "Don't listen to her. She's making shit up. She doesn't—"

"Keep your mouth shut, or I'll shut it for you," Antonio growled, then looked at me. "So what *things* are you talking about?"

"Oops. I thought you knew how he felt about your wife. I picked up on it at my first session. The way he looked at her; you couldn't miss it. And if the way she kept touching him, brushing up against him is any indication, the feeling was definitely mutual." I gave Antonio another sorrowful look.

"Is that true? Did you make a move on my wife?"

"Can't you see what she's doing?" From Antonio's expression, it was clear he had no idea what I was doing. "She's filling your head with lies, trying to turn us against each other."

I snorted a laugh.

"What's so funny?" Antonio hissed.

"The idea of me trying to fool someone like you is ridiculous. You're way too sharp. But it seems as if you and your wife are going through a rough patch. Don't be too hard on the doctor. There might have been a little hanky-panky going on, but nothing compares to the heat between those two." I cut my eyes in the direction of the bedroom.

"Are you saying my wife has something going on with that pissant?" He pointed his gun toward the hallway.

I shrugged.

"That's exactly what she's saying." I had to hand it to Riley when it came to the quick reversal. "There was never anything between me and Tiffany. But I've suspected for some time that—"

Lucas picked that moment to return to the room with Tiffany a few steps in front of him. "He must have slipped out the window and dropped to the neighbor's balcony. We took his phone back at the clinic, but it won't take him long to find a way to call the cops. We need to get out of here."

For a reporter, the man wasn't particularly adept at picking up on body language. Tiffany, however, was. She took one look at Antonio, passed the gun to Lucas, then moved to her husband's side.

"He's right, babe." She put her hand on Antonio's arm, but he ignored her and sent Lucas a death stare.

Still oblivious to the man's hostility, Lucas tucked the gun into the back of his jeans and continued. "Tiff and I can go to the clinic. We'll take the van in case we need to load boxes. You and Riley take the car to Kara's. There's duct tape in the trunk, so you can tape her up and leave her there; then meet us at my place."

The prospect of being left with two men who didn't seem like the kind of guys who would leave witnesses behind terrified me, but I had to stay cool.

"Hmm, hmm," I muttered in Antonio's direction. "Isn't that interesting? He and *Tiff* head off in the van while you and Riley stay behind."

"That's not what I said. Well, yes, it's what I said, but all I meant was—" Lucas stopped and glared at me, finally seeming to pick up on the tension in the room.

While he was giving me the stink eye, Antonio stuck the gun inside his jacket and flung Tiffany aside. Then, moving at a speed that belied his bulk, he slammed into Lucas, knocked him to the floor, and began pounding him with both fists.

Tiffany shrieked before hurling herself on top of the men, dislodging Antonio's gun in the process. I could feel Riley's breath on my neck as we both scrambled for it. I grabbed it first, jumped to my feet, and pointed it at him. He raised his hands and began backing up.

A cracking sound echoed in the room. "Oh, shit!" I waited for Riley to drop, but he made a dash for the door.

The room grew quiet enough to hear a low moan from behind me. Still holding the gun in what I hoped was a menacing stance, I turned. It took several seconds for me to figure out that the soft groaning came from Antonio. It took a little longer to see that the blood puddling nearby came from a surprisingly small hole in his chest and not from the woman trapped under him.

Lying next to the couple, Lucas was bleeding from his mouth and nose. He rolled to his side, whimpering with the effort, and pushed himself into a sitting position. Looking up at me, he wiped blood from his lip.

"Kara," he said. "Thank God you're okay."

What a total bullshit artist.

"Absolutely." I wasn't sure if I answered out loud or in my head.

"You are all right, aren't you?" He held out his hand. "Could you help me up?"

I stepped back at the same time Tiffany began screaming. "Somebody get this pile of blubber off me. I'm suffocating."

"If you don't stop screaming, suffocating will the least of your worries." I sounded like a cross between a gangster and a bad parent but didn't care. For the first time, I could understand the appeal of packing heat.

Grunts and groans replaced the screams as she tried to wriggle out from under her loving husband, who was no longer moving. While I'd been watching Tiffany, Lucas had gotten up.

"Don't move," I warned.

"You don't think I was really going to leave you here with those two, do you? I was just playing along until he dropped his guard." He reached his arms out to me.

"Stop right there." My Glock-related confidence was ebbing as I realized it wasn't the actual gun that held the power. It was knowing you could pull the trigger. From the lop-sided smile on his face, Lucas didn't seem to think I could, and I was afraid he was right.

You got this, sweetheart. Hold it with both hands and keep your finger on the trigger.

"Come on, Kara. This whole thing is part of my story, our story if you'll help me finish it. Exactly the way Michael wanted."

The mention of my husband's name conjured a picture of him, alone and bleeding. I squeezed my eyes tight to shut out the image. When I opened them, Lucas was lunging for me, for the gun. And the room exploded.

Chapter 39

"That is some shit!" Nina exclaimed from her seat at the head of my kitchen table.

The others remained silent, but from the looks on their faces, I was confident they shared the sentiment.

"You really shot the bastard?" Howard broke the silence.

"I guess you could say that. I squeezed the trigger, and the gun went off. But the bullet hit the overhead light. It came loose and fell on Lucas. Sparks started flying everywhere. Then the police burst in."

"Awesome," Nina whispered.

"Not all that awesome."

You might be able to fool these guys, but not me. I know exactly how you felt when you pulled that trigger.

Garnet was right. I experienced a rush at being on the giving end of fear—powerful, strong.

I never wanted to feel that way again.

"I can't believe that terrible woman was the mastermind of the whole thing," Betty said.

"Pretty much. She took the job with Riley so she could steal his prescription pad and forge his signature. Then she and Antonio would fill them and sell the drugs. Apparently, that wasn't lucrative enough for Tiff, though. When she uncovered Riley's work at the clinic, she figured she hit the jackpot. All they had to do was give fake medication to the vets and take the real stuff for themselves."

"Too bad you didn't get the chance to shoot her," Louisa spoke up.

"Getting squished by her husband—talk about poetic justice. It's a shame the police got there before she flatlined," Betty said.

"Also, too bad that bullet missed any of Antonio's vital parts." Nina added.

"You ladies are scaring me." Everyone but Betty laughed. She merely Mona Lisad me.

"And Lucas, he let himself get taken in by a pretty face," Howard said. "What a sucker,"

"That plus the prospect of getting rich," I said and shared what I learned.

Lucas had been working on a book about the plight of the veterans at St. Celia's when he met Tiffany. She seduced him, then brought him into the drug ring. Michael discovered Tiffany wasn't just screwing around with Lucas; she was screwing with the books. The night my husband was killed he was supposed to meet Lucas with the flash drive containing the evidence he'd gathered. For some reason Michael changed his mind. He came without the drive and started asking questions. Lucas panicked and shot him.

"I think that dude was the worst of the bunch," Nina said.

"He did try to keep Antonio and Tiffany from killing me immediately after Michael's murder."

Lucas had urged them to wait. He argued it would be stupid to give up a lucrative business and said I might lead them to the drive. Installing keylogger had been his idea. When they found out I was investigating the center, Tiffany pushed to get rid of me.

"Lucas came up with the plan to get me to see Riley. He talked Tiffany into infiltrating Barb's tennis team, where she convinced my stepmother that she knew this incredible doctor who everyone said was a miracle worker with depressed patients. When the plan worked, she had Lucas case my house, then sent Antonio to slip in and out to scare the crap out of me. It was her idea to have him rearrange my photographs. She was the one who sent the flowers."

Nina wasn't letting Lucas off the hook. "But he was the asshole who let that other asshole pump you up with drugs that made you think you were losing it. What was that about?"

"He wasn't as straightforward with the police about that. He stuck to his statement about only being in on the original scheme to make me and everybody I knew think I was having a breakdown. They weren't too worried about my finding the flash drive since they were monitoring my computer activity and could step in if I started putting things together. That changed when Andy discovered I'd been hacked."

I paused at the memory of how vulnerable I felt at the time, then took a breath and continued.

"This is where Lucas's story gets harder to follow. He said he didn't know anything was up until he overheard Tiffany talking to Riley. She wanted to send Antonio over to take me out of the equation, but Riley said he increased my meds and pretty soon I wouldn't be able to tell night from day."

"I don't believe that douche bag," Nina fumed. "And wasn't the phony-ass reporter the one who pushed the nun down the stairs? I hope they all rot in prison."

Lucas admitted Sister Mary Alice confronted him about Michael's death but insisted the fall was an accident. The police didn't agree and had reopened the investigation into her death. It wasn't looking good for him. That, combined with his confession to killing Michael, insured he would be spending twenty-five to life in prison.

Riley was another story. While the Russos and Lucas were facing lengthy sentences, there was no hard evidence against the doctor. His behavior was unethical, but there was nothing but the word of two felons and one lying journalist to implicate him in the drug-selling business. Without the flash drive, Riley might get off with a fine and a license revocation. I kept this depressing tidbit to myself.

Nina's indignation on my behalf plus the genuine expressions of concern on the faces of the others threatened to undo me. Seeming to sense my emotional state, Louisa spoke up.

"This is probably a good time for all of us to come clean. I'll go first. That day in class wasn't the first time we met. I thought you were pretending not to recognize me, and I was a bit miffed."

Miffed? She had been buzzing with hostility.

"Then I realized you didn't remember me, and I understood. You were still in shock when you came to the grief group. It's a common mistake lots of people make, coming too soon. I told Betty you wouldn't be back."

I turned to Betty. "You were there, too?"

"I missed the session you attended, but Louisa recognized you from your book cover and told me you'd been there. The grief group is what brought us to your writing class. Our counselor said we should each keep a journal. Recording my thoughts and feelings made me want to get better at writing. When I saw your name on the rec schedule, I talked Louisa and Howard into signing up with me."

"I wish I'd gotten to know you sooner." I wondered how things might have turned out if I had gone back to the group. "I'm glad I got a second chance."

"You might not be so glad when you hear what I have to tell you," Betty said.

"We all have secrets, dear." Louisa patted her shoulder. "But I'm not done. I've been a member of the group for years, ever since my daughter's death. She overdosed when she was sixteen. I blamed myself for not seeing how depressed and hopeless she had become. I needed my husband to tell me I was wrong, that she fooled him, too. But he couldn't even look at me. I lost them both."

Not much is more frustrating than for a writer to be unable to find the right words. Had my friends and family experienced this same helplessness when they tried to comfort me?

"I lost my husband, too," Betty began. "But first I lost myself. We were married less than a year when it started. His initial weapons of choice were verbal. I was too fat to be attractive, too dumb to get a good paying job. I married him because I needed a meal ticket.

"I made excuses for him. He worked too hard, his mother had been withholding, his father violent. Then he started slapping me."

She took a tissue from her purse and crushed it in her palm. "I rationalized it was only an open-handed slap, and he must be right when he said I provoked him. When he started using his fists, we both stopped pretending, and I knew he wasn't going to stop until one of us was dead.

"That night, the pot roast set him off. It was too rare or too dry. I can never remember. I was curled up on the floor, wishing I could see my mother once more before I died. The phone rang while he was kicking me in the back. He was so cool and calm when he went to answer it. I think that's what gave me the strength to drag myself to the closet. I don't remember standing or reaching the top shelf. But when he came through the door, I didn't wait for him to pick up where he left off.

"By the time the police got there, he was dead. Seems I hadn't taken any chances. I fired over and over until I ran out of bullets. Only hit him twice, but that had been enough."

Howard explained he had been one of the police on the scene and testified she acted in self-defense. After her acquittal, he invited her to join the grief group he attended to deal with the loss of his wife.

"Louisa and I got to know each other better, and the rest is history." He wrapped his hand around hers.

I watched the two of them, surprised I wasn't jealous. Instead, their happiness brought me joy.

"I guess that leaves me," Nina said.

I was tempted to tell her I already knew about her past and spare her the pain of reliving it. Then it occurred to me she might need to talk: to become the narrator of her story and take control of her life. The others must have sensed it, too.

"For a long time, I couldn't stop myself from believing I was responsible for what happened to Mom. Betty's been helping me understand we aren't as powerful as we think we are. We can't change how others act and we can't change the past. We have to work on the present and hope for the future."

"I don't know about the rest of you, but I could use a drink." Louisa stood. "I don't know if you drink bourbon, but I told Howard before we left that this was going to be a bourbon night—Makers Mark."

We were in the middle of our second round when the barking began. I followed the sound to the front door and had my hand on the knob when a high-pitched human howl stopped me.

Howard came from behind, shoved me away from the door, and commanded, "Get down and somebody call 911." He slid to the side and craned his neck to look out the peephole. "I don't see anything."

Then I heard it. A low growling whine.

"Rex!" I dashed past Howard, threw open the door and gasped. It was Todd. Despite the cool night air, sweat trickled from his sparse hairline giving his thin face an oily sheen.

Howard tugged at my arm and shouted for me to shut the door, but I was mesmerized by the wild look in Todd's eyes.

"What the hell are you doing here?" I asked when I recovered enough to speak. "If you hurt Rex—"

Before I could complete my threat, Rex poked his head between Todd's legs and grinned at me. Todd yelped and stumbled forward, urged on by Ira's shotgun.

Chapter 40

For the first time ever, Andy and Wanda agreed with each other. They thought I was crazy to speak up for Todd in court.

"You do realize the bastard tried to poison me," Wanda said.

But I could empathize with the poor guy. Of course, there was no excuse for attempted murder, regardless of how inept the attempt was. But as an assistant agent, he was always a bridesmaid, never a bride. Unable to finish his own great American novel, he became fixated on me. Far from the literature he longed to write, my books had something his would never achieve. Commercial success. He convinced himself Wanda might someday turn me over to him and had been frantic when it appeared I'd become too distraught to continue Garnet's adventures.

When he realized Wanda had no intention of letting me go, he drifted into what his doctor called a dissociative disorder. If I refused to bring Garnet back, he'd do it himself. It was unclear why he showed up on my doorstep, but I didn't believe he planned to hurt me. I agreed with his attorney that what the poor man needed was a little alone time in a quiet padded cell.

"So, Miss Nancy Drew. Why so glum?" Andy asked after we returned from Todd's sentencing. Without waiting for a reply, he set two beers on the table. "You solved not one but two mysteries. We should be celebrating." He raised his bottle.

Identifying Michael's killer satisfied me on a basic level but had done nothing to help me get through the long, lonely nights. And there was still the missing drive, the one that would put Riley away for a long time. But that wasn't the only reason I was feeling low.

"I'm sorry." I clinked my beer against his. "I can't stop thinking about Michael's project and what he said in the note about me changing our corner of the world."

"Let's take another look at the note. Maybe now that you're clear headed—at least, as much as you can be—it will make more sense."

I'd shown Andy the note and the piece of circular cereal the day after my dramatic rescue from Tiffany's gang. Neither of us had known what to make of it.

Even though I wasn't particularly hopeful, I trudged upstairs where I kept the note and the lone GoldieO in my jewelry box. I brought both to Andy and watched as he silently read my husband's last message to me.

"Let's approach this logically."

I rolled my eyes.

"We agree Michael probably wrote this before going to meet Lucas. It sounds as if he suspected something was off and that he might be in danger," Andy reasoned.

"But he went anyway," I whispered.

"Listen, there was no way he could know how things would play out, or he would never have taken the risk. And don't forget he wrote that note to tell you how much he loved you. He even took the time to underscore his love by sticking cereal in with it." He sighed and shook his head. "I'll never get straight people."

"Michael and I had our own—wait a minute. What did you just say? The part about underscoring his love?"

"I said he stuck the cereal in to—"

Before he had the chance to finish, I jumped from my seat and dashed to the cupboard. I snatched the half-empty box of Goldies from the shelf and began shaking it.

"What the hell?" he asked.

My hands were trembling as I fumbled with the flap. As soon as I opened it, I eased my hand between the slick plastic wrapping and the cardboard.

"Jesus, girl. If you're that hungry, I can—"

Cereal flew as I freed my fist from the box. I extended my clinched hand. Then I relaxed my fingers and stared at the no-longer missing drive.

Epilogue

"To closure," Howard raised his glass and the others touched theirs to it.

"To Nina for her courage," I added.

"To Nina," Louisa repeated.

Nina blushed and smiled. I couldn't remember the last time I'd seen her signature expression of gloom and doom. Possibly the day she told us the date of her stepfather's parole hearing. But it hadn't returned when she faced the prison board and had been nowhere in sight after parole was denied. I had the happy suspicion we might never see it again.

"To justice," Betty said.

Nina cleared her throat. "You all know I'm not the best at letting people know how I feel, and I'll probably mess this up. Anyway, knowing I could count on all of you changed my life. More than that. You didn't just change it; you saved it."

Howard sniffed into his napkin and put his arm around Nina.

"Enough of that. We need to get started," Louisa said.

"She's right. But first, we have to congratulate Kara." Betty smiled in my direction.

Finding Michael's flash drive gave prosecutors all they needed to put Riley away with the others. The information on the drive enabled me, along with Clive as my research assistant and a little help from Aftershock, who was back on the right meds, to finish telling the story Michael had died for.

Unseen Soldiers was due to come out next month, and we'd already received speaking requests from a variety of civic organizations including several veteran groups. I planned to donate my share of the book's proceeds to rebuilding St. Cecilia's with Clive as the director. I was pleased with our work, but the best praise I received was from my co-author when he said Michael would be proud.

"I couldn't have done it without you guys," I responded. And it was true, not only because of their honest critique of my work. But also, the way they'd help me get through the agony of my loss.

They brought me back into the grief group and taught me to use my sorrow to help others while helping myself, how to talk openly and honestly.

But I kept Garnet to myself. Not because I was afraid that if I told them about our encounters, they would assume I had lost my battle with insanity. My fear was that revealing my heroine might banish her from my life, and I had accepted I liked having her around and that sanity was a relative term. That sometimes, embracing your crazy was exactly what you needed to do to stay sane. As for Michael's appearance, that unexpected gift was too private to share.

"So, what did you bring to share?" Howard asked.

We had discussed my reluctance to return to fiction, and I told them I might retire Garnet. I hadn't, however, told them my character, as usual, had other plans. The minute I sent my final draft of *Unseen Soldiers* to Wanda, Garnet broke what had been a long silence.

What kind of friend are you, leaving a girl and her ivory breasts hanging?

I explained it would be better to leave our readers wanting more than to overstay our welcome. She wasn't having it.

Honey, don't you know? You can't stop being who you are.

That was easy for Garnet to say. Unlike me, she knew exactly who she was and what she wanted. Before Michael, those concepts were cemented together. I was a writer who wanted to create a world where a woman could take what she wanted without guilt. I wanted to be reliable, to know my readers could count on me to deliver exactly what they wanted. Michael's death was the seismic shift that had made me question my reliability as a writer and a human being.

Garnet reminded me that not only was I a writer but could also encompass the strengths of my favorite creation. So, I brought her back, or maybe she brought me back.

Garnet watched the rise and fall of Jean Pierre's chest. She resisted the urge to run her fingers across his strong jawline. Now was the time she should slip out of bed and disappear into the night. So why was she unable to tear herself away from his warmth? Had she broken her one unbreakable rule and allowed herself to want more than pleasure from her new lover?

She moved closer to the man who stirred more than her passion, touched more than her body. Shivering with fear and desire, she remembered her guiding principle: Always trust your instincts.

She sighed, then placed her hand on Jean Pierre's chest and fell asleep to the rhythm of his beating heart.

When I finished reading my passage to the group, I took a deep breath and waited. After a few seconds, I began to worry. Maybe I wasn't up to the task of making Garnet more than a sexy avenger. Perhaps it wasn't possible for my one-dimensional heroine to grow.

Nina interrupted my litany of doubts.

"Remember that day in class when I said you were Garnet because she was so freaking fearless? Well, I was wrong. That woman was brave because she had nothing to lose. This Garnet is someone who trusts her instincts without having any idea where they might take her. She's not afraid to love someone, despite the risk of losing that person. She's got real courage because you've got real courage. This Garnet is you."

Acknowledgments

The title of this novel reflects how important it is to surround yourself with people you can count on. I've been lucky in this area. In addition to the love and support of my family and friends, the Roswell critique group has always been there to help me to "make it better." I've also had the Wild Women Who Write—Gaby Anderson, Kim Conrey, April Dilbeck, and Lizbeth Jones—to encourage me to become my own fearless self. I want to thank the creative people at Black Rose Writing: Reagan Rothe for his patience and expertise and David King for his cover designs. I'm especially grateful to my dear friend Madonna Mezzanotte for a photo shoot that was fun and resulted in the best picture ever.

About the Author

Katherine Nichols, author of *The Sometime Sister*, lives in Marietta, Georgia with her husband and their two rescue cats and two dogs. In addition to her passion for writing, she enjoys reading, hiking, traveling, and hanging out with her four incredible grandkids. She is vice president of the Atlanta Writers Club and Sisters in Crime.

Note from the Author

Word-of-mouth is crucial for any author to succeed. If you enjoyed *The Unreliables*, please leave a review online—anywhere you are able. Even if it's just a sentence or two. It would make all the difference and would be very much appreciated.

Thanks!
Katherine Nichols

We hope you enjoyed reading this title from:

www.blackrosewriting.com

Subscribe to our mailing list – *The Rosevine* – and receive **FREE** books, daily deals, and stay current with news about upcoming releases and our hottest authors. Scan the QR code below to sign up.

Already a subscriber? Please accept a sincere thank you for being a fan of Black Rose Writing authors.

View other Black Rose Writing titles at www.blackrosewriting.com/books and use promo code **PRINT** to receive a **20% discount** when purchasing.

Made in the USA
Columbia, SC
06 April 2022

58599432R00140